Taking On Secrets

Kevin Pilkington

Taking On Secrets

ISBN- 978-1-7374758-1-1

Published by:

Blue Jade Press, LLC
Vineland, NJ 08360
www.bluejadepress.com

For Jack and Lillian

"Don't play the saxophone. Just let it play you."
-Charlie Parker

"Women are the mirror of all things."
Tennessee Williams

Chapter One

My parents were killed, murdered. At first, I wasn't sure who the killer or killers, were until I realized in moments of slow confusion that it could only be one person: me. I was the one who killed my parents – it wasn't anyone else. That is why on that June night, two weeks before graduation, I had my ear pressed against their bedroom door to see if I could hear them breathing. My father snored quite loudly and could be heard from my room even with both doors closed. Usually, I would sleep with my pillow over my head so I wouldn't hear him. I never understood how my mother wasn't bothered from sleeping next to all that noise. Now, I desperately wanted to listen to him snore again, but there was nothing but the loud sound of silence.

I was too petrified to open their door to see with my own eyes what I had done, instead, quietly began to sob as I headed back towards my bedroom. I didn't even care that the walls in the hallway were ablaze with flames turning into thousands of tiny hands trying to grab me and pull me into the inferno. Slowly entering my bedroom, I closed the door behind me and began walking from one side of the room to the other – back and forth – knowing I couldn't stop with hundreds of miles ahead of me.

Earlier in the evening, my friend from grammar school, Timothy Bake, stopped by. Tim went to Bronxville High School where there were no dress codes or short hair regulations like at St. Luke's. He didn't understand how anyone could go to a school where you couldn't dress the way you wanted, had to keep your hair short, and most importantly, had no girls. He said it was like joining the army without going to Vietnam and always brought it up even though he knew I couldn't choose where I went to school. Also, he constantly brought up all the girls he was getting and how it was so easy that it was getting a little boring. I found it annoying because he wasn't bragging and was just so matter-of-fact about it. What made it worse was I had a girlfriend and was still technically a virgin.

Tim was just less than six feet tall, very thin, and wore his straight brown hair shoulder length that he parted down the middle. He modeled his look after his idol, James Taylor, from the cover of the *Sweet Baby James* album that had the song "Fire and Rain." I was rather pleased Tim wasn't as good looking, but he loved it if anyone mentioned he resembled Taylor. Tim even favored wearing faded blue work shirts to help with the resemblance. I made sure to never say he even remotely looked like Taylor. It was bad enough he was getting laid all the time, so why help his ego out any further?

Tim opened the back door leading into the basement where the TV was and where he knew I'd be watching it while sprawled out on the couch.

"Hey dude," he said, closing the door behind him.

"Dude" was a new expression I couldn't seem to get used to. I would've been more comfortable with it if we lived out West or even on the Westside in NYC since it would've made more sense. So, I stuck with the old reliable, "Hey man. What's up?"

"Well, it's Friday night and thought it was as good a night as any; in fact, the most appropriate night of the week, to have some real fun."

I liked what I heard and quickly sat up thinking he must have a hot babe or two from his school lined up and was hoping he did since it was more than over with Flora. "I'm up for anything," I said enthusiastically.

He smiled. "Great. Be right back – got to go out to the car." As he put his hand on the doorknob, he stopped and turned to me. "Where are your parents?"

"Upstairs on the third floor and bedded down for the night."

He nodded his head then went out.

I looked in the mirror in back of the couch and smoothed my hair down to look more presentable for when he came back with a girl, or knowing him, girls. I figured he had them waiting in his car out front and had to make sure the coast was clear before bringing them in. His car was an old Volkswagen Bug – a very old black Bug. It was easy to notice the difference between his and the newer models that were a bit bigger with a round window in the back and chrome fenders. Tim's Bug had no fenders, was a bit rusted around the edges, and had a bar down the middle of the rear window. It was probably one of the first to come off the assembly line in Nazi Germany. Tim referred to it as the "Hitler mobile" and joked that the brakes were so bad that when he had to stop at a red light, he'd open the door and put his foot out on the road. He always bought old tires to replace the older ones that blew out, which meant they were always balder than the ones before.

After a couple of minutes, he was back, but with no girls in sight. I was disappointed and sounded it. "Thought you would be bringing a chick or two."

"Sorry dude. Got something better."

"The only thing that could be better than a chick or two is three."

He didn't seem to hear me as he headed over to the couch and sat down. He took out a corn cob pipe from his jeans, then reached for a small piece of aluminum foil from his top shirt pocket and placed them on the coffee table in front of him. He started to unwrap the aluminum, "Forget about chicks tonight. This will be a nice change and just as much fun."

I looked at the small brown square of what looked like a piece of dirt with tiny white specks on it. I forgot about girls and had an idea of what I was staring at. I started to get a bit excited and nervous at the same time. "What the fuck is it?"

"It's hash dude," he said, not looking up as he broke off a bit and started to place a piece in the pipe.

I never smoked hash or much of anything else for that matter. Everyone I knew was smoking grass. Once at a party, I took a couple of hits on a joint that was being passed around, but instead of getting high, it just made me paranoid. It wasn't a pleasant experience.

"Where did you get it?" I asked, as I watched him get it ready.

"Was in the City last weekend and ended up in the Village – Washington Square Park. Some dude sold it to me. Said it's good. Real strong shit."

"Ever try it before?"

He shook his head. "Nope. Only weed."

I started getting even more nervous. "I only took a hit or two of a joint once."

Tim looked up. "You know how to inhale, so you're all set. Just sit down and relax."

I sat down but wasn't relaxed.

"I'll go first. Going to inhale once or twice and let this stuff work its magic." He picked up the pipe, placed it on his mouth, then lit a match and placed it over the bowl. He took a hit and held it in his lungs before letting it out, then took another. "Okay dude your turn, but like I said, the dude in the park said this is strong shit so maybe take just one hit to see how it goes."

And that's what I did. After Tim handed me the pipe, he laid his head back against the couch, and closed his eyes. The pipe went out as soon as I started to inhale. So, I lit it again, and inhaled some more. I began to choke and cough and was afraid I didn't get enough into my lungs, so I took a few more hits. A few more than I should have.

Tim didn't move. He continued resting his head against the couch with his eyes closed. "I'm already gone dude." He sounded as if he was half-dreaming.

I wasn't. I picked up the pipe, lit it again, and took another hit – this time really sucking it down. It was right after that last hit that the room went pitch black. Bright yellow lights sped towards me. I yelled at them, but they separated, and each light moved around me just before they hit me. After a few minutes, another set came and the same thing happened. They would separate and move around me. After another two more sets of lights came towards me, I heard Tim calling in the distance.

"Dude, you are really fucked up. We gotta get back inside."

As he grabbed my arm to pull, I realized we were outside, and maybe in the street. I began to move, but his hand on my arm started to feel like a vice that got tighter and tighter until blood began spurting everywhere. Horrified I yelled, "Get your fucking hands off me! Can't you see you are crushing my arm? Can't you see all the fucking blood?!" I was out of it, but could still tell Tim was scared.

"Calm down dude. There's no blood. I'm fucked up, but you're really fucked up."

After he said that, I saw that the blood was gone. I calmed down a little and followed him back into the house. I vaguely remember him leading me over to the couch.

"Try to calm down dude. Just relax. Try to relax. You'll be okay. I got to get my ass home. Call you tomorrow."

As soon as he left, I had my ear pressed against my parent's bedroom door, listening and convinced they were dead. But the more I walked back and forth in my bedroom, the moments of clarity began to get longer.

Around dawn, after I felt like I walked a few hundred miles, I realized how stoned I was and crashed exhausted onto my bed and fell asleep.

I stayed there until I was awoken by a knock on my door. My mother wanted to let me know that it was ten o'clock, breakfast was on the table. She was on her way out to go shopping, and my father was on the golf course. Her voice sounded so good. I was never more relieved knowing my folks were just fine. I was glad she didn't open the door, though, since I still had all my clothes on and probably looked like crap. Before I got up, I knew my days of smoking were over. It's what I told Tim when he called around noon to see how I was doing.

"You're a lightweight dude, and that was strong shit. Should've known that the white specks meant it was laced with something. I got some weed that should be easier on you. We can try it next time."

"Fuck no! I'm never smoking any of that shit ever again. I thought I killed my parents after you left."

"Woah dude! Really? Murdered your parents?"

"Yeah. Murdered my parents."

"Man, you better stay away from all forms of happy weed." After a couple of moments, he added, "You must have some weird, deep psychological shit going on man."

Being analyzed by the newly certified Dr. Bake was annoying. "Thanks, Freud. Talk to you later," I said, then hung up probably more exhausted than irritated.

Two weeks later, Tim was on the Hutchinson River Parkway on his way to a record store in the White Plains Mall. It was raining and it seems that this time, his tires were completely bald when his Bug skidded and went off an embankment. He was killed instantly. Since I'd never known anyone who had died before, this was my introduction to death. I was shell-shocked and couldn't sleep at all the night one of his cousins called to let me know about the accident. Reading about guys our age who were drafted and killed in 'Nam was bad enough, but no one at eighteen is supposed to die – not in this country or on their way to a record store. To me death always seemed distant; an act in Vegas where a magician makes someone disappear. I started to blame God because he was available and began thinking of Him as a Vegas magician, the Great Higher Power, in a gold cape who needed to brush up on his act.

I saw Tim the week before the accident. I was riding shotgun with my dad on our way back from placing bags of fertilizer for my mother's garden in the trunk of his purple chariot. It was the name I secretly gave his purple El Dorado Cadillac with the white vinyl roof. It was rather ostentatious looking to say the least. When we came to a red light on Main Street, I saw Tim at the corner. He looked like he was waiting for someone. I decided not to call out to him because I was embarrassed to be seen in the chariot. His hair was cut shorter and he had on jeans and a blue shirt with a striped beige and blue tie. The beginning of a moustache was making itself visible. I wanted to tell him he looked just like James Taylor on his new album, *One Man Dog* – the one with "Don't Let Me Be Lonely Tonight." I now wish that I had called out to him knowing that was the last time I would ever see him.

Chapter Two

In the summer of 1969, the Vietnam War was still raging, and so were my hormones. I was eighteen, a senior in high school, and Flora Kilkenny, my first girlfriend, wouldn't let me near *kiki.* It was the name she gave her vagina; in fact, she gave names to all the other parts of her body I was interested in. I found it annoying, but put up with it. It was the summer that I learned that I could put up with a lot, if I wanted something bad enough. So, to make Flora happy and the parts I wanted accessible, I used those names whenever we fooled around. "Baby, come here. Let me squeeze that *boom-boom*," I'd say while I stared at her butt as she climbed out of her dress. "What beautiful *tuties*" I'd happily whisper as I glared at her small, firm breasts. But the name I found most annoying, was the one she christened my penis with: *pookie*. It was an embarrassing name. What was even worse, she named it after her dead schnauzer; who accidentally hung himself when she was a kid. But how the name ended up swinging between my legs, was my own fault.

It seems firecrackers literally scared the piss out of Pookie, the dog, and drove him crazy. On a July 4th weekend ten years earlier while the Kilkennys were on a picnic, Pookie started running around the house as soon as the fireworks started popping. It must have been a loud one that made him run up to the second floor and take a piss near the open window facing their backyard. An even louder one to made him jump through it. Apparently, he fell into a clothesline and somehow got twisted in it. When the Kilkennys got home that evening, they found him hanging against the side of one of the trees the clothesline was fastened to.

The first time Flora told me the story over the phone, I sort of laughed. I said it wasn't an accident; the dog committed suicide because he couldn't stand his name. Flora wasn't amused. She said it was the most insensitive thing she had ever heard, that she would never speak to me again. I shouldn't even think about calling her "ever, ever, ever." She then burst out crying before slamming the phone down.

My shock at hearing Flora's reaction along with her slamming of the phone, was followed by anger. I took the receiver away from my ear, held it in front of my face as if it were a small Flora doll and yelled, "It was only a stupid joke. Go ahead. Take off. See if I give a damn. If you think I'm goin' to call you, you're out of your fuckin' mind." I slammed the receiver down so hard I would have hurt my hand if I wasn't so mad. Then I took off on a trip, the same one I always went on every time I got really upset: pacing around my bedroom. Since this time it was over a girl, I began talking out loud to myself. "Great. I'll never call her if that's the way she wants it. Who the hell does she think she is? She's not the only chick in town." I stopped to look at myself in the mirror just to make a point. "There are hundreds of chicks around for the Kissel." Point made. I left my reflection to continue on my journey. "My dad's right. Why get myself tied down to one dame?" I stopped near my window, surprised and realizing that I just used the word "dame." It was the word my father used from time to time, and the same one Bogart seemed to use in all his movies. But should I use it? At that moment it seemed important, so I said it aloud, "dame," then listened to myself as I said it again, "dame." It didn't sound quite right or feel comfortable in my mouth. Different era I figured and not appropriate I reasoned that I'd better stick to "chick" and then started pacing again. "Yeah, why get tied down with one chick? There are hundreds of chicks in this town." By the time I reached the mirror again, I was on a roll. I was feeling good and convinced three months with one girl was long enough. It was time to let the other girls in town enjoy me. Why be selfish?

I found myself in front of the mirror again. I stared into it while letting myself know that even though my ex-girlfriend initiated things, I was breaking it off and in command. "Time to move on big guy," I said smirking. I saw myself as a 6'2" and muscle-bound man, even though I was 5'8" and a rather slim teenager, "because you're not just anybody." I continued. "Not just anyone. You're made in the USA. You're a Kissel." To add punctuation, I threw a few jabs to prove my strength and power then repeated, "Yeah. You're a Kissel." The phrase had a nice ring to it. I thought it sounded like a car commercial. But then decided it sounded more like a truck commercial. I smiled, thinking I was a truck of strength. No one better mess with me, not even a girl, no matter how hot she may be. Satisfied, I walked over and threw myself on the bed. I looked at the ceiling for a moment before I let out a long sigh of relief and closed my eyes.

Half an hour later I was curled up on my bed like a fetus, crying like a baby. I realized my relationship with Flora was too new to end after only three months. There weren't many chicks in town, or at least chicks as good looking as Flora, and I was already horny. The girl I was ready to throw away about thirty minutes before was the same girl who introduced me to the wonderful world of sex. It was the best sex ever. Of course, I never had sex before, but it still didn't diminish the fact that it was the best sex I ever had. And now after three measly months, she was closing the amusement park, turning off the lights, shutting down the rides, and locking the gates.

I felt like it had been months since I had spoken to her, years even since I had seen her, rather than thirty minutes. For a brief second, I panicked. Both hands were gripping the bed covers and squeezing them in my fists. I couldn't remember what she looked like. Her eyes, no, her entire face, had faded into a white blur, but just as quickly, I found her again and placed the eyes, nose and mouth back where they belonged. As soon as the portrait was complete, I relaxed, let go of the covers, then focused on myself. In some ways, this was worse for me than the momentary panic I had just experienced. It was the first time in my life I began to look at myself without the need for a mirror to do it. The ceiling would do and what I saw when I stared deep into it, was that I wasn't the truck of strength I pumped myself up to be. However, I wasn't going to turn myself into a total weakling either. Why completely beat myself up? Besides, I already knew at eighteen that there was an entire world outside my door just waiting to do it for me. So, the strength thing, I reasoned, was still there, but I down-sized it into a car of strength. Something in the way of a '63 Volkswagen Beetle that needed a lube job. I did promise myself that if we ever got back together, I would never call her vagina, *kiki*. It was a silly name that took some of the heat away. But, of course, she would have to call me, because I wasn't about to call her. Depression quickly set in since I never got inside her, although I got my tongue in there, which counted for something. I remembered the first time she let me lick her *kiki* and later asked what it tasted like. "Chicken" I said. She didn't find that funny either. To me, tasting it never seemed like enough, it was just a warm-up for the headliner who never arrived. Still, it did give me a better understanding of a strange play I was studying in my senior honors English class at St. Luke's Catholic Prep. The play was *Waiting for Godot*. I envisioned Brother Murray asking me to stand and interpret the Godot character who never arrives. "Well Brother," I'd say, "it's like cunnilingus. It tastes great, a little like chicken, but you know it's just a warm-up for the main event." Brother Murray would be nodding his big bald head in agreement, looking scholarly and interested in my unique interpretation. "Now, take my girlfriend. She has this sweet-tasting vagina, but she never lets me in it. Never. So, you see, I too, am waiting for Godot. In fact, she shouldn't call her vagina *kiki*; Godot would be a more appropriate name. The day I get in there will never arrive."

Brother Murray, I imagined, would then turn his gaze upward to the crucifix hanging in the classroom the way he always did when contemplating a student's answer. Then I imaged, he would look at me and say, "Exactly, Mr. Kissel. A very creative and insightful interpretation. Please be seated."

This, of course, was pure fantasy, but it made me smile. I needed something to smile about in my hour of discontent. The thought of what Brother Murray would have done in reality made me shutter. Murray was a Jesuit and like all Catholic orders, taught solid Catholic doctrine: sex outside of marriage was a major mortal sin, right up there with murder and masturbation. I was already an avid practitioner of the latter and began in earnest as soon as I heard how to do it, although I still had to work on my timing. Two out of three wasn't bad I thought, and the only thing I knew how to kill was time. So, I could never be a murderer. However, I heard the *Jackal*, a nickname for Brother Jacklyn who taught Advanced Theology, say in class one time that a Catholic was allowed to kill in a just war. I have been described as an excellent student and enjoyed nothing more than engaging faculty in debates, whether political, historical, philosophical or moral. As soon as I heard the Jackal make this comment, I saw the green light for debate. I raised my hand, stood up by my desk and said, "Brother Jacklyn, then there are obviously thousands of Catholics committing murder every day since there is nothing moral about our commitment to the war in Vietnam." The Jackal looked uncomfortably at me and in an annoyed voice said, "Don't be a wise ass, Kissel. Sit down."

End of discussion. I sat down, of course, perplexed and reasoned politics and religion don't mix. They were the old water and oil cliché, but sex was another issue that seemed to outrage the Catholic clergy more than killing. If I had told Brother Murray what I had fantasized about, he would have walked down the aisle, slapped me on the side of the head as hard as he could, then expelled me from school.

"Benjamin."

For a minute I thought I heard someone call my name. I lifted my head off the bed, and gave the room a quick once over. I didn't see anyone, so I decided it was just my imagination and went back to staring at the ceiling again.

"Ben."

This time I did hear it, and it made me jump a bit. It sounded like it came from the direction of my desk.

"Over here."

It wasn't someone calling me; it was something. It was the phone across from my desk sitting on the corner of my bureau. I thought that maybe I didn't hang the phone up all the way, but when I looked closer, I saw that I did. I sat up on the edge of my bed and stared at the phone.

"Come here," the phone continued now that it had my attention, "lift the receiver off me and call her," it said in a rather coaxing manner.

"First of all, it's Benjamin, not Ben." It wasn't that I was snobbish. It's just that by insisting on my full name as a kid, I was able to avoid all those Big Ben jokes that I hated. Now, I simply preferred Benjamin.

"Okay, Okay Benjamin."

"And I'm not going to call her," I said with all the forcefulness I could muster, "She's got to call me. She might have hung up on me, but I'm doing the dumping here."

The phone quickly became exasperated and tried reasoning with me. "Look. Flora is the best-looking chick in town. You were an insensitive jerk to make that crack about her dead dog, and more importantly, you haven't gotten into her receiver yet pardon the pun. So, use me. That's why I'm here. Call her. Say you're sorry. Lie if you must, but patch things up and get on with things."

I thought over for a moment what the phone had just said then answered in a defeated, but realistic, tone. "Maybe you're right."

"Of course, I'm right. Now get off your '63 Volkswagen Beetle lube job needing ass and call."

As I walked over to the phone, my heart started pounding, and my hands became sweaty. I decided I needed to get myself revved up first before I could make the call. I went over to my record collection and pulled out the new Beatles album, *Abbey Road.* I put it on my portable record player and moved the needle down to Ringo's first and only drum solo. I flailed away with him on my imaginary drums. Then, I took over for John, Paul, and George on the various guitar solos that followed Ringo's drum break. Of course, thousands of girls were screaming as I twisted and contorted my body over my air guitar.

As soon as the guitars stopped their frenzy, I went back over to sit on the edge of my bed again to listen to the Beatles sing:

And in the end
The love you take
Is equal
to the love
you make.

They were right I thought. I was now ready to make the call.

"Hello."

I was in luck; it was Flora and not her mother. I knew I had to talk fast to keep her from hanging up, so I jumped right in, "I'm sorry. Really sorry. How dumb and insensitive of me," I blurted into the phone. With that urgent bundle of words out of my mouth, I stopped to listen. Nothing. I heard nothing. There was no click. The first hurdle cleared. She was still listening. I went for the next hurdle, "In fact, I love the name pookie. It's adorable." I lied, but these were drastic times and called for drastic measures. I listened. More silence. Which simply meant more room to work. I was Joe Namath deep in my own territory, in control and moving the Jets up field. I needed some acknowledgment though. "Flora? Flora are you there?" Of course, I knew she was, but I had to get her in the game.

"Yes. I'm here, Benjamin," she said in an annoyed voice sounding a lot like my mother when she was annoyed at me.

"I'm really, really, really sorry," I said, not sure if I was asking for forgiveness or begging for it.

More silence, then, "You are?"

Daylight. Her voice sounded forgiving; I knew at that moment there'd be more chicken in my future. I didn't miss a beat. "Yeah, I really am. How dumb of me to make a joke about a pet you loved."

Half scolding and half forgiving she said, "You really are sorry aren't you, Benjamin?"

It was time to let go of the urgent and pleading tone in my voice and relax. "I really am."

Another lie and lying did disturb me since in every aspect of my life. Up until then, I prided myself on being truthful. It was something my mother drummed into me as a child, and it stuck. Since my father had polished the fine art of bullshitting, being truthful took on a greater significance. But, lying to Flora simply felt right. And more importantly, it worked. I remembered listening to an alcoholic that the Jesuits invited to speak to the school in my junior year about the evils of drinking. He said that he had his first drink at age fifteen and immediately liked the warm feeling it brought, first to his right shoulder and then to the rest of his body. More importantly, he liked the security it brought. From there, it was all downhill. He told us how he drank throughout high school, got kicked out of college, and ended up begging for money to buy his next bottle. However, I didn't exactly see myself at age thirty destitute and begging change from strangers so I could buy my next lie, I could see parallels. My lie to Flora was my first, bringing me a similar warm feeling and I liked the security it brought too. I was hooked.

"It really is a cute name," Flora said. Her voice losing all signs of a chill.

For some reason, I had an erection and felt as if I hadn't fooled around with Flora in years. I wanted to get things moving in the direction of sex, so I lied again, but it didn't bother me this time. "Since you like nicknames so much, call me Pookie." I thought she'd love that idea.

"Oh, no. I love your name Benny," she said with an abundance of girlishness in her voice, "I would never call you *Pookie*."

Close one I thought, but I bristled at hearing Benny. No one ever called me that. She never even called me that. If I wasn't trying to smooth things over and get into the wonderful world of sex, I would have put an end to Benny. Flora knew it too, but also knew she could get away with anything since I wanted her naked as soon as possible. So, she took advantage of the situation, knowing I was horny and I would be until she let her dress fall around her ankles. I was a used '63 Volkswagen Beetle.

It was time for me to push things along. "Ya know, Flora, I really missed your body," I said, making it sound like I actually hadn't seen her for some years.

Flora didn't question the time element, and said coyly, "You have?"

"Yeah, I have."

"Well what should we do about it then?"

I could hear her smiling, "Get together tonight."

Flora was silent, playing hard to get and I knew it, but it still made me a little nervous. I couldn't keep the urgency out of my voice, "Come on, Flora I really miss you." I then elaborated with the appropriate terminology. "I miss your *tuties*, I miss your *boom boom*. I want to kiss your *kiki*." I heard a little giggle that put me at ease.

"I guess I would like to have *hotty* too."

Hotty was a new one, but I would have been a fool to question its meaning; besides, it was a no brainer—another one of her dumb names for sex. I did have her admitting she wanted to fool around too, so it was time to set things up. "So, want to get together tonight?"

"Okay," she said immediately.

I was surprised she replied so quickly. My confidence came flooding back into my veins with such force there probably wasn't any room left for blood. Open the gates; turn on the lights; start the rides. The amusement park was reopened and ready for business.

Unfortunately, I couldn't leave well enough alone. I got a little cocky. "Like I said before, you can call me *pookie* if you want." I almost made the offer again to firmly cement my sensitivity in place.

"No. I couldn't call you *pookie*. You're too big for a name like that."

Great. Not another bullshit name, I thought.

"You know what though, Benny?"

"What?" Came out of my mouth a little more forcefully than I intended when I heard Benny. Luckily, she didn't notice.

"I am going to suck you tonight as a reward for you calling to apologize."

"Really?" I couldn't hide the joy in my voice. She had never put her mouth near my groin. For that matter, I'd never had a blowjob.

"Yep, I am," she replied sounding happy and confident. I almost yelped, "Great!"

"I'm going to lick your..." she stopped mid-sentence looking for a word to substitute for cock, dick or penis. Words she never used. Then found the right word and happily exclaimed, "I'm going to lick your *pookie* until you ejaculate."

It was a mixed blessing. I was finally going to get a blowjob, but she was going to suck my *pookie*, not my dick. Much of the joy left my voice, "*Pookie*, huh?"

She understood what I meant. "Yeah, isn't it a great name for it? You gave me the idea when you kept saying to call you *pookie*. Your thingy is more appropriate." She said excitedly.

"Great," I said rather blandly.

"Come by around eight. I think my parents are going out tonight. See you then."

"Okay." I hung up and stared at the phone for a moment, then walked over to sit on the bed. I couldn't leave things alone I thought. I put the *pookie* idea in her head. "My own fault," I said aloud then looked to see what time it was. Already 7 p.m. I had better take a shower and head over to Flora's.

As I climbed out of my clothes in the bathroom, I looked down between my legs and said, "She's going to call you *pookie* tonight. Try not to listen. I'm particularly to blame." Climbing into the shower, I turned on the water, adjusted the spray, and then reached for the shampoo. As I lathered my hair, I envisioned Flora going down on me. Hell, I reasoned, if calling it *pookie* makes her happy it's the least I can do. And when I could actually feel myself in her mouth, I tilted my head back to rinse the soap out of my hair and thought, "what's in a name anyway?"

Chapter Three

Although this was a first for me, I knew this wasn't it. I grabbed the sides of the mattress with both hands and lifted my head off the pillow. I looked down at the work area and in obvious discomfort, blurted out directions, "The teeth. The teeth. Not so—easy—much teeth." Flora immediately took her mouth off of me. Before looking up, she took air into her lungs since she was obviously holding her breath and glared up at me. Before making eye contact with her, I shot a glance down at my deflating erection to make sure she hadn't drawn blood.

"I'm doing my best, Benjamin," she said annoyed. "Do you think this is easy for me, that I even like sucking *pookie*, that I've done this with other boys?"

If she had done this with other boys, I thought, they would have suffered significant blood loss.

"I can't believe you sometimes; your insensitivity amazes me," she said before moving and throwing herself down next to me. She slammed her head against the pillow then lifted it and slammed it down again even harder before settling and then stared at the ceiling.

We were on the third floor of an apartment building my father had bought two years before. He said property was affordable in Mount Vernon and a safer investment than stocks.

The house was located in a predominately Italian neighborhood in downtown Mount Vernon where it rubs shoulders and shares the same sky as the Bronx. It was a three-story brick building with a flat roof. I referred to it as "the box" since that is what it looked like to me, and with Flora's fondness for nicknames, she adopted it as well. "Let's be really alone tonight," she'd say, "Let's do the box." It's where we went for total privacy, to the third-floor studio. Like the town, the entire building was rundown, and my father was in no hurry to spruce things up. He had bought it from a patient, who for some reason, needed to sell in a hurry. The box was filled with two rather loud Italian families who lived on the first two floors. The studio required so much work that my father could never rent it unless he had significant repairs done. So, it remained empty.

I was depressed and stared up at the ceiling along with Flora. Perhaps I was insensitive. Maybe Flora should be mad, but I just didn't feel like patching things up just yet. Besides, my mother always said I was a sensitive boy and considerate too. She said it so often I actually believed I was, and why shouldn't I believe my mother? She never lied. But maybe with a girlfriend, the sensitivity rules were different and a mother's criteria didn't apply. I was too "down" though to think it through. It had a little to do with Flora's lack of licking expertise, but even more so to do with the apartment we were in and Mount Vernon in general.

Take Ralph Kramden's kitchen on *The Honeymooners*, remove the kitchen table and place a mattress there instead and you had the third-floor studio apartment we were now in. It wasn't an exact replica, but it was depressingly close. It was the only place; however, Flora and I could go to be totally alone and totally naked. It's where we went to have *hotty* as Flora called it. When I found out the apartment was vacant, I went into my father's library, got the keys from the desk drawer and had an extra copy made. I heard my father say to my mother when they bought the house that it needed a lot of repairs and the top floor studio was so rundown that he would have to renovate it in order to rent it. I knew my father well enough to know it would never be renovated and anything needing repairs would continue needing repairs. So, it was safe to take Flora there from time to time to get really naked. At other times, we actually fooled around under my parents' feet, literally, in the basement at home.

My parents had this theory that as long as Flora and I were in their house, we couldn't possibly be tempted to have sex. It was a theory with holes. I would turn the TV on loud enough for my parents to hear, but not so loud so I couldn't hear them. Flora, who always wore a skirt on these occasions for easy access, would take off her panties, place them in her pocketbook, and then hike it up. I was a "bottom man"; a shapely butt and legs flipped my switch. Since Flora possessed both, she'd walk around on her high heels while I unzipped. Usually, I would be sitting on the couch; then, she'd come over and stroke me while I played with her. Whenever we heard my parents come down from the bedroom into the kitchen, which was right above the finished basement, whatever was held up was quickly dropped and whatever was zipped down, zipped up. We would then move to opposite ends of the couch and stare at the TV like proper Catholic teenagers. These minor interruptions would break the mood, and we actually would end up watching TV. To avoid what I referred to as "penis interruptus", we would go to the top of the box. If Flora and I were ever really going to abandon our virginity, it would take place there as well.

Out of the corner of my eye, I could see that Flora had closed her eyes. I was glad. Five minutes had gone by without her saying a word. With a little luck, I might be able to stretch it into another five or ten before starting the patch-up work. I looked around the studio and found it more depressing than the last time I was there. It was almost as depressing as Mount Vernon itself. I even tried to avoid driving through the town if possible. I disliked its blue-collar ambiance and all the amenities that went with its small dark factories, faded two and three-family homes, children using streets for backyards, yelping dogs on chains and billboards usually empty or advertising products that were no longer in existence. Even passing through on the train, it was easy to see that Mount Vernon was a bruise that was never going to heal.

Maybe it simply depressed me because of the fear it brought me—the fear of ending up there. The adults who lived in Mount Vernon never went to college and the guys my age who were graduating from high school in June were probably from Mount Vernon High. That usually meant they were dating the same girl since freshman year. Within a year or two after graduation, they would get married, then their first child would be on the way within a few months after that. The wife would stay at home in a small second-floor apartment. The husband would be the sole breadwinner; working two rather menial jobs anywhere from pumping gas to selling shoes. It amazed me how anyone in his right mind would choose such a lifestyle, especially at the age of eighteen. Why not go to college? It was the key to broader horizons, intellectual expansion, culturally diverse women and the most important of all, fatter paychecks. Of course, some didn't choose: The Mount Vernon way of life chose them. It certainly chose Chauncy Dance.

When in Mount Vernon, I couldn't help but think of him. Dance was on a full scholarship at St. Luke's in New Rochelle. I was competitive, but Dance was extremely competitive, which became the distance between us just being friends, rather than close friends. Dance was the academic leader of our year while I was a close second; more precisely the A to Dance's A+. At times, it bothered me, but Dance was extremely likable with a good sense of humor. Besides, with Dance as my only real competition, it made me work harder, even if it did make me feel like Avis, which meant Dance was Hertz.

Chauncy was a bit too good-looking for my taste. In junior year, he was already six feet tall, muscular, and had the kind of bright white teeth that made you want to search your pockets for sunglasses when he smiled. Dance was also allegedly dating some "beautiful chick," although I never saw her. He also had his sights aimed at Harvard, and if for some reason he missed, Princeton was his next target. I had not set my sights on such targets for two reasons: one, I simply didn't see myself as Ivy league material, and two, my father made it clear that I could only go to a school offering me a full scholarship.

So, it was surprising when Chauncy Dance didn't return to St. Luke's for his senior year. No one seemed to know why and none of the Jesuits knew anything either, although I suspected they did but wouldn't offer any information. Even Dance's parents offered nothing to the few of his friends who called to check up on him—they simply said he was away, thanked them for calling and hung up.

During the first couple of weeks at school, rumors started to circulate. One rumor was that Dance couldn't handle living in his parent's large, pretentious home built by D.W. Griffith when he shot many of his silent films in Mamaroneck. So, he decided to do the Kerouac thing and hit the road. Others said he joined the Marines to put an end to the war in Nam. Over time, the rumors became more creative and even outlandish. It seemed every week someone came up with a new story on where he was, or that there was a new sighting. Soon, everyone was playing. Even I got in on the fun and went with a couple of other guys from school to see *Easy Rider*, still in theaters. We wanted to check out if the tall guy in the New Mexico commune scene (who was smoking reefer a few yards behind Dennis

Hopper) really was Dance. We all knew in our heart of hearts that if a positive identification was made, the game would be over. After considerable debate and an extra bag of popcorn without butter, we decided that we weren't sure.

I started a rumor of my own: Dance was doing the expatriate thing ala Hemingway and Fitzgerald. He went off to Paris to start the novel he had wanted to write since he was born. That one went over big with the guys in the Literary Club. "Dance Fever" spread to the freshmen, sophomores and seniors as well, and eventually into the ears of Brother Aidan Muse, who was the Dean of Discipline.

Brother Muse was no more than 5'5" and somewhere around forty-five years old. He wore glasses that were as thick as his Irish brogue and was all muscle. He governed St. Luke's with an iron fist, literally, since that's what it felt like if you were one of the unfortunates to receive a blow from his famously clenched fingers. It was guaranteed that if you wore your pants too tight, hair too long, were disruptive in class, or broke any of the twenty-five rules listed in the Student Conduct Pamphlet, that you would meet Brother Muse's fist without a proper introduction. Of course, there were never any lawsuits brought against St. Luke's faculty like those that were popping up in public schools around the country. Every parent of incoming freshmen or transfer student had to sign an agreement that stated they would allow:

> "Saint Luke Jesuits, under the guidance of Brother Aidan Muse, administer the proper and just punishment to their son by whatever means they (the Faculty) deemed appropriate and necessary. It is unfortunate that the time may arrive when an individual student may need a physical reprimand in response to a wrongly

committed act. With the hand of the Jesuit directly connected and guided by the hand of God, all duly administered punishment will be divinely sanctioned."

When I read the document as a freshman, I knew it was St. Luke's way of having its own ass covered as it kicked yours. Once in Math class, Tony "Chick" Torricelli (the nickname was given to him because he could smell a girl any time one stepped foot on campus) sat with his head down through most of the class, but then quickly lifted it and started sniffing the air like a bloodhound. Everyone in class who noticed him then started whispering "Tony smells chicks." Sure enough, we find out later that an attractive nurse arrived on campus to talk about New Rochelle Hospital's Blood Drive. Tony told me that he saw The Conduct Pamphlet as more than having your ass kicked, it was a license to kill, like the one James Bond was given by his boss M. Tony was always getting into trouble for various infractions until it all came to an end for him in junior year. During lunch in a field in back of the administration building, he was joking around with a couple of friends, and in response to what one of them said, Tony pretended he was jerking himself off. However, he didn't know was that he was right outside of Brother Muse's office window. Later during class, Tony's name came over the loud speaker and was told by the secretary to go immediately to Brother Muse's office. I watched as Tony got up from his desk, and his dark complexion turned the color of milk. Everyone watched silently as he headed out of the classroom, feeling sorry for him yet glad it wasn't one of us.

I didn't see him later that day, but other guys did. Tony was cleaning out his locker. The side of his face was tattooed with Muse's fingerprints and his eyes were glazed over from crying or swelling; we couldn't tell which. Tony said nothing as he packed his books. Everyone knew it was the end of the line for him.

I, who never got on the wrong side of Muse, was still more shaken by the episode than I thought. That night, I dreamt that I woke up looking like Jerry Garcia of the Grateful Dead, complete with bushy black hair and beard. I knew Brother Muse would never allow that much hair and full beard, but it grew back immediately every time I shaved. I then found myself sitting in class and called down to Brother Muse's office. Fear made me shake as I awaited my fate. However, Brother Muse's office, however, was outdoors on the edge of a cliff with the ocean crashing below. In the distance was a black spot that became a man in Jesuit robes as I neared closer. At first, I thought it was Brother Muse, but it wasn't. Instead, it was Sean Connery. My mouth didn't move, but I heard myself say, "Who are you?"

Connery, sounding even smoother than he did in *Gold Finger*, said, "I'm Brother Bond, Brother James Bond," then he reached in under his robes, took out a gun and pointed it at me. My mouth remained shut, but I began screaming, "No!" Before Brother Bond fired his gun, I opened my eyes. I immediately felt relieved I was dreaming, but I jumped out of bed to look in the mirror to make sure Jerry Garcia wasn't staring back at me.

That same day, Brother Muse was strolling the campus grounds. Most of the students were outside during lunch break, and he walked over to a circle of boys who had their backs to him. The circle went four to five boys deep, all focused on something at the center. When Brother Muse tapped one of the boys on the shoulder to ask him what the "lads" were looking at, the freshman replied, "It's Life magazine, Brother, the issue about Charlie Manson. You know the crazy guy and his followers who killed the actress Sharon Tate," the kid said smiling.

Brother Muse lost his smile. "Really? Why?" He looked concerned, almost angry.

The look on his face confused the student then made him nervous when he answered, "Well, there is a guy in one of the pictures on the ranch that looks a little like Chauncy Dance."

Brother Muse's face went red as he began yanking boys with each hand out of his way and shoving others as he drilled towards the center of the circle. The taller boys were pushed with greater force, which caused them to bang into others who started yelling until they saw who it was. They quickly went silent. When Brother Muse got to the boys with the magazine in their hands, he grabbed it, looked at the cover, and ripped it up. Everyone was stunned, confused, and frightened by his anger.

"Lads. Back to your classrooms," Brother Muse yelled, making his voice deeper than usual, "Lunch break is over." Actually, there was another ten minutes left to the lunch hour, but no one would bring that slight technicality to his attention.

That afternoon an assembly was called for the entire student body, which was at least four hundred students, that was to be held in the auditorium. Faculty members sat with their respective classes, and only Brother Muse was on stage at the microphone. The Dean of the school, Brother Jonathan Book, wasn't there; in fact, he was seldom seen. He was usually off chasing money or any kind of financial support he could acquire from individuals and corporations to ensure St. Luke's future. Brother Muse was always around and involved. Even though he was second in command, he ran the show.

Brother Muse spoke after the entire school stood to recite the Hail Mary and sing the school song. He stuck out his arms in front of him and said, "Sit, my lads," then slowly lowered his arms as we followed his fingertips to our seats. I thought his brogue sounded thicker, which I had learned from previous experiences, meant he was madder than usual.

Brother Muse leaned on the podium and spoke with his chin jutting out at the audience. "I want to bring a grave matter to yer attention. Meself and da rest of da faculty have been aware of da game dat has been played on da campus over da past few monts. Da game refers to da whereabouts of a recently departed St. Luke's student. And a fine lad he was. Of carse, his whereabouts should be of no concern to you."

Great, I thought, *he's not going to tell us what happened to Dance.* The game lives on.

"However," Brother Muse continued, raising his voice for emphasis then lowering it, "when dat student did leave, he left as a good Catlick and was a product of a St. Luke's education for tree years of his life. And any young lad who leaves St. Luke's after tree years, leaves wit Catlick teachings instilled in his very fiber." He stopped to glare, then moved his head slowly from left to right, as if daring someone to stand up and contradict him. "Furthermore," he raised his voice again for emphasis before lowering it a notch, "I can't stand by and let a good Catlick lad, a former student of dis school be degraded da way he was degraded today at lunch."

I still didn't get it, nor did any of the other guys who were throwing quick, confused glances at one another.

"To say, even if it tis a game, dat one of our own, even if he didn't graduate, a Catlick school pupil, or for dat matter, any Catlick school pupil from any of our schools in dis contree, would be part of a murderous gang is like saying we are all murderers too!" Brother Muse's voice was growing louder until it was a few octaves below screaming.

I thought he sounded like the screaming banshee in one of Yeats' fairy tales we read in English class.

"There is no way a true Catlick would be a longhaired, hippie practicing free sex. Dat's right: free sex! Dey, of course, call it free love, but it's just an excuse to have free sex. Sex! And premarital at dat!" He stopped to glare at his captive audience for a few moments then continued in a lower tone of voice. "Just a murderous bunch of hippies at dat, killing da innocent because dis poor excuse for a human being, Charlie Manson, Satan himself, told'em to butcher dese people." He looked down at the podium and began moving his head back and forth. "I cannot, as a good Catlick, allow a St. Luke's lad to be defamed any longer." Then he looked back up at us again. "Dis foolish game will stop. Must stop. If any of da faculty reports to me dat dey hear of it again," he slammed his fist against the podium, causing an echo that reverberated in the auditorium like an empty stomach, "dare will be grave consequences." He stared out at them for a couple of moments before lowering his head as if in prayer and concluded with, "Amen."

So that's it. Brother Muse got pissed because it was a Catholic thing. No Catholic would be a longhaired, commune living, free-loving or a murdering hippie; and certainly not one who attended St. Luke's. The fact that Dance only lasted three years didn't seem to matter. I figured Dance really didn't matter either; it was the Church that Brother Muse was protecting, and more importantly, St. Luke's.

It didn't stop the boys from playing the Dance game. However, they were simply quieter about it. When they did play the game, they double-checked to make sure no faculty member was within earshot. Even as the students left the assembly, I heard someone to my right whisper that he thought he saw Dance over to the side of the stage behind the curtain. Someone in back of him picked up on it and said he thought he saw Dance too. I smiled.

After leaving the box with Flora, I noticed that my fuel gauge was almost on empty. I stopped at the Esso station two blocks away before taking Flora home. After I pulled up to the gas pump, I started searching my pockets for money as the attendant came over asking if I wanted it filled up. I looked over, but before I made it up to his face, I saw the name "Dance" stitched in gold script above his breast pocket. I looked up and into the face of Chauncy.

"Hey man," Chauncy said smiling. His hair was curlier and longer, and there were grease stains streaked across his face as baseball players wore under their eyes to block out the sun.

"Chauncy," I said, sounding surprised. "You're working here?"

"Yeah, it's a second job actually. I also work in a shoe store three days a week."

What's wrong with this picture? Chauncy Dance is bright, good-looking, and has it all. The guy who was aiming for the Ivy League is now working in a gas station, selling shoes, and in Mount Vernon, no less. It didn't add up. "Wow. Two jobs, huh?"

"Well, I need 'em. I got married," he said matter-of-factly, letting his smile go in the process.

"Really?"

"Yep, in October. We just had a boy a couple of weeks ago."

If it didn't add up at first, it did now since Dance just handed me the numbers.

"Yeah. She got pregnant, but we would've gotten married anyway," he said sounding as if he were trying to convince himself more than me.

"So, where you living, Chauncy?"

"Just about three blocks away on South Broad. It's a nice two-bedroom on the second floor of a private home."

I knew the street; it was as depressing as all the rest. I wanted to say it was nice, but I couldn't quite get that out. "Oh yeah. I know the street. It's not bad." I quickly added, "So, you had a boy, huh?"

"Yeah. Harley."

"Nice name."

"We named him after my wife's father since mine hasn't spoken to me in a year."

"Sorry," I said, really meaning it. I couldn't imagine not talking to my own father even for a couple of days let alone a year, but I could imagine how pissed Mr. Dance must be. I remembered Chauncy saying how his father wanted him to go to law school and then join his firm. Although Mr. Dance was a successful lawyer, the money he came from was old, and the blood, blue. All the dreams he had for his very intelligent and handsome son must have been crushed.

"Shit. He hasn't even seen the baby yet. But he'll come around eventually. And if he doesn't, fuck 'em."

Wanting to be supportive, I offered, "He'll come around. He will."

Dance stared off for a moment then came back. "So, how are things at old St. Luke's?"

I felt like telling him how there's a game about him, how the entire school got in on it, and the assembly about it, but I also realized last minute that it might offend him, so instead, let it slide. "You know, pretty much the same. Brother Muse is still kickin' ass but Tony got booted."

Dance half-smiled. "No great loss there."

I only brought it up because everyone liked or thought Tony was a riot, but obviously Dance thought otherwise.

"Ya know," Dance said, "I wanted to stay. I even went to the powers that be and told them of my situation and that I'd get a job. Since I was doing well academically, I could get through and graduate."

"What did they say?"

"They didn't go for it. They already knew my dad wasn't going to help me out, but their major concern was that I sinned and 'impregnated a young girl' is how they phrased it. I even told them I wouldn't tell anyone at school and that I was going to live in Mount Vernon. None of the guys would come to this town for all the obvious reasons. Besides, almost everyone is from upper Westchester. In fact, you are the first guy I've seen from school."

"They didn't go for it?"

"Nah. They figured I'd tell someone or somebody else would find out and soon the entire school would know. They would look like hypocrites if they rewarded adultery."

I jumped in with, "They are."

Dance smiled. "Basically, they said I broke the laws of the church and they couldn't make any exceptions. They told me to leave and said they'd pray for me."

"How very Christian of them," I added while shaking my head in disgust.

Dance said, "They're like my folks. It's all about appearances," He then bent over and peered in Flora's direction. "Is this your girlfriend?" he asked smiling.

"I better be," Flora said good-naturedly.

"Sorry. This is Flora."

"Hi. Nice to meet you."

Flora smiled sweetly back at him. "Hi."

Dance then looked at me, "Well I better get you some gas. How much do you want?"

I only planned to put in three bucks, but now that Chauncy was feeding the fuel, I told him to fill it up. It wasn't that I was trying to impress him. I was trying to help him out, thinking in some strange way it would help Dance look like a top-notch employee. I figured the guy now had a family to support, so maybe a full tank from a customer would help make Dance indispensable. It made little sense but it was worth a shot. Luckily, I had eight dollars.

Chauncy closed the hood after checking things out, finished up with the gas, then came back around and said, "That will be $7.50, Mr. Kissel."

I smiled at his formality and handed over the exact amount. "So, I guess I'll see ya around," I said, knowing in the back of my mind that I would never come back to that gas station. Maybe I had no right to, but I felt sorry for Dance.

"Hope so," Chauncy said, smiling then bending down to peer over at Flora and say politely, "Nice meeting you."

Flora smiled back. "Nice meeting you too."

As I started up the car, Dance stood up and stepped back a bit so he was out of Flora's ear range. He looked down at me and said, "Be careful," then winked.

I just nodded then pulled out of the station. I shot a quick glance into my rearview mirror and watched as Dance stared at the back of my car as I drove away before turning and walking into the garage.

I was lost in my thoughts about Dance as I drove, but Flora startled me out of my thoughts when she began snoring. I turned to look at her. She must have been exhausted from giving me half a blowjob, or was simply exhausted from the trauma of attempting one. Looking at her profile, I noticed something for the first time that made me take my eyes off the road for a more thorough inspection. Shit. Her face possessed a strong resemblance to her father. If she were to awaken at that moment to kiss me, I would feel like I was locking lips with him. I closed my eyes tightly at a stoplight hoping to erase that image and decided not to look at Flora for a few more minutes hoping that the resemblance would disappear.

I stared up at the stoplight and thought about Dance living no more than two blocks away in a second-floor apartment complete with a wife and baby boy. The reality of the situation sent a shudder through me. The guy who was shooting for Harvard, or Princeton, missed when he ended up shooting in his girlfriend instead, changing his life and future forever. It was just another case of premature adulthood.

For a fleeting moment, I decided I shouldn't do it with Flora after all. I could do without early fatherhood along with a two-bedroom apartment of my choice in beautiful Mount Vernon. I turned to look at Flora again, entertaining the thought that she was the enemy and that women in general existed to ruin men's lives. It was that Adam and Eve thing. Look at what happened to Dance. But those moments of insanity passed—I realized it was just fear again rearing its ugly head.

I looked at Flora's face again. The resemblance to her father had thankfully disappeared. I glazed over the rest of her too: her small firm breasts and her gorgeous legs. Although they were much shorter than her mother's, they shared the same shapely curves. Luckily, Flora's body looked nothing like a cathedral, but fortunately, like a house of worship.

I pulled over at a 7-11 to get some chips and decided to let her sleep a little longer. Then I would wake her up and open with a little packet of lies to make her feel better. Maybe say it wasn't a bad blowjob, and I wished she hadn't stopped, or something like that. I was beginning to think that I wasn't really lying, rather, it was more like avoiding the truth. It made life with Flora easier. I was beginning to understand that I liked all the amenities that went with her, though I didn't actually like her. She got under my skin more than she got on it. More fear set in. What if all women got under my skin and not just Flora, and that avoiding the truth was a necessary evil? Or did it then become a necessary tool for surviving a relationship?

I thought back to Chauncy and St. Luke's again. No wonder the Jesuits didn't know anything about Dance's whereabouts. They were simply embarrassed and didn't want the rest of the students to know that their best, a product of their fine Catholic institution, committed the greatest of all sins; not the taking of a life, but the creation of a new one before marriage. So, they banished him and pretended he never existed—just another case of ecclesiastical white-out. I was catching on. It wasn't God who moved in mysterious ways; it was the Jesuits.

During the first week of school that fall, before first bell, everyone was at their lockers getting ready for the day's classes. I heard two guys at the lockers in back of me saying someone spotted Dance in Alaska over the summer. One of them said, "Wow, that's far away." I closed my locker and arranged my books under my arm and mumbled out loud, "He's a lot farther away than that," then headed off to class.

Chapter Four

I couldn't believe it was over. This time it was mutual. However, it didn't make things any easier for me. I fell back on my bed with my hands placed on the back of my head, and stared up at the ceiling. Shock and disbelief were turning into reality and then acceptance. It had been an hour since I heard The Beatles had split up. McCartney had thrown in the towel. It had come over the radio as I was driving home from school. The details were sketchy as to why they couldn't go on, but it didn't make any difference how it happened since it could all be summed up in one word as far as I was concerned: Yoko. All the rumors about the guys fighting and all the other weird shit started as soon as she hooked up with Lennon. He really got weird when he left his wife for her. More importantly, The Beatles started turning out fewer songs since he was always off with her doing dumb stuff like the "bed-in for peace" in Montreal or posing nude with her on their album *Two Virgins*, which was certainly no Beatles album. The cuts I heard on the radio consisted of Yoko screaming in a high-pitched voice like a wounded animal. One day in Sam Goody's, I was able to slide off the brown cover to the album that hid their nude bodies. I couldn't believe how bad she looked with her large breasts sagging near her waist. It couldn't be her looks that he was interested in.

I turned over and looked out the window. I never found Asian women attractive and now in protest, I vowed to myself that I would never date one as long as I lived. Except, perhaps, if it were Nancy Kwan. I loved how she looked in that scene in *Flower Drum Song* where she sings in her bedroom wrapped in only a white towel and dancing around in Betty Boop high heels. It's the point in the movie where she realizes she's in love with William Holden. Every time the movie was on TV,

I'd watch it until that scene was over then turn it off. I never knew how the movie ended.

I decided to call Flora to see if she heard about the breakup and to share my grief. After the third ring, Mrs. Kilkenny picked up. "Hi, Mrs. Kilkenny, it's Benjamin."

"Oh. Hi Benjamin," she said sounding actually pleased to hear my voice. "What can I do for you?"

I liked how she always asked me that when I called even though she knew it was obvious I wanted to talk to Flora. I wished I could surprise her and say, "I want you, Mrs. Kilkenny and your beautiful legs wrapped around me," but instead, I proceeded with the norm, "Is Flora there?"

"She's not. She went to the store for me, but will be back any moment."

I could hear her take a drag on her cigarette. I closed my eyes to better see her lips wrap around the filter and then the red ring left on it when she took it away from her mouth. "Just tell her I called then."

"Will do. By the way did you hear The Beatles split up?"

I was surprised to hear this question since it came from a parent and thought their generation typically avoided rock music, especially Beatlemania. "Yeah, I'm really bummed out about it."

"So am I," she answered like she meant it. "Their latest stuff is truly amazing—Sergeant Pepper's is already a classic. Don't you think?"

"I was more amazed that a parent actually listens to The Beatles. Mention The Beatles to either of my parents and they still think insects first. Sergeant Pepper's is definitely a classic."

"These things happen. We shouldn't be too down though; their music will be with us forever. Anyway, I'll tell Flora you called."

"Thanks, Mrs. Kilkenny."

After I hung up, I went back to my bed to lie down. I was impressed with Flora's mom for digging The Beatles and for being upset about the day's sad turn of events. I thought about her some more. I thought about how she elegantly held her cigarette, the gentle swerve of her hips when she turned, leaving me to sit on her sofa, those few brief moments when I came by and could stare at her legs, before Fiona's father's face came in to keep me company. I began wondering how it would feel to make love to a woman her age, and then not just any woman her age, but Mrs. Kilkenny. I felt embarrassed fantasizing about my girlfriend's mother, when the phone rang. I picked up the receiver and heard Flora yelling.

"Stop it, Benjamin! You sick jerk! How could you think about having sex with my mother?"

I shut my eyes tightly to shake Flora's imaginary phone call out of my head then stared back at the ceiling again and thought more about Mrs. Kilkenny. Why not think about screwing someone her age since I hadn't screwed anyone my own age yet? And why not Mrs. Kilkenny? I had always been attracted to her and it always bothered me that she ended up with a cathedral face. She deserved better, and younger.

Just then, the phone rang, and I waited to see if it would ring again to make sure it wasn't my imagination this time. The second ring followed, the real thing. I jumped up to answer.

"Hi, sweetie."

It was Flora. "Hi,"

"Mom told me you called. What's up?"

"Did you hear the bad news? The Beatles split."

She sounded relieved. "Is that all?"

Her response pissed me off. "Don't you care? One of the greatest groups in the world called it quits!"

Hearing my tone made her voice stiffen, "To tell you the truth, I don't care."

I could feel another argument coming, after an already long series of little tiffs. She was getting under my skin again; all I wanted was a little understanding. It's what I got from her mother, but of course I should've known better than to get it from her. I upped the tone in my voice an octave. "I can't believe you don't give a shit about this."

She fired back. "What I give a shit about is when this damn war will be over. When will Nixon end it? This year or next? When will there be a cure for cancer? When will men see women as equals? Will the Ferguson boy down the street, who was hit by a car last week, lose his right leg or not? These are some of the things I care about. So, excuse me if I could care less if the stupid Beatles are breaking up!"

I had to admit to myself that, that put it into context. The Beatles breaking up didn't make the cut, but that wasn't the context I was putting them in anyway. It was the wrong context, just like I realized Flora was the wrong girl for me. All I wanted was for her to share in my disappointment, that there would be no new songs from The Beatles in the future. But she never could relate to me, so why did I expect any different from her now? I didn't want to argue with her again; I just wanted to get off the phone. Besides, Mrs. Kilkenny already gave me what I wanted to hear. In a non-confrontational tone, I said, "Well, your mother was upset about their break up."

Still sounding annoyed and bristled for battle, Flora said, "She doesn't give a damn about it."

I hoisted the white flag, "Whatever." There were a few moments of silence then I added, "I gotta get goin'."

Flora didn't miss a beat. "Me too," she hung up.

I looked down at the phone and saw Flora's face with her mouth open. It became a Flora phone, something like the Mickey Mouse phone I had when I was much younger. I placed the receiver into her open mouth as if I were gagging her, so that I couldn't hear her voice then went back to bed and laid down. *Why?* I thought. *Why them? Why couldn't it be the Stone's breaking up? Damn.*

Chapter Five

Definition of SAINT

[1]saint ***noun*** **\ˈsānt,** ***before a name*** **(ˌ)sānt** ***or*** **sənt**

1: A person who is exceptionally meek, charitable, patient, etc.
2: In certain Christian churches a person officially recognized as having lived an exceptionally holy life, and thus a being in heaven and capable of interceding for sinners.

This was the basic definition of a saint I came across in the dictionary when I began my research paper on various saints for theology class. When I first read it at my desk in my bedroom, I heard my mother come in the back door and into the kitchen directly below my room. As I listened to her move around, I thought that maybe I should add my mother to the list of saints I was going to research. She certainly fit the dictionary definition, and I pretty much canonized her myself freshman year when the concept of sainthood was first discussed. I kicked around a title. Perhaps: "What Makes a Saint: A Study of the Lives of St. Teresa, St Cecelia and St. Hillary Kissel." I liked the ring of it with my mother's name tacked on. I read the definition again and had known for some time that my mother was "exceptionally meek"; too meek. She certainly was around my father and even more so in social situations.

Once, after studying late for an English exam on King Arthur and the Round Table, I went to bed and awoke to go to the bathroom. My parents had gone to a party and had returned around 2 a.m. Their door to their bedroom was ajar. I was walking down the dark hallway on my way to the bathroom when I heard my father scolding my mother because she had called him

Mr. rather than Doctor Kissel when ordering a drink from a waiter. "After all Hillary," he said sounding more like an annoyed father, rather than a husband, "I'm a dentist- a medical professional and should be referred to with the proper title." It was at that moment when I was sixteen, while standing in the hallway with a bladder full of piss and a slice of light emanating from my parents' room, that I realized that my father was a fool. There was something pathetic about a man who didn't just want a title – he desperately needed it. I pictured my father getting out of his big green Cadillac in a suit of armor. My father had knighted himself but didn't realize he was simply Doctor Kissel of the Round Belly. When I heard my mother answer, "You are absolutely right, dear. I wasn't thinking, it was my mistake." I closed my eyes, and with a mixture of shame and regret, whispered to myself, "Mom don't."

Doctor Kissel loved to talk about his accomplishments and possessions, which I discovered were more often than not fictional. My mother never uttered a word to the contrary, at least not to me, that her husband was an artist as well as a doctor: a con artist. When I was around twelve, we were at a barbecue at the Branfords' our next-door neighbors. I overheard my father telling Mr. & Mrs. Branford about a ranch he owned in the Southwest, that he later sold to buy a farm in Vermont, just a holler from the Canadian border. My mom stood by smiling, nodding her head and laughing at appropriate intervals, but, of course, never uttered a word. At home, when I asked my dad when we could go to the farm in Vermont, my father smiled and asked, "What farm, son?"

"You know the farm you bought after you sold the ranch."

My father's smile left to make room for the puzzled look that appeared. "I have no idea what you're talking about, Benjamin."

Confused, I replied "You were telling the Branfords about a farm you bought in Vermont."

A smile returned to my father's face, and in a comforting tone, he said, "You're mistaken, son. You have quite an imagination, but are obviously mistaken." Then put his hand on my shoulder and squeezed it gently, adding, "But if I do buy a ranch or a farm, you'll be the first to know."

I turned and started to walk away.

"Benjamin," my father called after me.

I turned, "Yeah dad?"

He corrected me, "Yes, father."

"Yes, father," I replied grudgingly.

"You should never eavesdrop on peoples' conversations. Especially the conversations of adults."

"But I wasn't eavesdropping," I responded, sounding exasperated in the process.

"Never mind son, go along now."

I turned and walked out of the living room, through the dining room and into the kitchen. My mother was at the table polishing silverware but was looking out the window as her hands slowly massaged a plate with a cloth. When I entered, I pushed the door with a little added force in an attempt to get my mother's attention. It worked.

"Benjamin, dear, what's wrong? Why that long face?"

I walked over to her, "I don't get it, Mom," I said quietly enough so my father wouldn't hear me.

My mother put the plate on the table and began to stroke my hair, smoothing it against my skull as if it had been sticking up, which it never did. "Don't get what, dear?"

"The ranch and the farm," I said, as if she should know.

She was puzzled, "What ranch? What farm?"

"The ones Dad said he bought when he was talking to the Branfords at the barbecue. You know, you were standing right next to him when he was talking about it."

She stopped smoothing my hair, turned and picked up the plate again, looked at it, then began polishing it once more.

"I asked Daddy if we could go to the farm in Vermont."

My mother seemed more concerned with polishing her silver rather than answering any of my questions about the farm. She seemed to be rubbing harder, really making the plate shine. "What did your father say?" she asked putting the plate gently on the table.

"He said I didn't hear it correctly and that he never said he had a ranch or a farm."

Mom stopped rubbing, looked at me and smiled. "If your father said he never said it then you must believe him."

"But, Mom," I responded, as if I were gravely wounded, "you were standing right next to Daddy when he said it. Didn't you hear him?"

My mother constantly reminded me about the importance of truthfulness when I was a young boy. She even told me that she always made a special effort not to lie to anyone. Later on, I figured it must have been her way of trying to make partial amends for my father's chronic bullshit. Since it was in her nature not to confront, contradict, or argue with anyone, least of all her husband, I stopped going to her to set the record straight. However, I did learn that when she was forced into a position where she had to go along with one of my father's lies, she found her own way to move around it. She found a formula that worked for her and one she could obviously live with. It simply consisted of keeping her husband's creative truth alterations in his mouth and not placing them in her own. So, she ended this conversation with the formula. "Enough of this nonsense, young man. If your father said he didn't say it, then you'll have to believe him. You'll just have to be satisfied with living here in Bronxville. Now let me finish my polishing."

In time my mother's formula worked for me, too. Every time I wanted her to set the record straight, and she came back with a variation of, "If your father said," I knew it meant *your father is bullshitting again.*

I did occasionally worry about lying to Flora. Was this how my father started? Was starting to lie more frequently a bad habit like smoking pot? According to everything I read about drugs and was forced to read at school, smoking reefer leads to harder stuff. I pictured myself rolling up butts of Flora's hair, inhaling it, then with my eyes glassy, enjoy every lie I told. So, if my lying to Flora was like smoking pot, then my father was doing heroin. The way he bullshitted, it had to be heroin or coke or something. My own lying to Flora, though was necessary to make life with her easier, it wasn't an excuse; at least I wasn't lying to myself. But why did my father? He lied to everyone. It must have made life for my father easier. But "easier" was as far as I got when it came to Dr. Kissel, and as far as I wanted to go.

"Charitable and patient..." I read those two adjectives again. I was thinking about how to begin my research paper, but I wasn't ready to separate my mother from the definition. She possessed these two qualities as well; as far as I was concerned, she had the market cornered on saintly attributes. She was overly charitable when it came to Dr. Kissel's looks, or maybe it had to do more with that "beauty is in the eye of the beholder" phenomenon. Every time I got dressed up to go somewhere lately, my mom would look at me and say proudly, and a bit whimsically, "You look so handsome! More and more like your father, every day." To look like my father was an esthetic goal I hoped never to accomplish. My father was on the short side, no more than 5'5," with a large hooked nose like the Indian on the back of a nickel. I figured there wasn't much my dad could do about the beak he was born with, but he was the archaic designer of his waistline. Dr. Kissel loved to eat; the size of his waistline was in direct proportion to the size of his appetite, which was extra-large. Each year, his belly grew. It made him look rather comical since his face was somewhat thin and so was his chest, then right below his man boobs was where the expansion took place. All supported by two thin sticks which resembled legs if viewed from appropriate angles. When I was a child, my aunt gave me a book with Humpty Dumpty. At the age of two, I pointed to the picture on the cover and said, "Da Da!"

My father's beauty maintenance consisted of a haircut every ten days and a manicure. There was never one hair out of place, as if his barber used a type of epoxy glue to accomplish this feat to ensure that the hair formed a precipice over his forehead and was strong enough to rest a dish on it if necessary. To ward off invading gray hairs, a jet-black dye was applied to his glue hairdo. His nails were always waxed and buffed to a hard, glossed shine; it made his chubby fingers look like they ended with thin pieces of broken glass. He also spent a lot of money on clothes, much of which was purchased at Brooks Brothers, and much of which I liked. The hair, nails, and clothes were a trinity my father believed would camouflage his obvious sins. Of course, it didn't, but he thought it did and that was all that mattered, so why diet?

This was the abundance of male pulchritude that sent Mrs. Kissel's heart a fluttering. Her favorite movie star was Rock Hudson; "Now there's a man," she would say. "Any woman would give her right arm to be with Rock, but he must simply have thousands." I also heard her once say, "Did you see your father in his new Brooks Brothers navy suit? He looked so handsome, as handsome as Rock Hudson." Now there was something to argue about, but I let it go for all the obvious reasons. I liked to think it was my charitable mom at work again who was a clear example of the expression "love is blind." This didn't separate her from any of the saints the church canonized, however, because after all, they acted out of love for God who (it was clear to me) created an imperfect world that was filled with every imaginable human suffering.

My mom went to the 6:30 a.m. mass every day. Like the mailman, she went through rain, sleet or snow. She usually drove, but if it were icy or snowy, she simply put on her boots and walked down the hill, past Bronxville High School, across Pondfield Road and over to St. Joseph's. The drive took ten minutes; walking in the snow took twenty, or through ice and snow around thirty. She liked to sit in the first pew to be up close to the action. Going to church every morning constituted "an exceptionally holy life," as far as I was concerned. Sometimes during the winter, the sound of my mother's footsteps would wake me as she walked down the stairs and headed out the back door. It would be pitch black in my room except for the bright green face of the electric clock on the table next to my bed. I could almost hear the brittle sound of the snow and cold outside as if the entire world were ready to shatter if you set foot outside your door. I would lift my head off my pillow and stare at the clock until its face came into focus so I could make out the time. When my head would hit the pillow again, that's when I felt closest to my Higher Power. Since I had at least another hour until I had to get up for school, I'd whisper, "Thank God," then go back to sleep.

I discovered my mother was connected to the church in a much more formidable way than by faith alone. The year before, I was invited to a Halloween party. I decided to go up into the attic to rummage around for some old clothes in hopes of putting a costume together. The storage space was filled with boxes and clothes my parents no longer wore. There was stuff from the 40's and 50's complete with a musty smell to prove their authenticity. I had a good time opening up boxes labeled with my mom's handwriting. I began to admire her script, each letter of every word she wrote rolled like large waves on the blue ocean of her pen. Shoes, shirts, dresses all seemed to float in on the tide as I pulled each box in front of me to examine their contents. I soon forgot I was searching for a possible costume, as it began to feel more and more like Christmas morning—every box a present with gifts from the past.

I worked my way through fifteen boxes; the most interesting were the ones filled with photos of my mother's childhood. It was fun discovering the three-year-old version of my mother's face in a photo where she stood between her tall parents and holding their hands on the front lawn of their home. I never knew my grandparents, Elgin and Eleanor Fig, who both died before I was born. Although my mother said she loved her parents very much when I would ask about them, she rarely mentioned them or brought them up in conversation. I knew very little about them except that Elgin Fig worked for an insurance company in

Weehawken, New Jersey where my mom grew up. He died from a heart attack just four months after Eleanor died from pancreatic cancer. When they died, my mother was just ten years old and was raised by her aunt, who had never married.

I held the photo closer to get a better look at my grandparents. Being an only child with dead grandparents, I always felt short-changed. My dad's parents had died by the time I was five. I didn't remember them other than a vague blur at a dinner party. I envied my friends who had brothers, sisters, and all kinds of relatives at family gatherings. I always wished I had a younger brother who I could have bossed around and teased. It seemed to be the inalienable right of all older brothers. My father often talked about mom and himself. Sometimes he brought up his father, a pharmacist, who owned many drugstores throughout Connecticut, including one in Hartford, where my father was raised. I learned to edit my father's stories which probably meant my grandfather worked in a small local drugstore. Since my mother rarely spoke of her parents, I was naturally more interested in them. They both looked to be on the tall side, with strong angular facial features. I hunted for hints of my mother's face in theirs as she may have ended up with her mother's nose and her father's mouth, but that was where the resemblance ended. My mother was no more than 5'1", certainly not the height of her parents, but it was an old photo, and she was only three, so they may have just looked taller than they actually were. My grandmother was more handsome than pretty in a print dress. My grandfather was dressed in a dark double-breasted suit with slicked-back hair that shined in the sun. He wore wire-rimmed glasses, the kind that were coming back in style ever since John Lennon appeared wearing them on the cover of Sgt. Pepper's.

I put the picture aside and rummaged through the box for another. There were a few more photos of my mother at various stages of her childhood, but no more of the Figs. The rest of the box was filled with carefully folded baby clothes that were my mother's. I closed the box then straightened up the other boxes, putting them back in their original arrangement. As I got up to leave, I noticed the end of another box that was sticking out from behind an old door, leaning up against the wall. I went over and pulled it out. It was much smaller than the other boxes and unlike the others that were merely folded, this one was taped shut. It was very light and, of course, I ripped the tape off immediately curious as to why it was quarantined from the rest of the boxes as it was hidden and securely closed.

Inside the box were more family pictures of the Figs, a few of my mom as an infant then all the way up to age eight or ten. I glanced at them, figuring they meant a great deal to my mother, who simply had the box taped to ensure their safety. But when I picked up the last photo, it became clear why this was an essential box. It was an eight-by-ten formal picture of my grandfather, a headshot, which looked like it was taken sometime in the early 20's. He had the same slicked-back hairstyle as he did in other photos, with the John Lennon style glasses and dark suit. The only difference was the collar; it was the white round collar of a priest. At first, I thought maybe it wasn't my grandfather because it actually resembled Father Cavandish, the parish priest with whom my mother was close friends with. He led the 6:30 a.m. mass she attended every weekday. Father Cavandish tended to turn up on holidays for dinner or just dessert. He even came to my birthday parties up to about age ten, but still sends me little gifts on every birthday since. Usually, he sends pens or a book on some saint, but the only worthwhile gift was two tickets to a Giants football game that I attended with my father for my 12th birthday. Then, I turned the photo over and read: "Father Elgin Fig, '21" written in the top right-hand corner. I recognized the letters, the waves in the handwriting as it was my mother's.

I didn't hear my mother walk up the attic stairs and jumped when her voice broke my concentration.

"What are you doing up here, Benjamin?" she asked smiling.

I looked up at her from one of the boxes where I was sitting holding the photo in my hands, "What the hell is this about?"

"What did I tell you about using profanity in this house?" she said sternly letting her smile disappear as she walked towards me.

"Sorry," I replied, to get the quick apology out of the way, then handed the photo to her. "Grandpa Fig was a priest?"

My mother took the photo from me and stared at it, then sat on the box next to me. She stared at the photo again. "Yes, your grandfather was a priest."

"Wow. You never told me that."

She continued staring at the photo "No, I never did."

"You said he was an insurance salesman."

She kept staring at her father. "He was after he met your grandmother and left the priesthood."

I let it sink in for a moment and then said, "In religion class, they say a priest can leave the priesthood, but in the eyes of the church, he is always a priest."

"That's right. Once a priest, always a priest."

"Did you know he was a priest when he was alive?"

My mom leaned over and pulled the box in front of her. She placed the photo under the other pictures where it was originally, making sure grandpa was buried again, then closed the box and looked at me. "No, I was too young. My Aunt Meady told me when I was seventeen."

"Around my age."

"Yes."

"How come you didn't tell me?"

"For a few reasons, dear. The first is the most basic. All women should have a sense of mystery about them. You'll find that out for yourself soon enough. I guess this was mine. The second is I would never tell your father."

"So, I'm the only other person who knows?"

She smiled, "That's right."

I felt privileged that I was being told a secret my mother was sharing with me alone, even if I stumbled upon it by accident.

"Of course," she added, "Father Cavendish knows too."

"Why him?" I asked, raising my voice an octave or two.

My mother, responding to the incredulous tone in my voice, "He's my priest," as if to say *why would you think I wouldn't tell him?*

So much for privilege, I thought, though I responded, "Of course."

Now that I knew about Grandpa Fig, and after a few moments of digesting it, it didn't seem like such a big deal that my mother found it necessary to hide it. But why didn't she at least tell my father? "Why didn't you want Dad to know about Grandpa?"

She turned to gaze at old clothes hanging from a rack against the far wall. "Because your father has problems with the Church, well, the Catholic Church at least. He believes in God, but not in the Church's teachings or what the Church stands for. He finds it full of hypocrisy. It would have given him more reasons to voice his displeasure with it, and I just couldn't handle that. He only agreed to get married in the church because I refused to marry in a civil ceremony. To be truly married, I had to be married in the eyes of God, which meant a Catholic ceremony. Of course, he has other reasons to be unhappy with Catholicism, but now is not the time to get into them. Besides, I will not speak for your father."

I knew my father wasn't very religious. In fact, he never went to mass, not even on Christmas when everyone gave in and went. He also was never friendly to Father Cavendish the way he was to our other guests. I figured the visiting priest wasn't important enough for my father to care. Perhaps if Monsignor or Bishop Cavendish visited, my father would have been sufficiently impressed and much more cordial, but knowing my dad found the Church hypocritical made me feel closer to him. I had been looking for something, anything, to connect with my father as I got older and Church hypocrisy was a good place to start.

"Another reason I didn't want anyone to know is more personal. My faith and my relationship to God has always been the most important relationship of my life."

Hold on, I thought, *what about our relationship?* All of a sudden, I was jealous of God. I fought the urge to ask, w*hat about your relationship with dad and me?* But, I thought better of it and didn't interrupt my mother.

"It has always been the very core of my life." She stared down at her hands resting on her lap. "It has gotten me through some difficult times and brought me great comfort."

My mother always made me uncomfortable when she talked about God and the Church. She tended to sound like the Jesuits at St. Luke's and I felt like I should have my pen and paper out taking notes.

"You see, sweetheart, it's more than just belief." She went silent for a few moments before she continued, "I wish you would get closer to Father Cavendish. He's a wonderful man who possesses so many answers. He would be the first to tell you priests are just God's representatives here on earth. He would also tell you that priests are just as human as we are, flaws intact. He helped me understand my father's position when he met my mother and became her lover."

This last phrase excited me, "You mean when he was a priest, he was grandma's lover?"

She slowly nodded her head.

"So much for the vow of chastity," I blurted out, grinning without thinking.

My mother raised her voice and said in a daring tone, "Benjamin."

I realized my mistake, "Sorry, mother," I answered, my lips back in a straight line.

She was quiet out of annoyance over my remark, then continued, "That is exactly the point I had to struggle with."

"What point?" I asked even though I knew what she meant.

"That my father was a priest who broke his vow of celibacy and sinned. It was very difficult for me to accept this. But after years of prayer and counsel from Father Cavendish, I was able to accept that my father was human and allowed to contain flaws. Since he was a priest and continued to be one in the eyes of the Church, I came to understand that I was connected to God in a much more unique way than the average Catholic." She looked in the direction of the clothes again, but this time seemed to look through them. "I also realized I am truly blessed to be to be a daughter of the Church's spiritual fathers, figuratively and literally, a daughter of a priest." She no longer saw what was in front of her but rather what was in her mind. Her face brightened at what was in her mind, and she added, "Sometimes, I think of myself as God's granddaughter."

She was starting to make me uneasy. I felt like asking, *how can you feel fortunate?*

Before she got up to leave, she looked at me. "So, there it is; I only ask that your father doesn't find out. I want that to be your promise to me."

It was a simple enough request. "Sure, mother."

She got up and walked back out. I put the boxes back where they were stored and headed back to my room. I sat at my desk and looked at the last part of the Saint definition again, "...lived an exceptionally holy life and thus being in heaven and capable of interceding for sinners." The exceptionally holy life certainly fit her; she always said Bronxville was like heaven. She obviously intervened when it came to her husband's bullshit and his not going to church. *Yep*, I thought, *she fits the bill. She's a saint.* I wished I could write about her, especially with all this new information.

Before starting my paper, I thought about my mother not wanting my father to know about Grandpa Fig. It made sense to me. If my father had known, he would have told everyone that his father-in-law was the Pope.

Chapter Six

I thought that I might have finally lost my virginity in the Kilkenny's playroom, as Flora's family called it, but I wasn't sure. It was once a garage attached to the side of the house that a previous owner converted into an extra room. It was paneled with dark, inexpensive wood almost entirely covered with family photos, Mrs. Kilkenny's diploma from the College of New Rochelle, and abstract watercolors painted by Flora. I disliked the abstracts that were done in very pale yellows and pinks because you had to look very close to make out what she actually painted. Flora wanted to major in art at her mom's alma mater. I had seen some of her larger watercolors and oils she kept out back in a shed, but they were just larger versions of those hanging in the playroom and almost anemic in their lack of color. They all needed paint transfusions, but her father thought he gave birth to a female Picasso. I once read the great painter liked to say that if he ran out of reds, he used blues. I imagined Flora exclaiming, "If I run out of pale yellow, I use nothing."

Once, I found Flora staring at a rather large matted canvas in the backyard that she had resting against one of the trees Pookie, the schnauzer, was found tangled among the clothes lines. As I walked towards her, I asked, "Are you starting a new painting?"

Flora turned around slowly and looked at me as if I cursed the entire Kilkenny clan, who were rooted in Dublin. Her face turned red with anger and she answered me through clenched teeth, "No. It's finished."

As I walked closer and squinted my eyes to get a better look, there it was, whatever it was, in very pale pink that was almost flesh-colored. If I hadn't gotten up close, the abstract would never have appeared.

There were photos of Mr. and Mrs. Kilkenny as a young couple, pre and post-marriage. I had to admit Flora's father looked pretty much the same, except his hair was ink-black, as was his wife's. My favorite photo was the one where Mrs. Kilkenny is posing in what looked to be in a photographer's studio. Since it was probably taken in the early 40's, it was in black and white and reminded me of a still from a film noir production with light and shadows placed strategically around her. She was wearing a suit with shoulders that were as straight as airplane runways. For some reason, I liked the still and admired the actresses who starred in the movies of that time: Betty Grable, Claudet Colbert, and Linda Darnell, who dressed similarly. It was as if architects had built the suits, not fashion designers, paying more attention to lines and angles. Mrs. Kilkenny's lips, although probably red, appeared black as her hair, which was pulled back tight and away from her face. Then there were those legs – long and graceful as a hymn. *If only I could perform some magic,* I thought, *like a modern-day Merlin, put Flora in the photos, then hocus pocus the young Mrs. Kilkenny into Flora's shoes.*

All the rest of the photos were the Kilkenny's with a relative or friend, and Flora would always be at the center of attention. Most were of Flora by herself or with her father beaming at each other, oblivious of the camera. The mutual admiration of the two of them made perfect sense to me. After all, Flora was her dad's one and only, but what annoyed me was Flora's inability to think for herself. Her admiration for her father bordered on hero worship. According to her, Mr. Kilkenny was the smartest human being on the planet. She would often preface a not-so-original thought with, "My father says" or "My father thinks." Out of disgust, I once said to her during one of our many disagreements, "I know what your father thinks, but what do you think?"

Flora's face would briefly blush for as long as it takes a quickly moving cloud to pass over the sun before she would grit her teeth and reply with, "We both think the same way." I would have paid anything, even given her my Abbey Road album, to hear one original thought come out of her mouth.

Of course, Flora detested the war and wanted it to end, but felt we should be there because "my father says the threat of communism must finally be stopped." It took everything in me not to engage her in a discussion as to why the U.S. should get its ass out of South East Asia immediately. I knew I'd have to insult her father in the process, which would do nothing to end the war, but would pretty much end our relationship. So, I learned to side step the most important issue of our time by simply saying, "I just wish it would end," knowing Flora would agree with me.

I found myself looking at the various pictures again on the playroom wall an hour after Flora called to say her parents were spending Saturday afternoon at a friends on Long Island and that I *should* come over. After she answered the door, she ran up to the bathroom, leaving me to wait in the playroom. As I scanned the wall, I realized it was the first time since dating Flora that I didn't have to sit across from her father in the living room waiting for her to get ready. As a result, I was totally at ease and ready to "fool around" with Flora as soon as she came downstairs. Although, any kind of sex wasn't mentioned on the phone when she called, but it was implied since she told me that her parents would be home late that night. I was very relaxed and anticipating up close and personal time with Flora. While I was waiting, I noticed the wall had a new acquisition: a small diploma. It was between a photo of Flora on a pony around age five or six and Mrs. Kilkenny's college diploma. This smaller one had been awarded to her father after completing, it said, a six-week course at Dale Carnegie. It wasn't a diploma after all, but rather a public speaking certificate. I reread it to make sure I was right. Why the hell would he want it up here? I thought. I didn't hear Flora come in behind me and was startled to hear her voice.

"My mother wanted my dad to hang that up," she said with a slightly apologetic tone in her voice.

I turned to look at her with a look of momentary shock, which she interpreted to my not hearing her come into the room.

"Sorry I made you jump," she offered.

It's true she did startle me, though she misconstrued the look on my face. I was more surprised that she too might have thought her father's latest six-week accomplishment didn't deserve to be hung on the wall. Could I be detecting a crack in their mutual admiration wall? I obtained a bit more enjoyment than her comment warranted perhaps, but I had never heard any displeasure or hint of dissatisfaction in her voice with any aspect of her father since I knew her. I wanted to stay on the subject. "Where is your dad's college diploma? It would make more sense to have that up near your mom's."

Flora gazed at some of the other pictures. "He never went to college," she said somewhat defensively.

If she made this announcement about anyone else it wouldn't have made any difference, but this came as a surprise to me. I figured the arrogant little know-it-all must have had not one, but a few, graduate degrees since he was such an expert on just about everything, or so his daughter made me think. Of course, the guy should have taken a class in social conversation, not just a six-week class, but also a twelve-week class. My forty or so minutes waiting for perpetually late Flora in the living room with her old man puffing away on his cigarettes, saying only the mandatory minimum, was becoming cruel and unusual punishment. I had to splice together what I saw through the smoke in the chair across the room from him and his ideas and philosophies that flowed from his daughter's mouth to get a clear picture of Mr. Kilkenny. The portrait I created I disliked more than any pale abstract Flora had painted. Mr. Kilkenny was a conservative hawk who looked arrogant in his smoking chair and believed his daughter was beautiful and gifted since she came from his golden sperm. Therefore, no guy was good enough for her. He had difficulty with social interaction, had no use for small talk, pontificated on all subjects known to man, and disliked his daughter's first young suitor. Or, as I liked to refer to myself, with a nod to my favorite Williams' play, Flora's *gentleman caller*. I knew Mr. Kilkenny wasn't guilty of all those negative attributes, but perhaps I was too young to think otherwise. As far as I was concerned, Flora's dad was guilty on all counts. "Really? Your dad didn't get a college degree?" I said, trying not to sound so pleased.

Flora jumped right in to come to her father's rescue. "He couldn't. His father had died when he was fifteen, so he started working to take care of his mother and younger sister." Her voice then went a few octaves higher when she added, "And don't forget; it was the Depression."

Adding the last bit of information was Flora's way of emphasizing that her father wasn't just a hero; he was a super-hero. I knew all about the Depression from my father, more so than from history books. He always brought up how there were long bread lines for the hungry folks who were out of work. I was tired of hearing about how tough times were back then. My father constantly brought it up and used it as a way to instill guilt just in case Catholicism wasn't doing the job.

When my father got angry with me, he'd point out how lucky I was not to have grown up during the Depression. How lucky I was to live in a beautiful house in an expensive neighborhood and have all my needs taken care of. He never took off his belt when he was angry when I was younger the way some of my friend's fathers did. Instead, he took out the Depression and beat me over the head with it. Now, I was going to use it for a chance to make my own point. "Wow, during the Depression, too." I replied, making sure to sound impressed with Flora's father's accomplishment.

Flora lifted her eyebrows and nodded her head a few times in the process. She was impressed that I was impressed with her father, then gave me a now-you-understand smile as if to say *that's why he doesn't have a diploma hanging up there near mom's.*

I was actually setting her up for my next comment. "Ya know, that's exactly how it was with my dad."

Flora stopped nodding and lost her smile as a somewhat alarmed look came over her face. She offered a concerned expression – one that possessed a bit of confusion and perhaps a touch of fear. It was almost as if she was afraid to hear that my father might have achieved heroic deeds as a teenager as well. "How do you mean?" she asked.

"His dad died when he was twelve and he had to help support his mother."

Flora cast her gaze back at the pictures on the wall then looked at me. "Really?"

"Yep." I made my point and said more by saying less. Since Flora knew that my father went to college then dental school, I didn't have to elaborate. It was just another way of saying *my father is stronger than your father,* or at least how I would have said it ten years earlier. It felt good to show her that there were other heroes in close proximity who, perhaps, achieved greater accomplishments than her father. It's true that my father had all kinds of part-time jobs throughout high school and had two years of college before he was drafted into the Army, who paid for his dental training and rush job. When the war broke out, Uncle Sam needed dentists to work on various Army bases so they gave him a crash course in dentistry. He was rushed through a year and a half program, after which he received a diploma, and then was told to start drilling. No one, except my mom and myself, was aware of my father's dental training, and I wasn't about to share that bit of information with Flora. My father was still basically a drill-and-fill dentist. If a patient required anything more extensive, he would send them off to a specialist, or simply, a better dentist.

"That's great," Flora said, rather absent-mindedly.

Mission accomplished. Her father was knocked off his pedestal, or at least out of his chair in the living room. I looked over to the far end of the room, with a window as long as the couch underneath it. It's where the gravel driveway led up to when the room was still a garage, but where the Kilkennys now parked their newest used car when they were home– a big old '64 Ford that was the color of an Army tank car. I walked over and sat on the couch, then looked at Flora. She was still looking at the pictures but was obviously aware of where I went. When I patted the cushion next to me and said, "Come here, babe," she turned and smiled, then walked towards me. When she stood in front of me, I ran my hands up her legs and then nested them on her butt. It was no surprise that she wasn't wearing panties since she was wearing a short blue skirt and white polo shirt. It was a similar outfit she wore when we were in my parents' basement, so all she had to do was hike up her skirt to fool around, then drop it if we heard one of my parents come down. I laid back, unzipped my pants and with Flora's help, pulled my pants and boxers down around my ankles. Then she stroked me, smiled and said, looking at my erection, "you are really hard," then pulled her short skirt up around her waist and got on it like she was riding a horse so that she could slide back and forth on my dick. She slid back and forth without me penetrating her. She braced herself with her hands on my chest, at first sliding back and forth slowly and then picking up speed. We both closed our eyes and started moaning. It was around then that things got a little hazy for me.

Flora started sliding faster and faster as she began going up and down and slamming herself harder than usual on me. Since my eyes were closed, I didn't see that my erection would stand slightly at attention when she lifted herself off me before slamming herself down again. She did this a few times until *pookie* stood up a little too straight on the upswing and stayed there when she was on her way down. Flora yelled in pain, jumped off of me, and stood a foot from the couch. Before I could see what happened, I bolted upright and stared at her. Flora was looking down between her legs, still holding her skirt around her waist. Dark red blood was streaming down and onto the shag carpet. Flora looked up at me, "You broke it!" She shrieked. "You broke it!" Then looked down as the blood seeped into the deep carpet.

I was perplexed. I didn't know how it happened at that moment and I certainly didn't feel myself penetrate her. "I'm sorry," I said, upset and concerned. I was surprised at the amount of blood and it scared me a little, but not as much as it scared Flora.

She lowered her voice. "You broke it." She kept looking down at the blood with her legs frozen stiff. Then she looked at me; I couldn't take my nervous eyes off the blood flow. “You raped me!” she yelled. “You raped me!”

Hearing this snapped me out of my concern from staring at the blood. “What are you talking about?” I yelled back at her with a mixture of rage and bewilderment. Before either one of us could continue, I saw Flora’s eyes widen as she shot a look out the window. “My parents,” she whispered loudly, then dropped her skirt, quickly rubbing her barefoot over the blood on the rug, then turned and ran out of the room.

Panic grabbed me then started to squeeze as I shot upright and looked out the window to see the Kilkennys slowly pulling into the driveway in their car. I crouched down onto the floor, yanked up my boxers and pants simultaneously, zipped and buckled in record time, then went over to the bloodstain and quickly started rubbing it with my hand. Although the rug was a thick shag and a maroon color that almost matched the stains, I thought I needed water to make it blend more. I frantically started hurrying over on all fours like a dog so I wouldn’t be seen, and reached the dining room before getting up and running into the kitchen. I grabbed paper towels near the sink, ripped off several sheets, and soaked them with water. I ran back through the living room then got on all fours again and hurried back over to the stain. I rubbed it with the wet paper towel as hard as I could. I heard the Kilkennys at the front door fumbling with the lock as I surveyed the carpet, then stuffed the wet paper towels that were light red into my pockets. It looked like something had spilled, but not necessarily blood, or so I had hoped. I heard the Kilkennys say something, then the doorbell rang.

I hurried out of the playroom, and through the dining room until I was in view of the door. I walked quietly towards it and opened it. “Hi,” I said as calmly as I could.

"Hello, Benjamin," Mrs. Kilkenny said rather coolly, which was unlike her usual warm greetings. Cathedral face just looked at me as they both entered the house.

As I closed the door behind us, I asked, almost too friendly, "Having trouble with the lock?"

Neither of them said anything as Mrs. Kilkenny hurried up the stairs. Her husband walked slowly into the dining room then made a left for the playroom. I felt my stomach drop as far as my ankles as I heard Mrs. Kilkenny knock on Flora's bedroom door and say, "Let me in, Flora." I met Mr. Kilkenny's eyes as he re-appeared and walked slowly towards me. He always seemed to move slowly. He was one of those guys that I couldn't picture running or even walking at a quick pace, but now he seemed to be moving in slow motion. When he finally reached me, he calmly, but with a firm tone of conviction said, "I think you better go home, son."

Another wave of heat rushed through my body like a brush fire. Her father meant business, and using "son" meant it was serious business. He had never used that word before in our brief, strained conversations during our forty-minute waiting periods in the living room. Calling me "son" meant he was pulling rank, that he was the adult who was making it clear I was the wrong boy for his daughter. To his credit, he said nothing else as he turned and walked towards the door until he added, "And son."

I turned to look at his face that had turned a deep red. It was at that moment, staring into his face, that I disliked him most.

"You better not come back."

I had planned to walk out quietly, like a dog with its tail curving under his balls, but when I heard him add his final order, any fear or guilt I had been feeling vanished quickly. "You know my name," seemed to shoot out of my mouth as if I had no control over it. I walked a bit closer to Mr. Kilkenny, whose face grew redder out of fury, and perhaps a bit out of distress. It was apparent he didn't expect me to return a verbal volley and underestimated my nerve. I stopped a few inches in front of him and glared into his red face. I was surprised how small he looked and sensed he was a bit edgy, which made me feel more confident, but just as quickly felt embarrassed. I was, at that moment, an intruder menacing a small man in his own home. It quickly calmed me down, but I added firmly and as emphatically as I could, "I don't intend to." Feeling in command of the situation, I turned and walked slowly out of the door, knowing Mr. Kilkenny would have nothing to add.

Chapter Seven

I needed a full scholarship to attend college. My father made that quite clear to me since he didn't want to shell out a dime for tuition. He said he lost a lot of money in the stock market and simply didn't have the money for tuition. I heard him say to my mother once that he didn't believe in the stock market and that going to the track and betting on horses made more sense. So, it was up to me to try to get a free ride. The schools where I would have to board didn't offer me scholarships. Even though I had a 3.0, I didn't do that well on standardized tests and didn't score high on my SATs. The two schools I hadn't heard from were St. John's University on Long Island and Eugene Lang College in the City. I'd have to commute every day, which was fine with me. My mother wanted me to attend a Catholic school, but since none of the Catholic colleges offered me scholarships, it was down to St. John's and Lang. She was praying St. John's would come through with the cash. She was afraid that if both schools offered me full scholarships, I might turn down "the Catholic university of higher learning" as she referred to it on several occasions. When I told her I preferred Lang because it was in the city, she made an appointment for me to see Father Cavendish. I really didn't care what the priest thought. I believed it was none of his business, but I went to see him because it would have upset my mother too much if I didn't. What made it worse was that the appointment was at St. Joseph's and on a Saturday afternoon.

I rang the doorbell of the rectory that was situated in the back of the church. I waited for a minute or two until I heard footsteps and a little old lady in her seventies or eighties answered the door. She was no more than five feet tall in a dark dress with tiny white flowers. "You must be Benjamin," she said as she stepped aside to let me in. Closing the door, she added, "Please follow me." I noticed she was a bit hunched over, making those flowers look like they were growing from a tiny hill on her back. I once read that your sense of smell diminishes as you get older, and apparently, hers was obviously gone. Her perfume was so intense I thought she must have marinated herself in it. As I followed her down a narrow hallway, I kept thinking *why the fuck did I come here,* even though I knew the answer. She took me to the last room at the end of the hall and stopped at the door. She opened it and told me to have a seat as Father Cavendish would be with me shortly. I thanked her as she turned and headed back down the hallway, but her perfume followed me in the room where I sat in a medieval-looking wooden chair facing a large oak desk. I began to examine the room and started to feel nauseous from the lingering smell of the old woman's perfume. The room was rather sparse, dark, with heavy curtains opened just enough to let a whisper of light in. A large wooden crucifix hung on the wall in back of the desk facing me, and in the center of the room was a medium-sized red Indian rug. There was also a desk lamp turned on to help the sun, which seemed to struggle in a vain attempt to help illuminate things. I found the room incredibly chilly. I always hated cold rooms, but at least the chill this time helped battle the old woman's perfume until it was gone.

"Benjamin," Father Cavendish exclaimed as he came into the room.

I thought it was strange that I didn't hear his footsteps echo in the hallway. He seemed to simply appear. He thrust out his hand for me to shake before he headed to his seat behind the desk.

He looked at me the way my father's eyes did when he took a quick inventory of me after he came home from a hunting trip. Every year my father spent two weeks in Canada hunting deer. The brief once over always made me uncomfortable, and here it was again. It had the same effect, even if it was from a different kind of father.

I noticed that the priest had stopped slicking back his hair and started to let it grow a little longer around the ears. With his gold wire-rimmed glasses, he was looking more contemporary these days. Cavendish must've been in his late forties or early fifties, but with the grease out of his locks and not a speck of gray finding a home anywhere on his head, he could pass for a man ten years younger.

The priest leaned back in his chair, "You are looking more and more like your mother every time I see you."

It could have been worse. I was grateful he didn't say I looked more and more like my father. The priest leaned forward and placed his elbows on the desk so that he could clasp his hands together. Suddenly, I felt strange as I realized that I had never been alone with him. Over the years when Father Cavendish stopped by at one of my birthday parties as a kid, I vaguely remember saying hello, and a few other pleasantries when he stopped by the house at Thanksgiving or on Christmas. But now we were alone, one-on-one, and what made it even stranger was that we were on the priest's turf. We weren't on my sacred ground: my parent's house.

I shot a quick glance at Cavendish's hands. Why was it that there was no mistaking the hands of a priest? They all had the same distinguishing characteristics; always scrubbed until almost white and relatively soft looking. Their fingers would slowly turn up at the ends so that they almost appeared to curl backwards. They looked like the hands of men who were in drag – at least in the photos I had once seen in a book I flipped through in a bookstore – that were trying to be feminine, but too masculine to fool anyone.

"How's your father doing?"

"Just fine, thanks."

Cavendish added, "It sure would be nice to see him in church one of these days."

"You better start praying now, Father."

The priest smiled as he leaned back in his chair. "I have faith, Benjamin. I have faith."

I smiled and replied good-naturedly, "I guess faith is a good thing to have in your line of work."

Cavendish was still smiling but seemed to be studying my face.

He changed the subject. "So, your mother tells me you are waiting to hear from St. John's."

That's right, I felt like saying. Let's get this over with. I'm doing this as a favor to my mother, and it's a big one since I'm sitting here in a rectory on a Saturday afternoon. Any other eighteen-year-old would've been out doing what we do: watching or playing football, smoking a joint, chasing girls. But, here I sit about to discuss the necessity of a Catholic university education.

Instead, I said, "That's right. I haven't heard anything yet."

"And your mom says you're waiting to hear from another school?"

"Eugene Lang."

"Ah," he said as if it were both a problem and a moment of clarity. "And your preference is?"

"Whoever gives me a free ride."

He looked at me, a bit puzzled.

"You know...a full scholarship."

Cavendish nodded his head in acknowledgment as another "Ah" came out of his mouth, then added, "Won't your father offer any financial support?"

"No," I answered forcefully, making it clear that I didn't want to discuss my father's financial situation further.

The priest understood and moved on. "Eugene Lang is an excellent school. Isn't it part of the New School in the Village?"

I nodded.

"You're not considering going away to school? Your mother said you applied to Boston College and Georgetown."

"Neither offered me a full-ride even though I got into both."

"That's puzzling. You're an excellent student."

"Yeah, an excellent student with low SAT scores."

Another "Ah" came from him as he leaned back into his chair.

A few moments of awkward silence followed as I began to look around the room, waiting for the next question as the priest stared at me.

"So, do you know what you plan on majoring in?"

I stopped examining the room and met his eyes. "No, not yet."

He smiled. "You mean you're not thinking of dentistry like your dad?"

Being a dentist was not on my list of things to do, and if it was, I certainly didn't want to be a dentist like my father. By the end of grammar school, I was beginning to realize my father's skills as a dentist were suspect. When I was twelve, I used to play with Addison Crumbley before his family moved to Greenwich, Connecticut.

One Saturday, when I was playing catch with him in his backyard, I took a break to go inside to use their bathroom. I went through the basement and got to the stairs that lead to the kitchen but stopped when I heard Mr. and Mrs. Crumbley. Mr. Crumbley was a dentist who had a practice in Byrum, a town between Rye and Greenwich. Mrs. Crumbley never referred to her husband as a doctor the way my mother referred to – or, more aptly, had to refer to – my dad. I decided to wait for a few moments hoping they would finish talking and leave the kitchen. Then with the coast clear, I'd hurry up the stairs, across the kitchen and into the bathroom. Although I wasn't very shy, I was shy enough not to want to be in the presence of adults unless it was absolutely necessary. As I waited, I heard Mr. Crumbley mention my dad, then lost the rest of what he was saying as the faucet sink turned on. When it was turned off, I heard him say, "I wonder how Bruno Kissel keeps his practice going."

I listened closer.

"He is strictly a drill-and-fill man."

Mrs. Crumbley asked, "What does that mean, sweetheart?"

"It means he basically can't do anything more involved than a cleaning or filling a cavity. If there's anything more involved, he refers them to another dentist or a specialist. Last month one of his patients came to me on her own in a lot of pain over a tooth he had worked on. It turned out he placed her filling too close the nerve, which created all kinds of discomfort for her."

"Oh, that's a shame," Mrs. Crumbley said, the way my mother sounded when she was only half listening.

"Another one of his patients came to me after Kissel crowned her front teeth. As a result, she had bleeding gums. After examining her, I had to give her the bad news that the crowns he put in were too heavy, and her gums would continue to bleed if they weren't removed. Each tooth had to be re-crowned with a lighter weight enamel."

Strangely enough, hearing this didn't hurt my feelings or make me angry. Nor did I want to run in and defend my father – mainly because it might be true.

Mr. Crumbley sounded incredulous. "He keeps losing patients, and what does he do to change matters? He works only three days a week, and the rest of the time he goes golfing or takes hunting trips."

My father worked on Mondays, Wednesdays, and Fridays, but it meant nothing to me at twelve. I just figured everyone's dad worked three days a week. I never gave it much thought then or as I got older, although I was always suspicious of my dad's dental expertise from that day forward.

Once in the Bronxville Pharmacy, while looking for aspirin my mom sent me to buy, I overheard an older woman complaining about her problem with the bridge in her mouth. She said to the man with her – her husband, I assumed – that they needed to find a new dentist since she'd had it with that "God awful Dr. Kissel. I swear my mouth has been worse ever since I started going to him!" I hurried out of the pharmacy without buying the aspirin.

When I was a freshman at St. Luke's, one of my best friends was Gunn Norton, whose father was also a dentist. He once complained that every time he wanted to do something or go somewhere with his father, it fell on a weekend that his father was away at a dental conference. He said his dad went to these conferences to keep up on all the "new dental stuff." He asked if my dad went to the conferences. I replied that my dad preferred hunting trips, although he once brought back a tooth from a black bear. Gunn was kicked out of St. Luke's during junior year when he came to a dance drunk. The joke at school the following week was that

Norton got booted out of school because he went to the dance with his "gun loaded."

After hearing the Crumbleys leave the kitchen, I decided not to run up and use the bathroom even with the coast clear. Instead, I walked back outside across their backyard lawn towards a large oak. I kept looking at the grass, which suddenly annoyed me because it was perfectly manicured, like a country club golf course. I went back behind the tree where I couldn't be seen and emptied my bladder.

"I think," I said to Father Cavendish, "I'll wait and see before I decide what my major will be."

"I guess one dentist in the family is enough. It certainly is a major commitment – four years of college then dental school. Except for a dentist like my father who was rushed through dental school in a year and a half by the Army."

Father Cavendish leaned forward again and returned to our pressing topic. "Although Lang is an excellent school, its one and only drawback – and it's a big one in my book – is that it's not Catholic." He smiled and looked at me to see what my reaction might be or if I had something to say before he continued. I had no reaction or response so he continued. "I know it all depends on the larger scholarship but your mother wants you to continue your studies at St. John's so your spiritual life will continue to mature under the proper guidance. To build on the Catholic foundation St. Luke's has constructed for you. Of course, it goes without saying, I hope you will follow that path. Prep schools like St. Luke's construct avenues that lead towards Catholic institutions of higher learning like St. John's, Georgetown, Fordham, Notre Dame or any Catholic university of that caliber."

I was glad the priest wasn't going to beat around the bush. We both knew why we were here. Besides, the sooner I could wrap things up, the sooner I could leave and salvage what was left of Saturday afternoon.

I didn't favor one school over the other and would choose whichever gave me a full scholarship. Although after visiting both, I was leaning towards St. John's. Its campus had large green lawns and basic nondescript buildings with students moving about the campus but never overwhelming it. In short, it appealed to my suburban sensibilities. There was the mandatory cross here and there, but at least it didn't wear its Catholicism on its sleeve. There were no priests in sight, nor were there any teaching the classes I sat in on when I visited. The chapel was in back of the campus, built under a promenade that made it almost hidden. It didn't feel anymore Catholic than Lang with its one building on 12th Street in the Village and the other a block away on Fifth. The buildings didn't stand apart from the rest of the city and seemed to disappear in its urban camouflage – meaning there was no campus. As far as I could tell, the only real evidence that school was in session were the students on the streets and in front of the building on Fifth with books in their hands or backpacks. They all seemed to be in a hurry, or maybe they were trying to stay in step with the fast pace of the city.

I didn't want to tell the priest that I was leaning towards St. John's. I wanted my mother to think Cavendish had something to do with it because I knew it would please her. I could tell how pleased she was when I said I would come to the rectory. She always wanted me to become closer to Cavendish and confide in him the way she had ever since I was born. There was no way for me to get close to this priest or any other priest but, again, if it made my mom happier, it was an easy talk to complete.

"There is also a danger that is hidden and subtle in non-Catholic universities, Benjamin."

"Really? What's that?"

Cavendish placed his hands on his lap where I couldn't see them, looking concerned, and went on.

"Many university professors are atheists and talk against the existence of God, organized religion in general, and specifically the church."

I got the very same warning in all the religion classes at St. Luke's, but I acted surprised anyway.

"Really?!"

The priest nodded his head slowly. "They often plant seeds in students' heads against God and try to destroy religious teachings," he said, waiting a second before adding, with a slightly elevated tone, "Catholic teachings."

I injected with, "I could never be an atheist, father."

He raised his eyebrows at my comment with an expression of satisfaction and asked, why not?

I couldn't help but grin a bit, then replied, "Because atheists don't have any holidays." I wasn't quite sure why I said that, and obviously, it was a bad joke with bad timing.

A look of concern spread across his face, "Benjamin, this is no laughing matter. It's an issue of real concern for a young man of your age about to embark on his college career. It's also a concern of your mother's. We both feel you would be less inclined to find such professors at St. John's and more likely at Lang."

Who the hell put you at the controls of my life – isn't that my parent's job? I wanted to say.

"Well, to tell you the truth, Father," I said, "if I get a full scholarship to both, I'm leaning towards Lang."

The priest stared at me for a few seconds, "I see," he said, sounding slightly discouraged. "Well, if you do, I hope you can recognize the type of professor I told you about."

I felt like saying thanks for the tip, but I've had a lot of practice with bullshitters. Between dealing with the secular bullshit of my father and the ecclesiastical bullshit of St. Luke's, I think I can recognize any other bullshit that comes my way.

We ended our meeting talking sports. Cavendish started telling me there was no way the Jets would win another Super Bowl victory with Joe Namath, who got lucky the first time around. It was the way Namath lived his life off the field and the wrong message he was sending the youth of America that Cavendish couldn't support. I told him I hoped they would win another and probably would, if Namath stayed healthy, but they might need a miracle this year. I joked that the priest should understand the concept of how important miracles were, especially when they applied to sports. This made him laugh at least, and I decided not to get into how Namath wasn't sending the wrong message or any message for that matter. I figured he was just trying to win football games and live his life the way he wanted. It wasn't worth getting into an argument over it, one that might upset my mom if she heard about it later, so I let it go.

Father Cavendish walked me to the front door with his hand on my shoulder, getting in a few more good words about St. John's. When we reached our destination, we stopped to shake hands. He told me how glad he was that I came by and that his door was always open if ever I wanted to talk again. I hurried down the stairs and heard the door close behind me, then hoping I'd never walk through it again.

Chapter Eight

Since the best St. John's could do was offer me a partial scholarship and Eugene Lang came through with a full ride, this meant my mother was disappointed, and my father thrilled. It was the end of my Catholic education for my mother, and for my father; it meant getting something for nothing. Father Cavendish stopped by one afternoon under the auspices of wanting to congratulate me on my scholarship. His hair was even longer than the last time I saw him at our meeting in the rectory. I assumed the reason for his visit was probably arranged by my mother when he began warning me about nonsectarian colleges where professors are atheists who teach against the existence of God. It was the familiar ground he covered in our last meeting, so I started to zone out until I was almost sure I heard the word "groovy" and knew he had to leave. It was a word I detested. I prided myself on never using it and always felt embarrassed for anyone who did so I interrupted him. I told him I needed to get to the library to work on a final paper and that my mom would be home later around seven if he wanted to come back. I then ushered him out the front door, and although we never used it, I bolted down the latch quickly as if I was afraid that he would come back and try to break in. It was an absurd notion which at that moment, felt logical and made perfect sense.

Later that week, my father came home after playing golf and wanted to have a quick chat about something in the living room. It was the "something" that made me nervous. I hurried down and found him already sitting in his smoking chair, which was an oversized leather chair I wasn't allowed to sit in. He didn't want me sitting on the cushion that had formed the perfect indentation after years of use and was now custom fitted to his butt. Next to it was a small table with his humidor and ashtray. I knew enough to wait while he performed his lighting-up ritual as he would never begin any conversation until after it was completed. He removed a cigar the size of a small club from the humidor and examined both ends before he slid the length of it under his nose to inhale its aroma. He grabbed his cutter and clipped off the top so he could draw from it then lit the cigar with a wooden match. He started puffing until smoke pumped out of his mouth like small clouds ready to block the sun streaming through the window behind him. He then tilted his head back to blow out a rope of smoke that was long enough to tie around his vast waist. After he was satisfied, he began.

"Benjamin, I just wanted you to know how proud I am of you for getting that scholarship." I was sitting in the chair across from him that no one ever seemed to sit in. It was a bit stiff and uncomfortable from lack of use, but when I heard him say he was proud of me, I was so relieved and relaxed that the chair became the most comfortable in the room. I was also a little surprised since I never heard my dad say he was proud of me, he might have thought it before, but it's just that he never said it. He never handed out compliments because that was my mom's department. I should've figured saving him around twenty-eight thousand on tuition was what it would take to make him proud of me. At that moment, it was worth every cent. I beamed, "Thanks, dad."

He took another puff on his cigar. "So, this is what I was thinking." Another puff then, "The city is a wonderful place to live at any age, but especially at your age. I love the city and still go down quite a bit." This was news to me. I didn't ever remember him making trips to the city, especially if the weather was good and he could be on the golf course instead of in his office.

"Didn't know you liked the city so much."

He took the cigar out of his mouth and turned it to see how long the gray ash was. He once told me the longer the ash stayed on, the higher the cigar's quality and the cooler the smoke. As a kid, I always watched the ash get longer and longer and waited for it to fall off, but it never did until my father wanted it to when he would knock it onto the ashtray. I was always disappointed that it never made it to the rug. I knew what to expect now when he flicked the ash off.

He watched it drop into the tray. "Oh sure. I've always loved the city and have been going down more than usual lately."

"Really? For what?"

He didn't answer my question, which meant it wasn't really that important or simply none of my business.

"So, this is what I've been thinking. Since you have a full scholarship, and if you can make enough money this summer to cover most of your expenses, I'll help you out with rent."

Hearing this, I sat straight up in the chair and moved to its edge before almost falling off. I couldn't believe what I was hearing. First, my father was proud of me, then wanted me to live in the city, and he would give me money towards rent. If I knew this was coming, I would have been convinced there was a God years ago. At that moment, it was too much to take in all at once. My surprise and excitement seemed to jump out of my mouth on its own in one word without any help from me. "Great!"

My father smiled. "I think it would be good for you to get out of the house, away from Bronxville, and to fend a bit more for yourself."

I was on board with all of it. I was excited and nodded my head in agreement as if it needed to be fastened tighter to my neck.

"I'm convinced it's a good move for you and I'll just have to convince your mother of that."

My head stopped nodding when he mentioned my mother. I tensed. "You mean Mom isn't okay with me living in the city?"

He smiled, "I thought about you living there this morning. I didn't get a chance to talk to her about it."

"Oh," I said sounding more disappointed than I intended. I didn't want my mother to put up any roadblocks.

"Don't worry, I'll convince her it's good for you. Which it is."

I nodded again.

"The important thing for you now is to make money this summer. Like I said, I'll give you some towards the rent, but I won't pay for it all. Alright?"

He then relit his cigar that had gone out and puffed two smoke rings shaped like donuts fat enough to dunk in a cold glass of milk. "I made some good investments for a change in the market over the past few months. I can put a little of that money into your rent."

I wanted to say, *but I thought the stock market was like going to the track and betting on a horse. Isn't that why you bought the building in Mt. Vernon as a safe investment?* But I didn't since I'd only overheard him say that and he never said it directly to me. I didn't care though, how he got the extra money. I only cared that he was willing to give it to me. Maybe, I was the horse he was betting on this time. In any event, I was grateful and again said, "Thank you."

Sitting there across from my father with the warm sun painting the living room a golden yellow, I was grateful for the pride resting somewhere in his chest and a new world was waiting forty minutes away by train. I couldn't help but feel now was as good a time as any for the rest of my life to begin.

That summer, I didn't get a job – I got three. I first worked with a landscape company making sure the large Bronxville lawns looked like expensive green carpets. After, I worked in town doing anything the owner wanted me to do in the hardware store. I also spent most of a sweltering August working for a restoration company painting the outside of a large clapboard house off Kimball Ave. On weekends, I took the train into the city to look for an apartment with the *Village Voice* under my arm. I would scan the rental section and try not to get distracted by the last three pages that advertised escort services. There were photos of girls in all shapes, sizes, makes, and colors who wanted me to call them at the phone numbers locate below their breasts or other private parts that were blurred or blocked out by a black square. Some of the photos looked professionally done, while others looked like a friend, or even a pimp, took them. On occasion, I would fantasize about dialing one of the numbers, and our conversation would last anywhere from a few minutes to the entire train ride. The last imaginary phone call I made turned out to be Flora, which surprised the hell out of me. I recognized her voice. She admitted it was her, and after my saying how disappointed I was in her, she broke down. After we broke up, she was despondent and knew she could never meet anyone like me again. Of course, she was right. I understood how she ended up here following the loss of the greatest guy she ever knew, turned to drugs, and finally the last three pages of the Village Voice. That conversation was the longest and came to an end when I reached Grand Central.

Since I still didn't know the city very well and knew the subway system even less, I took a bus down 5th Avenue towards the Village. It would take me a while before I stopped feeling like a tourist and got used to the city's sights, sounds, and pace. Growing up just forty minutes away suddenly felt like it could've been forty thousand miles away since everything was radically different. Although I'd come in on occasion over the years, they were quick trips to see a movie or play, so I never really paid much attention to how the city breathed since I had a destination to get to. Now I was going to live here, the city was my home. I wanted to find out as quickly as possible how it all worked. I liked the look of the 42nd Street library that took up an entire city block with the two lions sitting out front, seemingly tamed and quiet in their concrete fur. The traffic lights thru the city were strong enough to stop all the traffic, even the buses and trucks when they turned red. The apartment and office buildings were as tall as the clouds, and the Empire State Building on 34th Street reminded me of a giant syringe sticking its needle in the sky. The yellow cabs the color of egg yolks constantly drove past along the street, and the flat iron building standing alone on 23rd looked like a slice of birthday cake. I loved it all!

The bus let me off at 5th and 12th. I strolled the four blocks and turned on 8th Street. The street between 5th and 6th was jammed with mostly younger people hanging out -- hippies, tourists, those like myself -- from the surrounding 'burbs, and shoppers. Cars had to move through slowly because so many pedestrians kept crossing the street. There was the smell of weed in the air, although I couldn't see anyone smoking it. On the corner of McDougall that ran into 8th was the 8th Street Bookstore. According to the *Voice,* it was one of the better-known bookstores where many known local writers went to buy, browse, or hang out. I couldn't see it, but closer to 6th, Jimi Hendrix's studio he built called Electric Lady Studios. It was still hard to believe that the greatest guitarist in the world would create and record music across the street from where I might be living. It was almost too much to think about so I quickly let the thought go since I hadn't gotten the apartment yet. There were also a few "head" shops selling water pipes and rolling paper, but most were shoe stores. In fact, I had never seen so many shoe stores. Their windows filled with all kinds of bizarre-looking footwear like boots and platform shoes in bright florescent colors of pink, orange, and purple. I saw sneakers with heels and thigh-high red, patent leather boots. There were one or two more traditional shoe stores or at least carried shoes that I recognized, but it was obvious 8th Street kept much of the city on its feet and walking.

I found the apartment building I was looking for in the middle of the block. It was a pre-war brick that was the length of three brownstones, which was rather long since most were narrow, traditional tenements. I opened one of the two large black doors and walked into the foyer where I pushed the buzzer with "super" next to it that I found. After a few minutes, the door opened and a man no taller than 5'2" appeared wearing a matching dark blue shirt and pants with a dirty white patch over his breast pocket labeled "Super." He looked in his late sixties, but I was never good at guessing a person's age. His head was entirely bald and shined to a high gloss as if he waxed and buffed it. He had a full smile filled with a set of yellow stained teeth that seemed to stretch and reach the corners of each ear.

"What can I do for you, Son?"

I held up the *Voice*. "Wanted to see if your apartment is still available."

"Oh, yeah, it is. Let me show it to you."

He pushed the door back for me to enter and put his hand out to shake mine. "I'm Dominic Creech, but you can call me Dom or Creech. It's what most of my friends call me. And your name is?"

"Benjamin Kissel."

He closed the door. "Nice to meet you, Mr. Kissel."

I followed him up the stairs. "Benjamin is fine."

He stopped on the top step and turned. "I prefer to call tenants Mr. or Mrs. or Ms. It's a formality I feel is appropriate. If you rent here, it's Mr. Kissel." He exposed his yellow teeth again, surprisingly revealing one or two more than last time, then he continued, "The apartment is in the front on the fourth floor." As he fumbled with the keys outside the door, I wanted him to hurry since the scent he exuded – a mixture of beer, sweat, and cheap cologne– was making me nauseous. Once the door opened, I put more distance between us, and he encouraged me to get a feel for the place. "Yeah, go ahead and take a look around."

To the left of the entrance was a kitchen big enough for a small table with two chairs. The living room was next. It was kind of box-like with a window that faced the back. The building wrapped around a square in the center so you faced the apartments across a small concrete courtyard below. A hallway with a window to the right let in all the noise from 8th Street. In the back of the apartment came the bathroom and a decent sized bedroom with another window facing the back apartments. When I walked back to the living room, Creech was bent over, looking out the window. "Look at this," he said.

I leaned over and looked into the apartment across the way. A young woman in pretty good shape was in her bra and panties standing at her kitchen sink. In a low, leering tone, Creech said, "That's 3J. She's a real looker."

She was a looker, alright, but I felt like a Peeping Tom and quickly straightened up to examine the living room again, although I really wanted to stare some more at Miss 3J.

When I turned around again, Creech had stopped looking. "There are quite a few more like her in the building. If only I'd lived here when I was a young man like yourself, Mr. Kissel."

I didn't answer but sort of smiled. I didn't want to talk to him anymore or be in his presence. I just wanted the apartment.

"What does a young fellow like you do for a living?"

"Actually, I'm a student."

"Oh, yeahhhh," he almost sang. "NYU?"

"No, the New School."

"Ahhhh." He seemed to have run out of small talk. "So, what do you think of the apartment?"

"It's perfect," I said, looking around.

"Can a young college man like yourself afford the rent? It's 180 a month plus utilities."

"I sure can. I have money saved and financial support."

"Sounds like parents are in the mix." A big, yellow grin followed.

I didn't address his comment, "If you have a lease ready, I'd like to sign it."

"I'll get the lease and be back in a few." He turned to leave, then stopped and turned around. "Ya know, with the view you have," he tilted his head towards the window and 3J, "I should tack on another fifty bucks." He waited to see my reaction, but before I gave him one, "Just kiddin'! Be right back." With that, he headed out the door quietly, laughing as his footsteps faded down the stairs.

The only problem with the building, as far as I could tell, might be him. The apartment was perfect. It was big enough for one or even two people, cheap enough for my father to kick in some bucks, and just four blocks from school. It only needed my clothes, a few bookshelves, a bed, and the girl from 3J.

Chapter Nine

She was the only reason I didn't drop a boring philosophy class I took in the fall semester of junior year. I even made sure to get to class early just to watch her walk in and take a seat in the front row like she always did. Once I got past the miniskirts she usually wore, I moved on to the rest of her outfits that were stylish, and probably expensive and her shoes. There were black shoes with six-inch heels, knee high brown boots, red platforms, purple pumps, gold buckles across the ankles, silver buckles, suede spikes, and more that were worn on Marla Davis's feet. She never seemed to wear the same piece of clothing twice. I didn't learn much more about ancient philosophers that I didn't already know, but I did become a Marla Davis fashion critic. I only knew her name because the professor was one of the few faculty members who took attendance before class. I couldn't tell if she was Spanish, black, Greek, or some other nationality, though it was clear she was exotic. Her hair had a wild, styled look as if it grew in all directions and was cut to stay that way. There wasn't a blemish on her skin, which was the color of a coffee with extra crème. Her clothes were just tight enough to suggest curves you needed to get close to rather than avoid.

I kept trying to figure out the best way to introduce myself and get some small talk going. It seemed like a difficult task since she always arrived right before class began and would hurry out when it was over. I had no idea it would take Joe Jr., a local diner near the school, to bring us together. It was a small diner. It had a few booths and a counter where I usually sat to watch the short- order cook work the long skillet and oven under it. He put on quite a show, like a conductor in complete control of his orchestra. His baton was a flat spatula that he would bang against the skillet before flipping. On each end of the grill was a large pile of hash browns and bacon he always took from to fill each shiny plate that passed by on the line, although neither pile ever seemed to deplete. He also kept a pot with oil in it that he would ladle out onto the flat surface for when he poured eggs, that he could crack open with one hand that would spit and dance before calming down. There always seemed to be a burger going, filling the air with its greasy aroma. From time to time, he would pull out the grill under the oven to check on some gooey Italian or Greek dish to see if it were done. It was fun to watch if I was alone, which I usually was since I stopped in before or after class for a quick cheeseburger or coffee. The burgers were just thick and greasy enough with sharp cheddar to make me crave them. I was disappointed when I went in one day before my evening philosophy class and all the counter seats were taken so I had to take the one empty booth near the window that faced the door.

I was sipping my coffee, watching outside of the window at the Village move about the day, when I looked back at the front door and into the eyes of Marla Davis. She stood for a few seconds looking around for a seat when she looked at me and, to my surprise, a glint of recognition spread across her face.

"Aren't you in my philosophy class?" Her smile was warm and relaxed.

I was happy she even recognized me since I could describe everything she wore for the past six weeks. "I am." I pointed to the seat across from me that at that moment looked big and empty. "Want to join me?"

"Thanks." She sat, looking a bit more casual than usual but still in style with a jean jacket, a white t-shirt, and black, high-waisted, pinstriped pants. "I'm Marla Davis." Her lips were full and her teeth were bright white: perfect. "Nice to meet you," she said, extending her hand across the table to shake mine.

It was soft. I didn't want to let it go and couldn't believe my good fortune. Marla, who I had been watching from across the room for weeks, was now sitting across the table from me.

"That's exactly what I need."

I looked down to see the coffee she was gesturing to and still recovering from her joining me.

"Yeah. I always need at least two extra cups before that class..."

"...To stay awake, right?" she giggled.

I matched her smile. "Yep. It's by far the most boring class I've taken here."

"It's not the subject matter. It's him."

I nodded. "He's the worst."

"I'm glad I'm not the only one who thinks so."

I enjoyed looking at her, large eyes set slightly farther apart than usual, her full lips, flawless skin, and the smooth, mellow tone of her voice. Just looking at her was like going on vacation. I had forgotten I was in a small, crowded diner on 6th Ave.

"So, is that your first or second cup you're working on?"

"It's my first."

"Then I'm not too late."

"For what?"

"Well, if we don't go to that boring class tonight," she glanced at her watch, "which starts in ten minutes, you won't need another cup of coffee to stay awake, and we can go for a real drink somewhere and skip class together. That is if I can talk you into it."

"You just did."

I went for my wallet. "Great! Let's go!"

She stopped me, “No, I’m the bad influence so coffee is on me.” She stuck her hand in her bag and fished out a couple of bucks to place on the table.

This was the first time a woman treated me for coffee or anything if I didn’t count my mother. It felt a little odd, but I appreciated the gesture.

We stopped in a small tavern with open doors and a lot of wood inside. I walked past it a thousand times and never even noticed it. We got a table in the back and ordered two glasses of wine. I was surprised by how interested she was in me and where I was from. I answered her questions as quickly as possible; where I was born, grew up, what my parents did, where I was living now, and why Eugene Lang. When I was done giving the CliffsNotes version of my boring life, I fished for the unabridged version of her story. She was born in Queens; her dad was black, and her mom was white with a touch of Japanese thrown in, which explained Marla’s exotic look. She was an only child, and her dad, a jazz musician and composed music, was on the road a lot and would spoil the hell out of her when he was home. They would go on “daddy” dates together, just the two of them, without mom, where she would get all dressed up. He would take her to lunch at the Russian Tea Room or for high tea at one of the hotels along 5th. He was just starting to make real money by scoring some European films and got some of his songs recorded by up-and-coming jazz artists – names that didn’t mean anything to me except for John Coltrane and Miles Davis. A heavy smoker and drinker, her father died of a massive heart attack at the age of 45. She was eight and remembered waking up the day after his funeral to a heavy downpour and running to get his raincoat to bring to where he was buried so he wouldn’t get wet. In high school, her mother remarried a guy Marla couldn’t stand, and when they moved to Boston, Marla stayed with her aunt in

Brooklyn. She finished high school and put two years of college under her belt before she got into retail, where she eventually started buying and selling clothes for various department stores. She bought some of the clothes she wore, but most were freebees. She also did a little catalogue modeling – "nothing serious." So, after a two-year hiatus from school, she decided to go back and get her B.A.

"Well, that explains all your cool clothes."

"Glad you think so."

"I do."

She stared at her wine. "At this point, I don't need the degree. It's just something I want to do."

"How many credits do you need?"

"Only about twelve, but I can only take a course or two a semester because of work. Which means at this rate, I should be done in another 30 years."

"What's the rush?"

"Exactly."

"You're 22?"

"Twenty-four."

"Ah, an older woman."

"As long as you don't say *old* woman," she offered, teasingly. "And how old are you?"

"Twenty-one."

"A mere child."

This was a playful response to mine but rattled me a bit since I didn't want her to end up thinking of me as a school buddy and nothing more, especially since I wanted more, a lot more.

"You dating anyone?" I asked, getting right down to it.

"You mean, do I have a boyfriend?" she said, sounding coy and playing with my question.

"Okay. Boyfriend."

"I don't have time for a boyfriend," she said, emphasizing boyfriend. "I work all the time and can just about fit in a class." A few minutes of silence, then, "Besides, I don't want to get tied down and get caught up in all the nonsense that goes with a relationship. I like to keep things loose. How about you? Dating any cute co-eds?"

She was playing with me, but at least she asked.

"Nope. Not seeing anyone co-ed or otherwise."

We both stared at each other for a few more seconds without saying anything until she broke the silence. "Didn't you say you live nearby?"

"Two blocks away on Eighth."

"Is it like a dorm? Do you have roommates?"

"No, it's not a dorm. It's a one-bedroom, and I live alone."

"Cool. Wanna show it to me? Or is it too messy?"

"Um, it's kinda clean."

"Okay, then show me what a downtown apartment looks like."

As we entered the building, Creech was sweeping the floor and only stopped to look at Marla. He smiled with his big, yellow tooth grin and greeted me with "Hellooooo. Mr. Kissel." I nodded and said to Marla, "It's on the fourth floor, unfortunately. There is no elevator."

When we were on the second flight and Creech was out of earshot, Marla said, "Who's that charming guy?"

"He's the super. Sorry about the leering. He's harmless."

We entered the apartment and stood in the living room. "So here it is," I announced as Marla looked around.

"It's really not bad," she said, sounding surprised. "It's clean too."

I chuckled. "Told you."

She leaned over and looked across the small courtyard to the other windows. "Bet you get to see some interesting things through those windows at night."

Unfortunately, 3J moved out soon after I moved in, but I did see a couple screwing, which proved strange to see in reality and not in a porn flick. There was also a couple that liked to walk around nude, smoke grass, and listen to the Grateful Dead. I could smell it every time it hopped on a breeze. I didn't want to talk about the other apartments since I was more concerned about what was going on in this one now. I was beginning to feel anxious about what to do next when she decided for me.

"I guess your bedroom is at the other end of the hall and there must be a bathroom right before it."

"Correct on both accounts."

"I'm going to go to the bathroom. While I'm in there, why don't you get under the covers, make yourself comfortable, and I'll come in as soon as I'm done, okay?"

She almost sounded like a parent telling a child what to do, though I was too stunned to say anything. With that, she gave me a peck on the cheek and guided me down the hallway. I went towards my bedroom as she went towards the bathroom. As soon as I heard her close the door, I hurried into my room and got out of my clothes, throwing them on a chair near the window. I checked my hair in the mirror over the bureau, then jumped into my bed and sat up against the wall with the sheet up to my waist, and waited.

After a few moments, I heard the bathroom door open, and Marla was standing nude in the doorway. Her breasts were big and round, so she seemed to follow behind them when she walked in. My eyes were moving quickly, racing over every inch of her to make sure I wasn't missing anything. She sat on the bed facing me with a faint smile, then lifted the sheet as if looking me over. "Not bad." I heard her say to herself - more good news. Before I knew what she was doing, she had leaned over and went down. For a brief moment, I braced myself, still scared from my Flora experience, but quickly relaxed. It was safe for me to close my eyes and enjoy it. It was better than I could have imagined, and right before I could embarrass myself, she got on top of me and started riding. It was amazing, and I never expected it, but how could I explain this to a close friend? I couldn't say I got lucky (funny how guys get lucky and women never do since they call all the shots) and screwed a beautiful woman. Then again, if this was another way of getting fucked, I was all for it. The rest was a blur if blur meant nothing ever felt this good in my entire life.

Later, we lay there quietly with Marla's head on my outstretched arm. It had grown dark. The window was open, and a strong smell of weed floated in on a breeze along with some Hendrix tunes. Marla, who I thought was dozing, shifted onto her stomach and propped herself up on her elbows. She looked me over and said, "Wow, you are really fair."

I looked down at myself, "Yeah, I guess. Can't help it though."

She quickly added, "I meant it as a compliment. It looks good."

"Thanks."

"As a matter of fact, I haven't been naked with anyone as fair as you since Nancy Piper."

I pushed myself up more in a sitting position against the wall. "Who is Nancy Piper?"

"She was my best friend in kindergarten."

"Oh, thought maybe you slept with her."

"I did on sleep overs."

"I mean..."

She giggled and stopped me. "I know what you mean."

I nodded.

"She showed me by accident that I was different...a different color."

"How?"

"We were out playing in her backyard and, like most kids, got covered in dirt, so her mom made us take a bath before dinner. We got in together and shared a washcloth, and when I saw how white Nancy's skin was, I started scrubbing mine even harder to get the dirt off my legs. When I saw that it wasn't coming off, I realized for the first time that I was black. No matter how hard I scrubbed my skin, it'd never be white like hers."

I nodded my head but wanted to protect the five-year old Marla from all the white kids, even the totally innocent five-year-old Nancy Piper. "But she didn't notice and stayed friends with you, right?"

"Oh, sure. But in high school, it became an issue."

"Whattya mean?"

"I went to a public school in Queens where most kids were black, but I wasn't black enough. They wouldn't deal with me because they said I was a white girl. And, I wasn't white enough for your people, who saw me as black. I didn't fit in anywhere there and decided I was neither black nor white. I was just Marla." She looked down at her nail and pushed back the cuticle on her thumb before looking up again.

"So, there you go, white boy," she added playfully. "A history of my racial past in five easy minutes."

I could listen, be sympathetic, but how could I really understand what it means to be resented because my skin color is different? I knew for some reason that her story would stay with me, even if she didn't.

"I'm the kind of person who wouldn't be welcomed on the streets of Bronxville... beautiful, wealthy, and white Bronxville."

Her tone had an edge to it this time. I wanted to diffuse it. "You're right. They aren't used to a beautiful, sexy woman walking through town."

"Good answer," she said, smiling again.

She was right; there were no blacks in Bronxville. It was the kind of town that had no sidewalks in front of neighborhood homes. This meant *we didn't want anyone from the outside walking our streets, looking in our windows, or enjoying what we bought with our money.* My neighbors didn't want to see strangers, and if they had to, it'd be better with a skin color that made them feel secure and understood.

She raised her voice an octave. "Could you imagine if you brought me home to meet your parents?" She didn't let me answer. "They would be so upset."

All I could come up with was a defensive, "No, they wouldn't."

The truth was, she was right. I could never remember a black person ever setting foot in our house for any reason. Once when I was fifteen, my mother and I were driving along when we finally spotted a parking spot and pulled in. We were about to get out of the car when an older, harmless-looking black man walked towards us on the sidewalk. When she spotted him, she made us stay in the car and pushed the lock button, securing the doors like some type of riot was inevitably coming. When the gentleman got closer, he smiled and touched the brim of his hat to acknowledge a passing white couple, clearly going out of his way to exude kindness, and strolled on. I was bothered by her overcautious assumption and said, "Mom, that wasn't necessary."

"You can never be too careful with these kinds of people," she said in her best I'm-teaching-you-about-life tone. Little did she know, she was teaching me much more – she was teaching me about prejudice and being fearful of anyone who doesn't look like you. She still used the word 'negro,' and my dad was fond of the expression "those people."

When I moved into the city, I became even more aware that Bronxville was a fortress with high walls to keep out the invading differences. It's why I loved the city and being at Lang since there were all kinds of people to be among and interact with, who came in all shapes, sizes, colors and from a city where Bronxville attitudes could never take root. The city was a place where black, brown, yellow, purple, and green lived and worked together, even though not always successfully, but they were at least trying. It was a city where I could be in bed with Marla Davis. If I was to see her again and again, and enough *agains* turned into a relationship, bringing her home to meet my parents would prove difficult.

She turned over on her back, and her breasts spread out over her chest while her nipples seemed to be floating on them. I couldn't keep my hands off, and as I reached over to touch them, she propped herself up on her elbows to look across at the clock on the nightstand next to me. She squinted her eyes, "What time does that say?"

"It's nine forty-five."

She jumped up and walked towards the bathroom and, without looking back, said, "Gotta get going. I have an early business meeting in Chicago and am taking an early flight out of Kennedy."

I enjoyed getting a good look at her ass. It shook a little as she walked. I was disappointed that she was leaving since I had hoped we could order something in and she would stay the night. I got up and back into my jeans and t-shirt, then walked to the living room while she put her clothes back on and got herself together in the bathroom. After a couple of minutes, she reappeared dressed and in fresh makeup. Her lips were red and looked even fuller. I wanted to kiss them, but thought better of it since I didn't know if this was goodbye for now or goodbye for good. "So, are you busy this Friday or Saturday?"

She smiled. "I'm always busy."

"Oh, okay." I might have sounded more disappointed than I intended and she picked up on it.

"Look, this was great, but I'm too busy with my job. I travel a lot and just can't get myself sidelined in a relationship or anything that resembles one. Let's just keep things loose, natural. If it happens again, great. If not, we had an awesome few hours tonight.

"Sure, if we hook up again, great. If not, we'll always have Paris."

This made her smile. "Good. Just as long as there are no expectations and we are clear."

She looked into my eyes, and I wanted to kiss her again but resisted. That would have been dumb, and I felt stupid enough.

"Are you listed?" she asked.

"Yeah."

"Well, I'm not." She searched through her bag. "Ah, here it is." She handed over her business card.

I looked down at it but didn't read it.

"Well, I'll see you in class," she said, walking to the door.

I opened it. She turned and smiled, then kissed me on the cheek.

"Yeah, see you in class," I answered.

I watched her walk to the staircase then closed the door, and listened to her walk down each step through the door. So, this is what it feels like when a girl acts like a guy. I didn't like it. It kind of hurt. In fact, it sucked.

Chapter Ten

I was walking down University after having dinner at a diner on 11th in early March. It had snowed two days earlier, and now it was rather warm, causing the snow to melt and kept the streets wet. The lights from the buildings and various shops reflected off the streets and streaked across them like abstract paintings hanging in the Museum of Modern Art. If there weren't bits of dirty snow left over, remnants of the later winter storm, you'd think it was spring or at least early March with a touch of May in it. As I walked, I was thinking about how I finally found an enjoyable class. It was an elective in advertising that I took simply because it fit into my schedule and not out of any desire to learn anything about the ad business. It was a copy writing class taught by a guy who headed up the creative department for Pruit and Gray, a firm on Madison somewhere in the 50s or 60s. He was impressed with the copy I wrote for fictional ads he assigned, particularly those pertaining to toothpaste, deodorant, toilet paper, ketchup, and feminine hygiene products. The professor during the first class reminded us that he wasn't an academic but rather an advertiser who taught this course during the spring semester on occasion for reasons he kept to himself. His name was Jack Sara. He insisted we call him by his first name, which took a little getting used to.

After we handed in our class assignments the week before, he asked me if I had ever considered becoming a copywriter. When I told him I hadn't given it any thought, he told me that when I graduated in May, I should put together a portfolio of my best copy, including what I had written for this class and see him at Pruit and Gray. He added he was always on the lookout for new talent. I thanked him, said I'd seriously think about it and left quite pleased to hear I was good at something I liked doing.

I started to think about Marla again. I always seemed to end up thinking about her. In a little over a year since coming to my apartment the first time, we had only gotten together a handful of times and always downtown. She usually called the shots, meaning we only got together when she wanted to and often for a cup of coffee or a quick dinner. At least twice, she said, let's go back to your place, which meant she wanted to have sex. If I suggested she stay over, she'd say she had a lot of work at home for her job or had to take an early flight. She was a buyer for a few expensive boutiques and had to fly to various cities to attend trade fairs, wholesale showrooms, and fashion shows. It helped her keep things between us casual as she wanted, and there were no signs to indicate that she was about to think of me as anything other than an occasional bonk buddy. I wanted a real relationship though. I wanted the kind of relationship where you go out to a movie on a Saturday night, wash and dry the dishes after supper you cooked together, talk about everything no matter how important or not, then say absolutely nothing to each other as you read *The New York Times* on a Sunday morning. However, it looked like I wasn't going to get it, at least not from her, and I wasn't going to push for it. If I did, I would just scare her away for good. So, if there were to be more between us, it would have to come from her.

Since I was never sure when I would see Marla after one of our brief get-togethers, or ever again for that matter, I kept myself busy with other girls who were mostly from school. They were all fine; they just weren't Marla. After a coffee, movie, or more sack time, I tended to let things slide and didn't call them back when I said I would. It's also why I had to sneak out of the diner earlier when I noticed a girl that I had gone out with about a month earlier.

I met her in the cafeteria at school, where everyone tended to share tables when it got crowded. She sat at my table and took out a wine book. I jokingly said that wine is what I should be studying, not psychology. It turned out she was taking an adult education class on wines. She was friendly with large dark eyes and skin so pale it was almost translucent. She said she was going to a wine bar near St. Mark's to order a glass of some burgundy that she would write a paper on. I was a little surprised when she invited me along and met her later at the Lazy Cork near Cooper Union. After a few laughs and two glasses on the subject of her paper, I walked her home. Her place was an old tenement on Avenue B across from Tompkins Square Park. Standing outside her building, I noticed an old-looking sign in the window on the ground floor that said: Dentist. "Glad to see you have a dentist in the building, although he must be pretty old by the look of that sign. Probably uses pliers when pulling teeth."

She didn't turn to look at the sign. "It's not a real sign. If you walk around the neighborhood, you'll notice a lot of old signs in the windows."

"Why's that?"

"They shot scenes from 'The Godfather' around here and placed signs in the windows to recreate the period."

"And they're still in the windows?"

"Yep. People left them as souvenirs, I guess."

"That's pretty cool. I've got to keep my eyes open for others."

"As a matter of fact, I watched them film the scene where Sonny beats his brother-in-law for hitting his sister. It was on 118th though, not here. James Caan is so sexy, but I think he enjoyed hitting that actor, who seemed nervous in between takes."

Before I could tell her that it might be my favorite film of all time and how lucky she was to see them film that scene, she said, "So are you going to put the moves on me or what?"

I liked what I heard, put my arm around her and went for her mouth. We stayed there with our mouths locked for a few minutes, and then she stopped and asked me to come up. She had a small, dark studio with one large window overlooking the park. She held my hand and guided me over to the couch where we sat and continued where we left off. Shortly after, she took her tongue out of my mouth and looked at me as if she were mad. In a loud whisper she said, "You want me to put it in my mouth. Don't you? Don't you?" She sounded like a little kid scolding another little kid. It was rather cute and playful, and I was ready to go. I just nodded my head yes. She helped me unbuckle my belt, pulled down my zipper, went down, and then went to work. And boy, did she work – stopping every few minutes to examine it as if it were the rarest of gems and whispering, "Beautiful, gorgeous." I never thought of it as beautiful or gorgeous, but I was happy to have it in working order.

After she sat up and I zipped up, we both sat there quietly and I realized I couldn't remember if her name was Beth, Bethany, or Betty. I decided to play it safe and not refer to her by name, but I did know that I wanted to get going.

She was the first to speak. "That was great."

"It certainly was," I answered and decided to begin my exit. "I should really get going."

She was leaning against me, but this made her slide over and sit upright. I started to adjust my shirt and belt and looked to see her staring at the floor with a rather anguished expression on her face.

"What's wrong? You okay?"

"I'm deciding."

"Deciding what?"

"If I should throw a tantrum or not."

I thought she was kidding. "Oh, really? A tantrum?"

She looked up at me. "Yeah, a tantrum."

She wasn't kidding, and I got a little nervous. "Why would you do that?"

"Because I wanted you to stay, sleep over, and make you breakfast in the morning. But now I'm thinking I should yell and start crying."

Rather than finding this unsettling, it saddened me, but I couldn't stay. I just couldn't be there any longer, so, I told her what Marla usually said to me.

"I have an early class tomorrow and still have a lot of work to do for it tonight along with finishing a paper for it."

This seemed to register with her. "Oh, okay. That's too bad. You'll have to stay next time and make it up to me."

"Sure. I owe you a sleepover."

She smiled. "Great."

With that, she walked me to the door. I gave her a quick kiss and said, "I'll call you in a few days."

"You better," she said warmly.

"Talk soon," I said and was gone.

Of course, I never called her back. I hadn't thought about her at all until I was in the diner and happened to look over and see her sitting at the counter next to the cash register when I went up to pay my bill. I hoped she wouldn't turn away from what she was reading and look my way. I handed over a ten-dollar bill and said, "thanks," when I got my change. I shouldn't have said anything, but it came out of my mouth from habit more than politeness. The sound of my voice made her lift her head and instinctually made me turn quickly and head for the door. I stopped when she called my name. I froze for a second before turning around to face her.

"Oh, hi." I still couldn't remember her name.

"You don't even remember my name, do you?"

"Of course, I do," I said, frantically trying to remember. Before I could embarrass myself more and come up with the wrong name, she shook her head back and forth as if to say, 'You're all the same,' then turned back to read her magazine. In a loud tone intended for me to hear she said, "Asshole."

With that, I became a dog who had been scolded, and with my tail between my legs, walked out the door. And it stayed between my legs as I headed down University. I really did feel like an asshole, a guilty asshole for not calling her back. I didn't because I wasn't interested in Beth or Betty or Bethany or whatever her name was, making me think of Marla again. I guess Marla doesn't really call me except on rare occasions because she isn't as interested in me as I am in her. That thought depressed me and made me feel worse. When I reached a magazine stand on the corner of 9th, I noticed the headline on the *Daily News* resting on a shelf all by itself. The other papers were sold out. It read, "White House Scandal." I walked over to flip the first few pages to read that Nixon's top aides could go to jail. I decided not to buy the paper and happened to look across the street in the direction of Knickerbockers. It was great restaurant I could never afford where a piano player would play jazz in the bar most nights. A few times when I walked by, I'd stop for a minute or two to listen to whoever was playing.

Before I was about to cross 9th, I noticed an attractive blonde walk out of the restaurant's front door. I couldn't help but notice her. She was quite tall, maybe close to six feet, and with her blonde hair piled up high, she may have been even taller. A long fur coat was open and draped over her shoulder, and underneath was a short dress that sparkled as it caught the reflections of the streetlights. She reminded me of the showgirls I'd seen on TV or in magazines and knew this would be the closest I'd ever get to one. She towered over the guy in back of her who followed her out the door. I wondered who the lucky guy was who landed her for the evening. At first, I couldn't get a good look at him, only noticing that he was on the heavy side and a good deal shorter. When he stepped around her to hail a cab, I got a good look at him and then froze. It was my father. He was talking and smiling back at her. He was wearing a white overcoat that made his stomach protrude out even farther than usual. He resembled a snowball with a cigar in his right hand. I didn't even try to hide behind a lamppost or car, nor did I try to see if there was a car nearby to crouch down behind. I was too surprised and just stood there watching rather than spying. My dad wasn't hailing a cab, but a black town car, that pulled up in front of them. He and the blonde laughed about something as he opened the door and followed her into the town car. I watched the black Lincoln car as if I were from another planet and had never seen one before and kept staring as it moved up University until it turned right onto 14th and was gone.

As I slowly turned to walk towards my apartment, thoughts started racing and ricocheting off the walls of my brain. Who is that blonde? Is she a friend or girlfriend? Is that what he meant when he told me that he loved coming into the city and came in often? The way he bullshits, she must think he's a multimillionaire. If it is a girlfriend, does my mother know? Of course, she doesn't. He would never tell her. My poor mom. Shit. I'm living a few blocks away, and he's out having dinner with some blonde. She is pretty good-looking.

Sexy even. What does she see in him? Maybe it's just a friend. Some friend's wife. Then where's her husband. Is he screwing her? Of course, he is. Maybe I should call him; *Hey Dad, saw you last night and you weren't with mom. Who is she? You sleeping with her? Mom know? Bet she doesn't. Mom's practically a saint. A fucking saint! How the fuck could you do this to her?*

By the time I reached my apartment, I knew I wasn't going to say anything to him, or at least not right away. When I lay down on my bed and faced the ceiling, I realized I really didn't know my father the way most of my friends knew theirs. I was never really that comfortable around him. Even as a kid, we never did anything together since he was at his office, playing golf, or maybe just playing. When I wanted to ask my father something or talk to him about something else, my mother would basically deal with it and tell me not to bother him. It seemed like she would have to make an appointment with him to meet in the living room and talk. Although I loved my father, I loved him from a distance.

Staring at a small crack on the ceiling above me, I admitted to myself that I didn't care that he seemed to be on a date with another woman and all that implies, but I did care that he was doing it behind my mother's back. She didn't deserve to be lied to or cheated on. Just because I loved my father, didn't mean I had to like him, and honestly, I hadn't really for years.

The next morning the phone rang loudly, waking me up. I looked over at my alarm clock – it was five a.m. I picked up the receiver and almost dropped it since I was more asleep than awake.

"Hello?"

"Benjamin?"

"Yeah. Who's this?"

"It's your mother."

It didn't sound like her. She sounded like she was calling from some far-off country. I cleared my head in a hurry and quickly sat up. I looked at the clock again. "Mom? Is everything okay?"

"I don't want you to be alarmed, but it's your father."

Now I was alarmed. "What's going on?"

"It seems your father had a slight stroke."

"Stroke! How bad? Is he okay?"

"He's fine. It... it was very mild."

I didn't think there were mild strokes. "Where is he?"

"He's at NYU's Hospital. I'm here now but need to go home and get some things for him since he'll be here another day or two for observation. He can't live without his cologne and wants his pajamas and toiletries."

"So, he's going to be okay?"

"Oh, yes. His doctor said so. But your father will need to change his diet and lose some weight."

I started to feel better after the initial shock of hearing he was in the hospital and thinking all strokes were fatal. "Where was he when it happened?"

"He was at a retirement dinner for a doctor friend of his here in the city."

"Who brought him to the hospital?"

"He brought himself. During dinner he said he experienced some slurred speech and didn't understand some common words. Being in the medical field, he knew the signs so he became concerned and brought himself to the nearest hospital, which was NYU."

There was no mention of a tall, attractive blonde woman who might have taken him to the hospital. At that moment, it wasn't important. I was relieved it was a minor stroke and grateful it wasn't worse. She said she would meet me in the lobby as soon as I could get there.

She would go home to get the things he needed and I could go to stay with him for a little while.

I didn't shower and got dressed in record time, before hopping in a cab, which was a first for me. I always took subways or an occasional bus since cabs were too expensive. I needed to get there in a hurry, and a cab was the only logical ride. As we drove over to 1st Avenue, I got to see the city in a way I hadn't before. It was a little past 6 a.m. now, and there was hardly any traffic except for the trucks making deliveries or a street cleaner – though it never looked like they cleaned much of anything. Most stores and shops were closed except for the occasional 24-hour diner. This was another first, watching the city wake with sleep in its eyes.

My mother was waiting, as planned, in the lobby at the hospital. She looked exhausted. I told her I didn't like her driving home but was pleased to hear that she had a car service bring her down and was picking her up to take her home. I told her to nap before hurrying back, but she said she had missed mass and needed to try and make the seven-thirty. Father Cavendish would be saying it. It sounded like an old movie she had seen on TV numerous times: the seven-thirty mass starring Father Cavendish. It was more important for her to go home and rest, though I knew it would be futile to try and talk her out of going to church, so I didn't try. As she was leaving the lobby, she kissed me and whispered, "Thank God your father will be fine." I nodded, walked her out to a black town car, similar to the one my father and the blonde got in only last night and told her to rest before returning. When I went back into the hospital, I realized I forgot to ask my mother what room my father was in, so I checked at the front desk and headed up to room 6B.

When I came out of the elevator on the sixth floor, there were signs with arrows pointing in the directions of various room numbers. My father's room was located at the end of a long hallway. As I walked, I made sure not to look into the rooms with open doors. When visiting a friend in high school who had his appendix removed, I learned that if you are nosy enough to look into a hospital room as you walk past, you deserve to see things you wished you hadn't, which are often hard to forget. I kept my head straight and only looked up occasionally at the room numbers until I reached my father's and entered slowly in case he was sleeping. He wasn't. He was sitting up with the help of a few pillows. As usual, and even in the hospital, his hair was perfectly combed and slicked back. Except for the hospital gown, which I'm sure he hated, he looked as good as he did the last time I saw him as he was exiting Knickerbockers. He greeted me with a big smile and almost sang my name, "Benjamin!"

I was relieved he looked so good. I had a strong urge to a kiss him on his cheek or forehead, but that would've been weird. We were never touchy-feely with each other, and any kind of physical affection would have been awkward and embarrassing for both of us. Instead, I stood at the foot of his bed.

"You look good. Thought you might be sleeping."

"I feel good, Son. As you can see, I'm wide-awake. I hope you saw your mother. She said she was going to meet you in the lobby."

"I saw her. She's on her way home."

"Probably on her way to church first."

"Probably."

"She'll return later with a few things I need, including my own pajamas."

"I figured you couldn't stand hospital gowns."

He looked down at them. "They're awful."

"Yep. The worst."

He looked up. "So, how are you doing?"

"I'm fine, but more importantly, tell me how you ended up here."

"Didn't your mother tell you? Fill you in?"

"She did. She said you were at a dinner last night and experienced slurred speech and memory loss."

"So, there it is in a nutshell, Son. Don't believe it needs retelling."

My father never wanted to admit, for some reason, he was ever sick. If he had a bad cold, he'd say it was the sniffles. If he had the flu, he'd say it was a bad cold. I'm not sure of the reasoning behind it; that's simply how he was. Even if he weren't feeling well, he would never admit that to anyone. I should've known he wouldn't tell me anymore than what he told my mother about his symptoms last night and how he got to the hospital. For a second, I toyed with the idea of saying I saw him coming out of Knickerbockers with a sexy, tall blonde. I quickly let that idea go. Now was not the time, and it certainly wasn't the place. I had no desire to add to his health issues. I wanted him up on his feet again and back home. "So, do you have to take any medication or be on a special diet? How long are they keeping you here?" Saying "special diet" was as close as I could get to saying "losing weight." He would always get annoyed if his weight was mentioned and always insisted he was in excellent health for a man who "wasn't meant to be thin."

"They're not going to put me on a special diet, but I am getting some medication. I'll be able to leave tomorrow."

"That's great." It sounded like it really was minor, even though I'm sure they wanted him to lose more than a few pounds. I stayed for about another half hour when an intern came in with a tray of needles and vials to perform a few blood tests. My father said with my mother returning in a few hours, there wasn't any necessity for me to stay. I told him if he needed anything else to call since I'm only a few blocks away, and if not, I'd come to Bronxville to see him on the weekend.

I didn't know what I expected to find when I got to the hospital, but I was exhausted with relief when I left. He was going to be fine. Outside the hospital on 1st Ave, I hailed a cab since I promised my father that I would take one, and when I got in and fell back against the seat, I happened to look over at the doorway entrance to the hospital and notice a black town car pull up in front of it. I thought it might be my mother until the back door opened, and out stepped a sexy, tall blonde with her hair piled on top of her head. She hurried up the steps, and as she entered the building, I suspected she was on her way up to Room 6B.

Chapter Eleven

I think her name was Nina. I met her in between drinks at the Madison Pub, an old gin joint just north of 79th and Madison Ave. You had to walk down a few steps to enter through its old wooden doors at the bottom of a three-story brownstone. It's been open since the mid 20's. It is totally out of place now sitting among the office buildings, expensive shops, and apartments, as well as the Carlyle Hotel a few blocks down. It's the kind of place that made you think just for a moment the city had a conscience and didn't forget, or neglect, its past just because there are greedy landlords are chasing higher rents and putting places like the Pub out of business. Inside it was dark, narrow, and paneled with names, some famous, some not, carved into the tables and walls. There was a jukebox with songs by Glenn Miller and Luis Prima broken and silent for years, and a few boxing photos over the bar. The bartender who had been working there for what seemed forever, liked to talk about all the famous folks who came in over the years including Ed Sullivan, Rex Harrison, the senator Pat Moynihan. Woody Allen came once but turned around and walked out when asked to remove his hat. As far as he knew, Woody never came back. Aside from its inexpensive, strong drinks, the Pub was known for burgers that might have been a touch better than the burgers at Joe Juniors. It was a debate I carried on with myself each time I came in.

I had come here a few times since I began working at Pruit and Gray as a junior copywriter for the past four months. After graduation, I took Jack Sara up on his suggestion to put together a portfolio and interviewed at his agency. I met with him again and then interviewed with one of his partners before landing the job. I figured since Jack liked my copy and myself, the interview was just a necessary formality. I became part of a creative team. They put me with an older, experienced writer in his forties named Bumpy Stackhouse. Bumpy liked to drink, and often came to work hung over, but the account executives never cared since he seemed to work best that way. He never told anyone his real name, but he did say he got his nickname in college from bumping into walls or anything that got in his way after a few drinks or what he called, "a few pops." So, I worked with Bumpy on brochures, leaflets, jingles, beer, toothpaste, laundry detergent, aspirins, socks in New York City, local radio stations in Westchester, print ads, and even a small car dealership in Yonkers. When we started to work on a laxative script, Bumpy said, "You simply have to write shit to sell shit. It's business." And that's what we did. Even though less than one percent of my copy ever made it before the client, I enjoyed the work. That was the downside – the upside was I got paid even if the client never used a word of what I wrote and they usually didn't.

Some of the creatives would end up at the Pub with Bumpy leading the charge on Thursday nights. Thursdays were also payday, which meant if you drank too much, you just had to get through Friday, one of the obstacles in front of the weekend when you would finally recover. At first, I resisted since I wasn't much of a drinker, but I ended up getting to know some of the other copywriters better. If I were truly honest with myself, it was one less night where I had to go home to an empty apartment. One night, I was drinking 7 and 7s, and the bar was packed and filled with smoke. Somehow, I ended up talking to Nina next to the jukebox. I first thought she worked at the agency but found out that she worked at a small shop a few blocks up on Madison that sold fancy soaps and perfumes. She had come to the Pub with a girl she worked with, but talked to a guy at the opposite end of the bar.

"Here's our newest fragrance," she said, as she leaned into me and tilted her head to the side for me to smell her neck. I guess I was a little more buzzed than I thought because when I leaned over to smell her fragrance, my nose hit her neck, making her giggle. She seemed buzzed too. She was about my height with straight hair that was cut short, but not as short as the print dress she was wearing. I thought she was cute, a word I had learned that women, for some reason, didn't think a compliment, so I made sure never to use it. She had a dark olive complexion, and when she told me her last name, it was so long I knew I would never remember it. A few drinks later, she wasn't just cute, but the most beautiful exotic woman I had ever seen. The liquor fueled the conversation and kept it flowing – even the most mundane bits of information shared were engaging, informative and at times, luminous. In short, we were shitfaced. Nina wanted to know where I lived and if it was a small apartment because of how important space was in such a crowded city. She repeated space so many times, I told her she was beginning to sound like an astronaut. She didn't find that comment humorous. She explained it was just that she was sure she lived in the smallest apartment in the city – a studio off of Lex just a few blocks away. She then offered to show it to me just to prove it really was the smallest! Of course, seeing it sounded like a brilliant idea so, I accepted her offer.

Outside of the Pub, the cool air cleared my head a bit. We both put our arms around each other, not out of affection, but to keep ourselves steady as we walked over towards Lex and 76th. We were quiet, but the liquor we consumed wasn't, and it seemed to find everything funny. It was as if the city turned into a comedian, a giant Henry Youngman doing his nightclub act of one-liners:

the one about the bus that rattled across town; the taxi blowing its horn at a guy on a bike; the dog on a leash that almost knocks the woman over who is walking it; the couple who had too much to drink trying to cross Park Ave. We laughed at all of them.

We made it to Nina's place, a small prewar apartment building with no doorman on the corner of 76 Street and Lex. I was grateful for the elevator since walking up three flights of stairs to her studio seemed, at the moment, a difficult task to negotiate. In front of her door, we stood wobbling as she hunted for her keys. It took a little over a year, it seemed, before she said, "got 'em," then held up her keys, then waved them back and forth as if she just caught a fish and was showing it off. Once we got inside, she stopped to spread open her arms as if she were greeting the sunrise and exclaimed, "Here, it is the tiniest apartment in New York City." She wasn't kidding. It might have been. Across from the door, her bed was against the wall, and I imagined that if we fell, our heads would hit the foot of it. To the left, was a sink and a small counter with a hot plate that served as the kitchen. To the right, a curtain was pulled back that exposed the toilet. She turned to me, and I said, "You're right. I've been in bigger closets." Before we could exchange any more pleasantries, we lunged at each other as if trying to devour each other's mouths and almost tore each other's clothes off in the process. I kept thinking I'm going to have sex with the most beautiful, exotic woman on the face of the earth with the last name so long it could reach New Jersey. I kept trying to get her clothes off, and she kept trying to help me, but all the booze was making it all rather complicated. We finally got out of them then fell onto the bed.

We were much too wasted to accomplish much. There was some licking here, sucking there, rubbing of this and some of that until we fell on our backs panting and faced the ceiling. After a minute or two, Nina turned to me. "Hey, do you want to see something really cool?"

"Sure. What do you have in mind?"

"I can make myself come."

"That doesn't really sound weird. Most everyone can do that."

"Of course, they can, but can they do it without using any hands?"

"You mean like a magic stick? Who are you, Kreskin?"

"Who's that?"

"The guy who does all that abracadabra stuff on TV."

"No. It's just something I learned to do on my own since fingers, penises and dildos don't get the job done."

I was starting to sober up more. "Well, as you can see, I'm a fingers and penis person and don't have a dildo with me."

"You have to watch since you won't see this too often...or ever," she said as she moved to the foot of the bed. She then laid down and faced me.

I propped myself up against the pillow to watch the magic show. Nina was even thinner than I thought, with small breasts that were cone-shaped and pointed up at the ceiling. Her skin was a dark olive color, but not darker than Marla's. Fuck Marla. I was training myself not to think of her since I only saw her once for coffee during the last few weeks after graduation. The other few times we were supposed to meet, she always offered excuses about writing a paper or traveling for work. So, I figured it would be healthier for me not to contact her and give up any notions of a real relationship between us.

Nina smiled at me and said, "Are you ready?"

"I'm just waiting for you to get things going." I was actually intrigued since I had never seen a girl masturbate before, with or without hands.

"Ok then. Here we go." She kept her hands at her sides, crossed her right leg over her left, and squeezed them together before releasing. She did this a few more times before switching legs, placing her left over the right, and repeated. She started breathing heavier but didn't close her eyes; instead, she kept staring at the ceiling as if she were in a trance. I began to find the whole endeavor a little creepy rather than sexy like I thought it would be. Her legs suddenly locked together as her entire body stiffened. Her eyeballs rolled back into her head until they disappeared, and only the whites of her eyes were visible. She let out a loud moan, and her body went limp.

I waited for her to say something, but she didn't, so I touched her ankle and called her name. "Nina?" She didn't respond. "Nina?" I said a little louder, but she still didn't respond. She was out cold. Maybe it was the booze, or she always passed out after she came, or it was a combination of both. In any event, the woman who lived in the smallest apartment in the city and was the most exotic woman I have ever seen after a few drinks, and with a last name so long it could reach Jersey, came and went. I kept looking at her while she was passed out. I don't know if I wasn't thinking much about anything, or avoiding what I was discovering about myself to be true. The reason I was in bed with a woman I didn't know was partly because I had too much to drink, and partly because I didn't want to go back to my empty apartment because I was feeling lonely. It was a feeling that was becoming more problematic over the past couple of months. Like a few of the other women I didn't know and had sex with, Nina wasn't the answer to filling that void. In fact, it had the opposite effect – I found that having sex with someone I had not even the slightest emotional attachment to made me feel empty and hollow, which was a lot worse than just being lonely. It was right there that I decided to leave it behind. I kissed Nina – who was still out cold – on the forehead and headed out the door.

Everything on Lex looked a little out of focus, and a major headache was taking up residence right behind my eyes. I was a little unsteady on my feet as I walked down a block to the subway on 77th. The city seemed rather quiet tonight as opposed to most other nights when it was noisy and seemed rather irritated with so many people on its streets and sidewalks. I often wondered what would happen if everyone in the entire city decided to come out at the same time – every high-rise and brownstone drained of its residents. Everyone would be crushed together, unable to move and make the city feel like a giant subway car in rush hour. I waited for the 6 train for only a few minutes when it pulled into the station. All the cars were covered in graffiti, and the one I got into had so much covering it, it looked like an abstract painting, but more de Kooning than Picasso.

I got off at Union Square, walked down Broadway, and then over on 10th since I liked walking past the old brownstones dressed in their original brick with windows so large you can drive a car through them. If the lights are on in any of them at night, I always looked in as I passed just to see how the twentieth century adjusted itself to a nineteenth-century living or dining room. As I was peering in a window, I was startled when a guy stepped in front of me. We were standing near a streetlight so I could see him quite clearly – I didn't like the fact that he was blocking me from walking. "Excuse me, man," I said as I started to walk around him, but he moved in front of me to prevent me from going any farther. I stopped, knowing things might not go well if I tried to pass. He was exactly my height, around my age, and had shoulder-length, greasy black hair and a Fu Manchu mustache that was rather sparse. A torn shirt was visible under his plaid jacket with wide lapels that was in style, but this one looked as if he cleaned the street with it and was wearing platform shoes that I hoped would go out of style tomorrow. Oh yeah, he smelled of booze and sweat.

"What's the rush, my friend," he said, grinning.

"No rush. It's late and I just want to go home."

"It ain't late. Relax."

I still had some leftover booze in me or I wouldn't have said, "Yeah, it's late. Besides, I was taught never to speak to strangers, and since I don't know you, that makes you a stranger."

This made the grin leave his face. He took out a knife from his jacket pocket.

"Okay, wise ass," he said, more nervously than threatening, "give me any money you got and that watch you're wearing." Then he held up the knife, "See the point I'm trying to make."

The point he was making was clear, and if it were another night, I would have forked over my watch and the thirty bucks I had, but the booze spoke up again, "You picked the wrong guy. I don't have a dime on me."

He stared at me for a few seconds, looking both nervous and annoyed, then raised his voice. "The fucker says he don't have any dough."

A voice from behind me answered, "I heard him."

I had no idea there was anyone behind me; whomever it was preceded to walk around me and stood next to Jim Bowie. We looked at each other. He was also my age, a little weathered with thin, curly blonde hair and wearing a jean jacket buttoned to his neck with the collar turned up. He had a thick beard but was not thick enough to hide the face of Chauncy Dance. I was both shocked and relieved. We stared at each other in a moment of recognition that felt more like an hour. All kinds of questions raced through my head, starting with *what the fuck happened to you?* Instead, I said nothing, nor did he. After the brief moment of shock, asking how he's been while he was in the process of mugging me seemed rather inappropriate. From the look of things, it was evident that not much had gone well for him over the last four years. I then wanted to help out my old high school pal, but not add to the embarrassment that was so evident on his face. I planned on saying, "I have thirty bucks on me – it's yours," which would have been straightforward and fitting for the occasion. Instead, I ended up sounding more like St. Francis, taking pity on some leper on the streets of Rome, "I have thirty dollars and I really want you to have it."

As soon as I said it, he looked down. He said to his partner, "Put the fucking blade away. Let's go." sounding both disgusted and annoyed. With that, he turned and started to run across the street. Jim Bowie didn't put his blade away but kept staring at me in confusion, not understanding why they weren't going to take my money. He yelled after Chauncy, "What the fuck are you doing, man? He's got thirty bucks!" He shot a quick glance over his shoulder to see if Chauncy was going to stop and come back. When he didn't, Bowie yelped, "Fuck." then put his knife in his coat pocket before taking off after Chauncy, slipping as he headed across the street on those dumb platform shoes that obviously weren't conducive for muggings.

"Stay in touch," I called out after him as he made his way around the corner.

I stood there watching to make sure he was gone, then started walking again. I was only three blocks away, but when I reached 5th, I was so wrapped up in my thoughts, I started walking uptown. How did the smartest guy at St. Luke's from a wealthy family end up probably on drugs and mugging people? I wondered what happened to his wife and kid? Couldn't his father forgive him for knocking up his girlfriend and give him a job? I knew those were questions I'd never know the answer to. Thinking about all of it scared me more than I should have been when I was getting mugged at knifepoint. Although the knife was in the other guy's hand, Chauncy was a lot more dangerous. He was the smartest guy I knew, who was supposed to have an Ivy League college degree and successful career in his future until a few poor choices got in the way. Looking at him was like looking into a broken mirror; I could make out some of my reflection, but not enough to recognize my face. *As long as I couldn't recognize myself, I'd be fine*, I thought. By the time I reached Fourteenth Street, I had realized I was walking the wrong way. I turned around and headed back in the right direction.

Chapter Twelve

Over the past couple of years, the price of microwave ovens had been coming down, and kitchen models have begun to outsell gas ovens. C.K. Appliances, who manufactured microwaves, wanted to tap into what they felt was a new demographic: single young women who were part of the Woman's Liberation Movement. Women were now applying to medical, law, and business schools and seeking jobs traditionally dominated by men. C.K. wanted to get a leg up on the competition and appeal to the "new woman" who had no time to cook, or *wanted* to. But with the low-cost microwaves, it was the quickest way for this new workforce to fortify themselves with hot, nutritious foods from their own kitchens as they headed off into a world they were trying to change.

Our art director pitched it to Bumpy and me, who had to write copy for an ad in *Ms.* magazine, the first magazine created, owned, and operated by women. It was extremely popular, had a wide circulation, and I was just happy to be working on it with Bumpy – except around noon time when he said he was going out to "drink lunch," which meant he probably wouldn't be back for the rest of the day. As the afternoon wore on, I wasn't pleased with any of the copy I was coming up with and was more than willing to take a break when Jack Sara called me into his office.

When I walked in, he was on the phone and motioned for me to sit in the chair in front of his desk. The window was open, and since it was near rush hour, the traffic on Madison was rather loud.

As soon as he hung up the phone, he said, "How would you like to get laid?"

I was startled for a second. What kind of question was that? Of course, I wanted to get laid – most guys my age did. Even though I promised myself no more going to bed with women I had no emotional attachments to, and this was the boss asking. I'd have to take one for the team, "Of course. Do you have someone in mind?"

He looked at me, then raised his voice a couple of octaves higher. "I don't think you heard me clearly with all the traffic noise coming in," he said as he got up to close the window. "What I asked was, how would you like to go to L.A.?"

"Oh, yeah, sure." This was even more surprising.

"Good, because it wasn't a question."

Of course, I wanted to go to L.A. I had never even been on a plane before but was eager to find out why I was going.

He sat back down behind his desk. "I'm sure you know who Mickey Green is."

"I'm pretty sure most everyone does."

Mickey Green was one of the more popular comedians in the country. Over the past few years, he made many appearances on the *Merv Griffin Show* and *The Tonight Show,* where he does his stand-up act. Mickey is in his late fifties with a large nose, greased back, gray hair, and always dressed in a black suit, white shirt, and black tie. He resembles a mortician rather than a comic. He tells short, self-deprecating one-liners, always ending with his catch phrase "give me a break" after the punch line. He got even more popular when HBO filmed his ninety-minute stand-up routine where he could say anything and not have to worry about being censored. When my parents first got cable, it was strange hearing anyone curse like that on TV, but Mickey was crude and even funnier. After that, his popularity grew when he wrote and starred in a movie naturally called *Give Me A Break* that amounted to a hit at the box office.

"Okay, this is why you're going to L.A. AT&T wants to get small businesses to come back, and I need to launch a new ad campaign. Mickey's people got wind of this, and he contacted them saying that he is a small business." This made Jack smile. "I guess he wants to star in some TV spots for them."

I was surprised Jack was sending me. "What do you want me to do out there?"

"I'm getting to that. Look, AT&T knows Mickey is way too crude a comic and feels he is not in keeping with their brand and image or, for that matter, the type of customers they're trying to attract."

"Who are they trying to attract?"

"Basically, upper-middle-class white guys who play golf or tennis on weekends and are driven to succeed."

"Mickey doesn't appeal to that demographic?"

"Of course not. They know he is blue-collar and vulgar, but he's famous and hot now, so just in case he comes up with something they can use, it might just payoff. So, they want us to test the water with him."

"Test the water? How exactly do we do that?"

"Yeah, that's where you come in. You are going out for ten days to work with him writing TV spots. See if he has any ideas they can remotely use, whip it into shape, and clean it up for use on the small screen. I'm sending you because there probably isn't a fucking snowball's chance in hell that any of his ideas will fly. I'm not about to pull any of my writers who are working on solid campaigns that need to be completed and send them out there to waste time. And since you're the new guy and low man on the scrotum pole, I'm sending you out to keep AT&T happy." He looked at me for a few seconds, then added, "Besides, you never know. Any questions?"

This sounded like a win-win opportunity for me. I get to meet and work with Mickey Green in L.A., and I was going to try like fucking hell to come up with scripts AT&T would want to use even if the chips were stacked against me. I could make a name for myself in the industry, ask for a raise, and no longer be the low man on the scrotum pole. I was excited. "When do I leave?"

"We booked you a flight out of Kennedy on Sunday morning and a room at the Beverly Hills Hotel where Green is staying and living. So, finish up what you're working on with Bumpy, and he'll keep working on the account until you get back. Keep your receipts for the meals and any extras."

It was music to my ears. "Great. Will do."

"If you have any questions during the week, you have my number. Just keep in mind that we don't expect much of anything to come out of this."

With that, I got up and walked back to my office. I was too pumped and excited to concentrate on microwaves, although I tried. I kept thinking about this great deal that had fallen into my lap. In six days, I'll be on a plane for the first time and on my way to L.A. – all expenses paid. It sounded more like a vacation than work. How difficult could it be to write with Mickey? He wrote his own jokes and a movie. I'll bring some ideas, blend them with his, and we'd bang it out together. We'll be Lennon and McCartney, Jagger and Richards; the ideas will flow – except we'll be writing a commercial instead of songs. And since we only had ten days, we would have to begin working almost as soon as I landed at LAX.

I couldn't keep my mind on the *Ms.* Ad. Of course, Bumpy never returned from lunch, and now it was almost 9 p.m. I packed it in and decided to walk home as far as I could since I was so wound up about L.A. Walking in the city always calmed me down or helped stimulate ideas for ads I was working on. Since I didn't eat dinner, I thought I might stop somewhere along the way. If I got tired, I'd just hop on the nearest subway. As I headed down Madison, I was feeling the best I had felt in a long time. I was excited about leaving for L.A. on Sunday and all the promise it held. Right before I reached 57th Street, I saw Marla walking out of a restaurant. She made immediate eye contact when she saw me. This would've added to my great mood, except that she was with some guy. Her usual friendly smile spread across her face.

"Benjamin!"

"Hey," I said as I shot a glance at her friend's face then down to his hand to see if he was holding hers – he wasn't. He looked older, maybe in his early to mid-forties, with a receding hairline and long, curly shoulder-length hair. He was ugly. Okay, maybe not ugly, but there wasn't anything special about him that I could see.

A few more minutes of awkward silence followed what felt like an hour. "This is my friend..."

She of course said his name, and of course, I didn't hear it. "Hi," I said as I put out my hand to shake his. He smiled and said something. "So, what are you guys up to?" I said although it was obvious since they just came out of a restaurant – probably a romantic dinner for two.

"Oh, we just had a quick drink and needed to catch up on some things," said Marla.

I think she implied she wasn't on a date for some reason, or there was nothing serious going on with them. I was glad she was trying to get that across, and relieved she inferred that they weren't a couple. At least, that's what I hoped she was trying to do.

"Where are you coming from, or going to?" She asked after a few more moments of more awkward silence.

"I just left work."

"Wow, you're working late."

"We work odd hours," I said. Then I added, "But I'm on my way to meet someone for a drink." I didn't plan on saying that, but I wanted Marla to think I had a social life and I might be meeting a woman instead of returning to my empty apartment. I looked down at my watch but discovered I wasn't wearing one and said, "I better get going. Don't wanna be late."

"Sure. I've got to get back too."

Another good sign. She didn't say, "We've got to get back." I looked at her friend or whatever he was and said, "Nice meeting you."

"Nice meeting you," he said, although it didn't sound like he meant it.

Marla leaned in and gave me a peck on the cheek. "I'll give you a call."

"Okay, great," I said although I felt like adding 'before a decade goes by.'

After that interaction, we went in opposite directions. I was feeling conflicting emotions. I was pleased to see her, and she looked great, but she might have been on a date, which pissed me off. Since I had not been trying to think about her and was so sick of her excuses about not getting together, I was mad that I had bumped into her at all. I felt like I had to get mad at someone or something, so I got mad at the city. Why, in this city, where there are thousands of people on the sidewalks – faceless, nameless New Yorkers who know nothing about you nor you them – do we seem to bump into the people we know and don't want to see? I wasn't sure if this qualified as a random act of violence, but I would argue that it came close.

Although I wasn't tired, I decided to hop on the subway at 51st and Lexington because I needed to get home and crash. After running into Marla, I was in no mood to get something to eat, but by the time I walked into my apartment, the mood lessened, and I was hungry. I stopped in front of the refrigerator, knowing full well a wasteland was waiting for me when I opened the door. I foolishly peered in at a container of Chinese food I ordered a few weeks ago. I hadn't thrown it away for some reason and now I was scared to open it. I reached for it and dropped it in the trash. On the shelf below it was a loaf of bread, and since I never cooked and lost my recipe for toast, I hadn't opened it. Even if I did, there was nothing to put on it. There was a bottle of ketchup and a bottle of beer. I had to put something in my stomach and ketchup was obviously out of the question. I reached for the Budweiser. I walked into the living room and threw my jacket on the couch before I sat down. I reached over and turned on the radio. I kept it on the same channel, 102.7, that played the best stuff. Tonight, Scott Muni, who used to be on one of those annoying AM stations when I was in grammar school before FM became popular, was playing new album releases. Joni Mitchell was singing about falling in love again from her latest album, *Court and Spark*, which came out about a month ago. I loved her but didn't care for the songs I heard from this album. *Blue* was still my favorite. After the song was over, Muni came back on and said he'd be playing the new Stones album, *It's Only Rock n' Roll,* and followed it with a few cuts from an album *The Heart of Saturday Night* by Tom Waits, a singer who I'd never heard before. Muni was excited about George Harrison who was beginning his first concert tour since The Beatles in '66. I liked a lot of his solo stuff except for the bubble gum sounding crap McCartney was doing with *Wings*. I figured they would have patched things up by now, and continued to hold on to that hope. It would only be a matter of time before they realize that the sum is much greater than its parts when it comes to The Beatles. I was convinced of it.

I looked down at what I was wearing and knew I had to get out of the clothes I was wearing all day. I got up, and as I headed towards my bedroom, the phone rang. I picked up the receiver and sat down on the edge of the bed.

"Benjamin?"

"Yeah. Speaking."

"It's Marla."

"The sound of her voice made me fall back on the bed. "This is a surprise."

"Really?"

"Yeah, really" I said rather coolly, although the simple sound of her voice was giving me a hard-on.

"Look, I was wondering if we could meet? I'd like to talk a few things over with you."

I glanced at the clock. "It's ten-fifteen. I figured you'd still be on your date."

"It wasn't a date. It was just a quick dinner with an old friend. If it's not too late, could you meet me in about an hour?"

This made me sit up. She wasn't on a date and wanted to meet tonight. If it were 4 am I would meet her. The suaveness I was trying to fabricate in my voice quickly evaporated. "Yeah, I can meet. Where?"

"Here."

I knew she couldn't have meant her place. "Where's here?"

"My apartment."

Her apartment. Another surprise. "Okay, your apartment."

"It's 115 East Sixty-Fifth on the corner of Second Ave. 1B on the 15th floor."

"See you in about an hour," I said, placed the receiver down, stared at the phone for a few seconds, and then jumped up. I took a quick shower, got dressed, and hurried out to hail a cab. The driver got me uptown in record time since he drove like he was in the car chase scene from *The French Connection.* When I got to her apartment, I looked at my watch and saw I was twenty minutes early. Even though I was anxious to see her and hear what was on her mind, I didn't want her to know that, so I went to the diner across the street. I took a seat at the counter and ordered a cup of coffee with a piece of apple pie. I forgot I was hungry until I wolfed it down completely, then ordered another. I checked my watch again then paid the cashier before hurrying over to Marla's building.

Surprisingly, I was right on time when I rang her doorbell on the 15th Floor. She answered the door wearing only a smile and a huge plaid shirt. She leaned up on her toes, and kissed me on the cheek before moving so I could enter. Her apartment was decorated almost entirely in white. A long narrow kitchen was to the right of the front door with a living room on the left. A white couch shaped like a horse shoe was placed against the wall next to some bookshelves. A large picture caught my eye, but then I realized it was actually a window with a view of the 59th Street Bridge. It was only about four blocks away but was so close it almost became a piece of art she had custom made for the room. Unlike mine, this was an adult's apartment, which looked like a college student was crashing in it. I walked over to the window, taking the view in. "This is a really beautiful place."

"Thanks. Glad you like it," she said from behind me.

The only drawback was the noise from the traffic on 2nd Ave. Even at this height and late hour, it was noticeable. I could only imagine how loud it must be during the day or at rush hour. I guess that's why I didn't hear her walk up next to me until she grabbed my hand.

"Let me show you the rest," she said as she led me over to a small hallway. "Here is the bathroom," she pointed out as we passed it on our right, "and this obviously is the bedroom." She led me in and stopped next to the bed. It, too, was decorated almost entirely in white with a smaller window and an air conditioner underneath it.

She took my face in her hands and pulled me down so she could kiss me. I began unbuttoning her shirt, and she started working on mine. She stopped to watch me as I pulled my shirt off, my chest felt like it was blazing and pounding, but it was her chest I couldn't take my eyes off of. Her breasts seemed to have grown even larger than the last time I saw them. I slid out of my pants in record time, and she immediately leaned over to start pleasuring me. I watched her for a few seconds before I had to lean my head back with my eyes closed and started praying – asking God to help me hold it. I could always hold it, but now I felt ready to pop, and this was my hour of need. *Please don't let me cum!* I had a lot more work to do. Suddenly, she stopped, then stood up, and the feeling of blasting off passed – I could regroup. She turned, and as she pulled the covers down on her bed, I couldn't help but look at her butt. I felt like I hadn't seen it in years. I can't say I could describe it, but I saw, at that moment, it was the closest a guy like me would ever get to perfection.

I followed her onto the bed as she laid down and turned on her back. I pulled her under me, and she guided me in between her legs. It was tighter than I remembered, although it wasn't the time to remember anything, or even think, for that matter. When I couldn't hold it anymore, I let out a loud moan; Marla quickly followed with her own. Just like that, it was over. I just stayed on top of her like a wet blanket and wanted to stay there forever. Instead, I rolled over onto my back, and she leaned over to drape her arm and leg over me.

Just like the 59th Street Bridge outside her window holding onto Queens, Marla's arm resting across my chest was a type of bridge connecting her to me for the first time. I felt like I wasn't about to let her go either. We didn't say anything for a while, and maybe even dozed off a little, until she kissed my shoulder, and I said, "So, what did you want to talk about?"

She kissed my shoulder again and then my ear. "I forgot."

I turned my head to look at her. "C'mon, you said you wanted to talk over a few things."

"Well, okay. I had been thinking about you and wanted to see you, and since I'm not taking any courses this semester, I just thought there'd be time for us to get together more."

I liked the sound of more. "So, you're not taking any classes to cut out time for us?"

"No, not exactly. I've been doing a lot of travelling, and I'll be doing even more over the next couple of weeks. Rather than kill myself and have to miss classes, I just took the semester off. Besides, as you know, I'm on the 20-year plan for a degree that I don't even need."

"I was beginning to think travelling for work and writing papers was a convenient way not to see me," I said, trying to sound playful.

"No, that wasn't the case at all. I explained to you when we just met how important my career is and a relationship just seemed like a roadblock that I wasn't willing to place in my own path. Along with school, it seemed like another hurdle I'd have to clear. Not being able to get together was because I really was too busy. If you are going to hang out with me, you have to understand that I don't bullshit. I'm nothing if not honest. Trust goes along with that. How about you?"

"How about me?"

"Are you honest? Trustworthy?"

I liked what I was hearing. She was laying down ground rules and beginning with the big ones: honesty and trust.

"Sure. I'd like to think I am."

Her voice got a little firmer. "Either you think you are, or you are?"

"Okay, okay. I am." I sounded as if she had a gun pointed at me.

"Good, it's important," she said matter-of-factly, then turned her head and faced the ceiling adding, "It's really important."

After a moment or two of silence, I said, "So, there seems to be an opening for me," as I placed my arm across her chest – a little bridge constructing of my own.

"It kinda sounds like you are applying for a job, but yeah, it looks that way."

"And just when I was trying to forget about you over the last few months," I said, sounding more serious than I intended.

"How'd that work out?" She asked teasingly.

"Not very well."

Chapter Thirteen

Spaghetti was now called pasta. You could buy yogurt frozen, and I had spent the last five nights sleeping at Marla's. As Dylan might say, "The times, they are changin'." All kinds of thoughts raced through my head as I gazed out the window of the plane I was on heading towards L.A. When we left the runway at LaGuardia, my fingers turned white, gripping the armrests of my seat, but so far, the sun was shining, and the flight was as smooth as an expensive glass of wine. I noticed a cloud shaped like a dog in the distance, maybe a Labrador, and there were others behind it looking like an entire kennel of clouds. Below my seat was nothing but farmland, fields stitched together in large squares like a quilt I could use to replace the one on my bed at home.

All the stewardesses were young, around 23 or thereabouts, in tan uniforms with round hats shaped like muffins balanced on the back of their heads. They all had long legs housed in miniskirts as though having great legs was part of the uniform. A blonde whose hair was short, straight, and cut, so both sides came to a point, brought breakfast on a tray. The older guy next to me, dressed in a bland gray suit that said more about him than he ever could, had been sleeping since take off. He opened his eyes briefly to tell her he didn't want anything, then went back to sleep. As she leaned over him, I helped her with the food tray she placed in front of me. Her smile consisted of perfect white teeth that were straight out of a toothpaste commercial – her smile was filled with all kinds of sunlight. Over the intercom, the captain said we had a perfect day for flying and would be landing in L.A. a little ahead of schedule. He told us the route we would be taking and said we would be landing in about four hours. I took my time eating my way across the entire state of Indiana.

After I finished my meal, another stewardess – with a butt that belonged in first class and not back here in coach – reached over Rip Van Winkle, who was still asleep and took my tray. I rested my head back and thought this might be my first time on a plane, but I've been flying for the past five nights. I had spent them meeting Marla after work for dinner, then sleeping at her place. I felt so high that my feet weren't touching the ground, that kinda thing. I was relieved when she called to meet for dinner, or dessert, again on Wednesday. By Thursday, it was understood that it would follow with me winding up at her place again. When I told her about Mickey Green and L.A., she, of course, thought it was a great opportunity. She was leaving for a trade show in Seattle on Sunday but would be back home on Thursday. I told her I would call as soon as I got back the following Wednesday.

I had taken out some notes from my briefcase, ideas for commercials to go over with Mickey later that afternoon. The plan was to check into the hotel, get settled, then go to his room. Everything had been arranged, and he was expecting me at four. I was hoping that after we got to know each other, or really after he got to know me a little, we could kick around script ideas then get down to writing first thing in the morning. It was important to make these commercials stand out, and with Mickey in them, we'd be halfway there. Humor is what makes TV commercials memorable, and with one of the hottest comics in the country, we had a real chance to make these AT&T spots stand out from the rest. I was anxious to get going and make it happen.

We landed in LAX half an hour early, just as the captain predicted. I grabbed my bag at the luggage claim and followed the signs to a taxi stand, then waited in line for about ten minutes before hopping in the first available cab. We took the 405, which we were on for about twenty minutes; it looked like any freeway except for the palm trees that took some getting used to. I had never seen a palm tree in person. They looked like tall, thin Rastafarians with their heads in dreadlocks swaying from side to side. Traffic was heavy with cars and trucks whizzing by, and it was easy to see how California moves. We got off the highway then turned onto a road where the homes were the size of museums. The lawns looked like expensive green rugs where you'd want to take your shoes off before walking on. I asked the cabbie what road we were on and when he said Sunset Blvd. We turned into the entrance, passing the famous green sign with white lettering spelling the name of the Beverly Hills Hotel in penmanship that would make any grammar school teacher proud.

The front of the hotel was large, pink, and expensive looking with its exotic plants and palm trees like they came out of a tropical desert. I paid the cabbie then grabbed my bags, before walking through the spacious lobby. I peered at the various art deco designs as I made my way to the front desk to check-in. I was given a key to my room on the second floor accompanied by a note waiting for me from Mickey Green. The note said he was expecting me for our 4 o'clock meeting and that I should go up to his suite after I got settled. I looked at my watch and realized I had a little over an hour to unwind, get my notes together, take a quick shower, and change my clothes. A bellboy, who was no bigger than a cough drop, took my bag then led me to one of the elevators, where we waited for a few minutes before it arrived. When the doors slid open, Charlton Heston walked out, smiled at us, and made his way through the lobby. I had to admit, it was a bit of a shock to see him come out of the elevator in a simple red shirt with a black handkerchief around his neck, not to mention, a toupee. As we rode to the second floor, I said to the bellboy, "Guess a lot of movie stars stay here."

"Yes, Sir. They have been since it first opened in 1912 and continue to. All kinds of celebrities."

He turned to smile, then picked up my bag as the doors opened and continued down the hallway to my room. Even with the curtains drawn, making it a bit dark, it was easy to see a large, tastefully decorated room. When the bellboy drew the curtains back, I wished I could bring it to Eighth Street and exchange it for my entire apartment. The bed was so large that Rhode Island could fit in it. There was a dark oak desk, and the bathroom looked like it had never been used. The bellboy said if I needed anything, I should just ring the desk and they would be happy to get me anything I needed. Before he left, I gave him the few dollars I had in my pocket and hoped it was enough. He thanked me and said to enjoy my stay. As soon as he left, I looked at my watch and saw I had about half an hour before going to Mickey's. I decided to take a quick shower and change my clothes before heading up.

I had brought my briefcase with me when I knocked on Mickey's door. It opened almost immediately, and there he was, dressed in a red and blue paisley robe, slippers, and possibly nothing else on underneath. His hair wasn't the slicked-back gray I had seen on television, but rather a relaxed mix of orange and gold, or something close to it – a type of accident that might happen if you try to color your hair at home and don't go to a professional. I put my hand out to shake his, "Hello, Mr. Green. I'm Benjamin Kissel."

He shook my hand and almost pulled me into his room. As I looked around, I saw it was a lot more like a suite of rooms.

"Mr. Green? How's the saying go? That's my father's name. I'm Mickey, but that's not really my name either. My real name is Chanoch – Chanoch Menachem. I was named after my grandfather. Of course, I couldn't use that – imagine a comedian called Chanoch Menachem? There's nothing funny-sounding about that, is there?" He was looking at me, smiling, as if he wanted an answer.

"I guess not."

"Of course not. That says immediately, 'I'm a Jew,' and there's nothing funny about being a Jew. So, I became Mickey Green. Just the sound of it makes you smile. Benjamin Kissel. Is that Jewish?"

"No, mostly German," I said.

"Got any Irish in you?"

"A little on my mother's side."

"Good. Irish is funny." Then he looked at me as if doing a quick inspection. "You're practically a kid. You must be a wunderkind or the agency wouldn't have sent you."

"I wouldn't say that."

"Modest. I like that. Proves you're not a Jew – we're never modest. Why be modest when it's easier to brag?" He pointed to a chair in the living room. "Come on over, kid and have a seat."

I sat on the striped cushioned chair, and Mickey sat across from me on the couch. When he sat, his robe opened around his crotch and there it was in full view: The Menachem penis. He didn't seem to care to adjust his robe or cover-up, or he was oblivious to it. Of course, it's one thing to tell a guy his fly is open, but this was in a league of its own. I said nothing and just made sure I kept my eyes above sea level.

"So, since we'll be working together, tell me about yourself."

I gave him the Cliff Notes version. He wanted to know how long I had been working at Pruit and Gray. I felt a little uneasy about answering since it hadn't been that long. "For about six months now. Started right after I graduated college." He was fine with it, if not enthusiastic.

"You've been a copywriter for only six months! Then you're a wunderkind. They sent me their hot guy, up and comer. Those AT&T fuckers will love what we come up with."

It was fine with me as long as he thought I was some kind of creative genius and not the low man on the scrotum pole.

"One other thing," he said, dropping the tone in his voice as if something important was to follow. "Is your lead singer getting taken care of?"

"Excuse me?"

"You know, your lead singer, your dick. Are you getting laid and sucked off enough?"

This was a question I wasn't expecting. "Yeah, I guess so."

"Married?"

"No."

"Good. Too young. I was married twice, bottom-of-the-barrel-stuff. Can't even remember their names. Girlfriend?"

"Yeah."

"How long?"

"Kinda new. Really just started getting things going."

"Great, great. But forget her while you're out here."

"Who do you mean?"

"Forget about her while you're out here working with me."

"Why's that?"

"Cause guys writing with me and are laying pipe with different broads who want to hang around Mickey Green are happier, which means their creative juices flow along with their best jokes and skits. It's just the way it is. So, if they're married or whatever, and forget they are, they always find their best stuff jumps out of their pens faster than gaucho juice out of their rods."

He stopped to see how I was digesting the set-up of our working conditions, then continued.

"Look, kid, I'm glad you're starting something up with your gal. That's fuckin' great, and I hope it fuckin' works out, but just forget about her while you're here. Stay loose, as I said, and we'll turn out some great shit for these AT&T ass wipes. Besides, I'll need help with all the broads that come after Mickey. I ain't braggin' or nothin', and it ain't because of my good looks."

He made his eyes pop out like I'd seen him do so many times on TV. A quick, strange sort of giggle followed that sounded like a muffled machine gun.

Of course, I laughed. One of the funniest comics in the country was sitting there in a paisley robe that was opened to expose his bare chest as well as his balls. His red and gold hair was sticking up as if he stuck his fingers in an electric socket. He was a little left of center, but what did I care? I was here to do a job, to write commercials. So, I was more than willing to tell him I'd forget my girlfriend so we could get to writing and work smoothly as a team. Any guy my age would be happy about Mickey's approach to writing and what was required of those who wrote with him. I already discovered that being with one person I had real feelings for suited me more than hopping into bed with a girl just to have sex. When it came to sex, I needed to specialize rather than freelance. I also had a sneaking suspicion that I was in love with Marla, but I wasn't sure since I had never been in love before. Not being sure still felt pretty good though.

"What girlfriend?" I said with a smile. I had to keep things in perspective. Even though I had no intentions of screwing any of Mickey's "star fuckers," having attractive women around who might want to simply screw me because I'm with a famous celebrity sounded a lot easier than having to go to Vietnam. That was the other way of getting screwed. Telling Mickey what he wanted to hear was the green light for getting down to work.

"Great, kid. Now that you are clear on how things work, we'll get some great stuff down on paper."

"Alright!" I said, enthusiastically. That's what's important -- getting stuff down on paper. It was clear Mickey was out there, and that's what probably made him funny, but since I was in his world, I had to play – or appear to play – by his rules.

"So, I have some ideas with me that I thought we could start working on tonight."

"Tonight!" he said as if I startled him.

"I thought since we only have a little over a week, we should get going as soon as possible."

"Naw, not tonight. There's a party I have to go to."

"A party?" I thought he'd be anxious to kick some ideas around, so I sounded more surprised than I intended.

"Whataya got shit in your ears?" he asked, good-naturedly, "Yeah, a party I gotta go to and you're coming with me."

"Okay, then how about we start working first thing in the morning?"

"Sure, sure. But it might not be the first thing since taking a leak is usually the first thing. And if I have a roommate, then comes a blow job, and then coffee.

Maybe we can get to work the third or fourth thing in the morning."

I didn't mean it literally, but he wasn't smiling – it was better just to nod my head in agreement. The door past the dining room opened and a woman walked out. She was wearing a white jacket with a matching belt wrapped around her waist. Her heels were so high she could've parachuted off of them. She was young – either pushing thirty or dragging it. She looked tired, and her hair was bright red, cut in a shag, and seemed like it was on fire in contrast to her pale white skin.

Mickey looked her way as she walked towards us. "Morning, hun."

"Morning, Mickey," she said as she stopped to search her pocket book to fish out the large black sunglasses she put on.

"Did you find everything alright?" He asked nonchalantly.

"Yeah, thanks." She replied, adjusting her sunglasses.

"Good. This over here is my friend Benjamin Kissel."

"Hello." She said, not looking in my direction at all.

She walked over to Mickey and placed her hand on his shoulder.

"See you soon," she said.

"You can bet on it." He turned to watch her walk out the door. "Every once in a while, I like a, redhead. They smell different." He turned to face me. "It helps clean out my sinuses."

I just looked at him because I didn't know how to respond.

"So whaddya think of that one?"

The best I could come up with was, "She had a pretty face."

He nodded his head as if he were contemplating my response. "Yeah. A pretty face goes a long way, but a great ass is everything."

Chapter Fourteen

After I left Mickey's, I was feeling a little down. It wasn't because he seemed a little out there, or slightly nuts, since so many of the great ones are, or that he wanted me to have sex with the star fuckers he couldn't accommodate. It was because he didn't want to get to work on the AT&T spots or at least explore some ideas that I had for him. It would just have to wait until tomorrow morning. In any event, I was exhausted when I got back to my room, so I just dropped my briefcase on the floor, and fell onto my bed. It must have been a combination of jet lag and being more nervous than I thought about meeting Mickey. I thought I'd rest my eyes for a moment, but instead, I fell asleep until the hotel phone rang. I was in such a deep sleep that the ringing startled me awake, and I thought I was in my apartment on Eighth Street as I fumbled for the receiver.

"Hello?"

"Hi. It's Chanoch."

"Who?"

"Just kidding. It's Mickey Green."

My mind cleared in a hurry. "Oh, hi."

"Are you ready?"

"Ready? You want to start working?"

"No, man. The party. The party we're going to."

I had already forgotten about the damn party. "Yeah, sure. The party. I'll be ready in about fifteen minutes."

"Okay, kid. I'll stop by your room to get ya and check it out to make sure it's to my liking. I make sure the people working on my team are comfortable."

"It's plenty comfortable, Mickey. I can come up to your place."

"No, no. It's on my way down and I have my driver waiting out front to take us there. See you in fifteen."

He hung up, and I jumped out of bed. I got out of my shirt that was wrinkled like an old man's face and hurried into the bathroom to comb my hair. I found some mouthwash in the cabinet and swished it around while I rolled on some deodorant. I put on the only white shirt I brought and decided my black pants looked clean enough to keep on. I took one final look in the mirror and knew I had no choice. It would just have to do, and as I finished getting dressed, I heard a knock on the door. I opened it, and there stood Mickey; his orange and gold hair was slicked back, and he was dressed in one of those Hawaiian short-sleeved shirts with palm trees all over it against a yellow background. His pants were bright red, and his shoes were white patent leather. His outfit was so loud that if I were deaf, I would've still been able to hear it.

"Here I am, kid. Dressed and ready to party," he said, with his arms open as he walked in.

"It looks like you are."

He gave the room a once over. "Not bad. Are you comfortable? If not, I can get you a bigger room. What the fuck? You're not paying for it."

"It's great. No complaints. I'm perfectly happy here."

He looked around some more, then at me. "Good, good." Then he looked at the bed. "Probably could fit a couple of broads in there. Ever have more than one at the same time? Whadya call it? A minute a twat or something like that?"

"No, never."

"Believe me, it's a lot of fun, but every time I do it, I'm like the Kentucky Derby – the fastest two minutes in sports. Fuggedaboutit."

I just laughed.

"That's funny? Didn't mean it to be. Gotta write that down." He paused to look at the floor and then back up at me. "The party's at Robert Evan's place, no more than ten minutes down on Sunset. Ya know who he is?"

"I think he's..."

"Yeah, the producer. He did *The Godfather* and the one that came out a month or two ago. He's probably the hottest producer out here right now."

"The Godfather is my favorite."

"Mine too. C'mon let's get going."

When we got into the elevator, an attractive woman's eyes lit up and she excitedly yelped, "Mickey Green!"

He smiled. "Hi, hun."

"I just love you!" She gushed.

"Oh yeah, how much?"

"A lot."

Mickey smiled. "That's never enough."

She looked at me for a brief second as I followed him out of the elevator.

"Bye, Mickey!" she said, sounding even more excited.

"Bye, doll," he answered, without looking back at her.

A limo was waiting for us in front of the hotel entrance. The driver got out to come around and open the door for us, "Good evening, Mr. Green." He looked at me and added, "sir," while nodding his head. It beat hailing a cab on your own and made me feel rather important. We drove ten minutes away to one of the mansions I passed earlier on Sunset. The driveway was shaped like a giant horseshoe curving in front of a large, white rectangular home that reminded me of the Frick Museum on Fifth Avenue. It was lit up, and easy to see all the expensive-looking cars parked along the driveway and on the lawn. There were Jaguars, Rolls Royces, Masseratis, and other fancy cars that I didn't recognize. I thought if I could steal one and sell it, I wouldn't have to work for a couple of years. If I stole two and cashed in, I could retire.

Mickey told his driver he would call him when we needed a ride back to the hotel. We got out and walked up the front steps. We entered the house through open doors the size of rafts and into a concrete and marble foyer with stairs leading up to another floor. There was a huge crystal chandelier over our heads and the doors to our left were open with the sounds of music, raised voices, laughing, and clinking glasses wafting through. Couples were making their way up or coming down, seemingly in slow motion. I couldn't help but stare at Liza Minnelli walking down in a short black dress with a drink and cigarette in her hand, laughing with a guy I didn't recognize.

"Sounds like a party to me," Mickey said excitedly. "Follow me, kid."

We walked onto what looked like a type of balcony with stairs on both sides of it leading down into a room large enough for The Lakers to play all their home games. I was glad someone in a white suit immediately greeted Mickey. It gave me a chance to walk over to the thick marble railing and take everything in before I walked into it. A circus of bodies was dancing in the center of the room, and pushed to the side were tables filled with food and couches filled with bodies. Some people were talking and others were going at it. I spotted James Caan talking to a blonde while a woman was sucking a guy off directly next to him. I was the only one who seemed to notice. On the far end of the room was a long bar where blonde and tan bartenders in white shirts were doing ninety – taking orders and mixing drinks.

Waitresses dressed in tight-hugging white jumpsuits that looked as if they were painted on – all of them beautiful enough to be models – walked around holding silver trays with glasses of champagne and neatly rolled joints resting side by side. If anyone wanted to get high in a hurry, all they had to do was take a couple of hits of the air in the room, which was thick with pot smoke. They wouldn't have to waste time lighting up.

The windows to the left ran from floor to ceiling and offered a great view of a pool and patio that was lit up by lights that weren't visible. More people were dancing out there, drinking, and getting out of the pool. The only difference was that they were all nude. There had to be at least two hundred people that I could see, and probably more where I couldn't. I started to recognize the celebrities inside. Elliot Gould was taking a hit on a joint; Karen Black was looking out the window before draining her glass, then walking out to jump in the pool without her dress. She looked even better without clothes. A waitress came up behind me, asking if I wanted a glass of champagne. The white jumpsuits they were wearing, that I thought looked like they were painted on, were actually painted on. They were sprayed in body paint. It was enough to make you thirsty even if you weren't, and I wasn't, but I wanted to play catch up and get a buzz going. I wanted to be a part of this party, even if I didn't want to be a part of it a few hours ago. All of a sudden, I wanted to dance, schmooze with celebrities, maybe even jump into the pool wearing only a smile, and forget that I had spent too many hours alone in my apartment over the past year. I grabbed a glass and drained it, then put it back on the tray where I drained another while the waitress stood there nodding approvingly. "Alright!" she exclaimed as if I accomplished something special or was on my way towards achieving it.

As she walked away, I grabbed another drink, then looked back to see if Mickey was still talking to the guy in the white suit. They seemed to be deep in discussion, and Mickey seemed to be listening intently. Even though I wasn't sure how I felt about him or if we could be productive working together, I liked how I was noticed just by walking next to him. I could see it in strangers' eyes that when they recognized him or called out his name, they looked my way as if trying to figure out who I was and if I was a celebrity too. I was surprised at how much I enjoyed being noticed. Maybe I was simply a little tired of feeling invisible.

"Hey, kid," Mickey yelled over all the noise. "Come here. Want you to meet someone."

I walked over, feeling buzzed from knocking down the champagne. The guy in the white suit was tall, good-looking with a dark complexion, and was wearing glasses as big as TV screens.

"Benny, this is Bob Evans, the movie producer and the guy who produced this awesome party."

Mr. Evans put his hand out to shake mine and smiled. "Robert, actually. Nice to meet you."

His handshake was firm, almost too firm. "I'm Benjamin, actually. Nice to meet you too."

"Mickey tells me you're a hot new writer. Let me guess, movie scripts?"

"No, I write copy for an ad agency. I'm out here to work with Mickey on a few TV spots."

Mickey jumped in. "He's hot, or the agency wouldn't have sent him out here."

Mr. Evans kept looking at me, but said to Mickey, "That's probably true. C'mon, everybody has a script that they want to sell."

"I'm sure that's true, but I just want to help Mickey write TV commercials."

He stared at me for what felt like an hour. "You're young, but you must be good or you wouldn't be here. Tell you what, when you get that movie script completed, I'd be happy to take a look at it."

I gave in. "Okay, when I complete my script, I'll bring it to you."

Mickey jumped in excitedly. "Kid, what an opportunity! This is Robert Evans – the hottest producer in town. Any writer would give his right or left nut to hear him say that."

Evans smiled. "I'm hot for the moment, so get the script to me as soon as it's complete. Mickey knows how to reach me."

"Will do."

"Have you guys checked out the upstairs? There's a lot going on up there too."

"Great," Mickey said, "I'll start upstairs and work my way down."

Evans turned to me before he left, "Nice meeting you, Bill."

I didn't bother correcting him. "Nice meeting you."

He said to Mickey, "So think about showing them what else you can do. I'll have my people contact your people."

A woman came over to Mr. Evans to kiss him on the cheek and started a conversation with him.

"C'mon, kid," Mickey said, "Let's check out the fun upstairs."

We started walking out towards the curving staircase that didn't seem to end. As we made our way up, everyone kept greeting Mickey as though he owned the place. We passed by Peter Sellers, who said a quick hello to Mickey but didn't stop to chat as I thought they might – England and America coming together for a quick laugh.

"He's overrated," Mickey said, "don't get his shtick." He didn't elaborate before bringing the conversation back to Mr. Evans. "You know, Bob was talking to me about appearing in a new movie he's putting together with Coppola directing, based on the Cotton Club in Harlem that takes place in the thirties."

It made me feel important that he told me what they were talking about, a preview of what was yet to come in Hollywood, and I heard it first.

"Although I'd be telling some jokes in nightclub scenes, it's basically a serious part." Mickey stopped halfway up the stairs. "I don't do serious. At least I haven't considered it."

I was still buzzed from the champagne and more than willing to offer some advice. "Why not do serious? Stretch a little and show what else you can do? Besides, you'll be playing a comic who's telling jokes. Sounds like the best of both worlds."

"That's good advice, kid," he said slowly as if he hadn't thought about it from that angle.

I thought *holy shit, I just gave Mickey Green advice and it made sense to him.* I wanted another glass of champagne to celebrate.

"He offered a lot of money, but I told him I don't even get out of bed in the morning for that kind of dough. It's always good to act like it's never enough. That's how you get more than enough."

"How did you leave it?"

"He said his people would call mine. But no more talk about business. We're at a party, so let's act accordingly."

While we began climbing the stairs again, I thought about how strange it was to have "people" do your heavy lifting, then all you had to do was show up. A large guy, rather heavy and looking out of place dressed in black with thick glasses greeted Mickey with a quick, "Good to see ya."

"That's one of your guys," Mickey said. "I like him."

"Why is he one of my guys?"

"It's Mario Puzo."

"The guy who wrote *The Godfather*?"

"Yep."

I turned to watch him head down to the room we had just left. In the past ten minutes, I had become a writer of movie scripts and placed in the same league as a legendary novelist. I was feeling more successful by the minute and beginning to like it out here. At the top of the stairs, a woman wearing a short white satin robe saw Mickey and hurried down to him.

"Mickey!" She squealed, throwing her arms around him, giving him a quick kiss on the lips.

"Hey, doll. Good to see ya."

"How have you been, Mickey?" She was in full party mode and obviously stoned by her lazy, red-rimmed eyes.

"Great, doll. Great."

"I'm running down to the pool, but I'll see you later, okay?"

"Sure, sure. See you later."

She looked at me trying to figure out who I was for a moment before going down the stairs. Mickey watched her hurry away. "Ya know, I think I went down on her about a month ago."

He looked at me with a confused expression as he tried to remember where he was with her.

"I'm almost sure it's her, but I'd have to look at her pussy to really know." He shifted his weight and continued, "Kid, do you like going down on chicks?"

"Yeah. Yeah, sure."

"Good. There's nothing like it. I don't get guys who don't."

"Really?"

"Yeah. Some comic buddies of mine say they don't like it. Redd Foxx. No, no, it was Nipsey Russell who said he never does. I asked him why not, and he said he wouldn't eat anything like that. After he's finished, he gets up and walks away."

"Okay then."

"Let's check things out over here."

We entered a type of living room with couches and plush chairs filled with everyone pretty much doing what they were doing downstairs. A guy was getting a blow job, but this time, he was leaning over and blowing another guy. Although it was quieter up here, I could still hear the music from below, the bass thumping against the soles of my feet. The room fed into a long hallway that looked like it ran the length of the mansion. On both sides of it, there were doors to various rooms; some opening as people walked in or out, others staying shut. As we made our way, I noticed a small group was standing outside one of the rooms looking in. Before we reached it, three giggling girls surrounded Mickey, each better looking than the other. They each took him by the arms and said that he had to go with them.

"I guess I'm being kidnapped, kid," he said, grinning as they led him away. "See ya later if I'm still alive." They walked him into one of the rooms down the hall and closed the doors behind them.

I just hoped they didn't kill him before we started working on our scripts. I wanted to get going on our work in the morning or early afternoon at the latest since it had to be around one or two in the morning by now. I stopped and stood next to the small group looking into the room, curious to get a glimpse at what was going on. A lot was going on. In the middle of the floor were about ten to fifteen people all sliding around on one another – a blur of blowjobs, girls on guys, girls on girls, guys on guys – nothing was open, all holes were filled. Unlike my fellow onlookers, who didn't move and kept staring like they were being paid to watch, I found it overwhelming and perverted. A waitress with the painted jumpsuit came by with a tray of drinks, although they weren't champagne. Even though I had no idea what they were, I took one in each hand, downed the one in my right, and placed the empty glass on her tray. Before, all the waitresses looked nude, but this one looked fully clothed. I followed her back to the living room, thinking I was definitely past the buzzed phase and on my way to shitfaced. I needed to sit down. I found a couch to fall into and watched the party move.

"Great party, don't you think?" A high-pitched, nasally voice said on my right.

I turned in the direction of the voice. It was coming from Truman Capote, who must have sat down in the chair near mine after I did, or maybe he was there, and I was drunker than I thought and hadn't noticed him. He was wearing a pink suit and white shirt along with small tinted pink sunglasses. There was no mistaking him or his voice. I had seen him on TV talk shows many times, and he seemed to pop up every other week on the *Carson* Show.

"Yeah, it's a good one."

"An Evans party is always worth attending."

"Wouldn't know. Never been before."

"And I've never seen you before. You wouldn't happen to be a Hollywood rent boy, would you?"

"I don't follow."

As soon as I said that, he pointed with his chin in the direction of a striking-looking guy walking through from the hallway with three younger guys – all tan and blonde – following him.

"That's Rudolf Nureyev, and the tan puppies following him are Hollywood rent boys. Robert brings them – or should I say, hires them – for his parties for people like Rudy to play with. You know, for people of my persuasion." He giggled girlishly. "Rudy is such an insatiable hound. I'm sure he went through all of them, but let's face it – he's an athlete and a beautiful dancer. Have you ever seen him dance?"

"No, never have."

"Well, he is exquisite and thrilling to watch. But enough about that, tell me your name and what you do. I'm sure you know mine and what I do."

"I'm Benjamin Kissel, and I'm not a Hollywood rent boy."

"I didn't think you were."

"I'm a writer."

"Oh, nooooo. Not another writer! I bet you have a movie script in your pocket."

"No, no. Not that kind of writer. I'm a copywriter. I'm out here working on some TV commercials."

"An ad man. You are quite young to be working on TV commercials. You must be hot! Well, you are, but I mean a hot, young writer for your agency."

I had too much to drink to avoid the truth. "Far from it. I don't even know how good I am or if I can pull off this assignment. My boss at P&G says I'm the low man on the scrotum pole."

"Come, come. I'm sure you are quite good. What's the assignment? Did you say 'scrotum'?"

Even when I aimed for the truth out here, I missed the target. "I'm here to work on commercials with Mickey Green."

"Mickey Green, the comedian?"

"The one and only."

"He is a Neanderthal but funny at times, I suppose."

I nodded my head in agreement, and then took a sip of whatever was in my glass.

"Well, Benjamin Kissel, I'm going to the bathroom to powder my nose." He placed his index finger on his right nostril and breathed in deeply with the other in case I didn't get the reference. "Care to join?"

"No, thanks. I'm doing great with this." I held up my glass.

"If you change your mind, the bathroom is at the end of the hall past the orgy room."

"Okay, thanks. By the way, are there Hollywood rent girls here too?"

"Oh, no. There is no need for that. If you haven't noticed, the women here are amenable to all kinds of sexual suggestions and recommendations. Rent girls would be a tad frivolous and rather gauche, don't you think?"

Chapter Fifteen

A brick wall felt like it toppled over on me as I walked by, or a large branch broke from a tree and crushed me. This was my first hangover. I woke up, or should I say, I came to lying on the bed in my hotel room still in the clothes I was wearing at the party. I wanted to look over at the clock on the nightstand and check the time, but no one was there to help me lift my head off the pillow. If I lived through this, I swore I would never take another drink again. When the phone rang, a buzz saw split my head in two. I leaned over and picked up the receiver just to make the ringing stop. I said, "hello," not recognizing the sound of the giant animal groan that escaped from my mouth.

"Kid, is that you? You sound like shit."

"I feel like shit, Mickey."

"You were wasted. Haven't seen anyone like that in a long time."

"Sorry."

"Nothing to be sorry about. It was a great party. At a party like that, it's your job to get wasted – you'd insult the host if you didn't. I was proud of ya. Did get you out just in time though."

"Whaddya mean 'got me out just in time?"

"After some young chicks cleaned my clock upstairs, I made my way down, and you were at the bar going at it with that young actor – what's his name? Tall blond, good-looking guy?" *Going at it with a good-looking actor?* That made me nervous.

"What do you mean 'going at it'?"

"You know, arguing. You were insulting the shit out of him. What the fuck's his name? Jay? John? Chris! That's right, Chris Walken. You kept saying he was the worst thing in the Anderson Tapes."

"I don't remember any of that."

"Yeah, you were getting into it with him, telling him he doesn't deserve to be in the same movie as Sean Connery."

"I did, huh?"

"Yeah. For a minute there, I thought Walken was going to take a swing at ya. Glad I got there in time. Got you out to the car, and my driver made sure you got into your bed. Hope he left your clothes on."

"Yeah, they're still on."

"So, Kid, how do you feel?"

"Awful."

"Send up for coffee. It'll get better."

"Think I will," I said, as I began to lift myself up slowly.

"Guess you're in no shape to join me downstairs in the Polo Lounge for dinner around nine?"

I looked over at my clock, which illuminated 8:00 in blaring red.

"You mean breakfast, don't you?"

"No, dinner."

"It's only eight AM."

"You mean PM." I looked at the clock again and saw a little PM in the bottom right corner.

"Fuck."

"Relax, Kid. We didn't get home until around five this morning and I needed the rest of the day to sleep, and you needed to sleep it off."

"Guess so." If I hadn't felt so awful, I would've felt disgusted with myself. The first full day we could have started working together was lost. There was no way I'd be able to work, let alone function, until tomorrow. One less day to create something worthwhile.

"No dinner for you tonight then."

"No, afraid not."

"Okay. Take it easy the rest of the night. Order up yourself a coffee, and then maybe come by my suite tomorrow at nine AM. I'll have breakfast here for us so we can start writing. Get at it right away."

Hearing that made me feel better. "Sounds good. See you in the morning. Nine AM sharp."

"See you in the morning," he said and hung up.

The last thing I remembered about the party was talking to Truman Capote and nothing about Christopher Walken – arguing with him or anything else. I slid myself back down, so my head was resting again on the pillow. I thought about Marla, whom I hadn't thought about for at least twenty-four hours. I remembered she would work at a trade show in Seattle that started today, which meant she was no more than an hour away by plane. I knew what it felt like to miss her when she wasn't really in my life, but missing her now was worse now that she was in my life. I guess now I knew what I was missing.

I slept through most of the night, getting up on occasion to empty my bladder of all the alcohol and even managed to change my clothes. By 6 AM, I was up for good. I took a shower, brushed my teeth, and began feeling human again. At precisely 9 AM, I stood in front of Mickey's suite ringing the doorbell with my briefcase in hand. Mickey answered in his robe and slippers again, although his chest looked whiter and his hair more orange than when we first met.

"Hi, Kid. How ya feeling? You certainly look better than the last time I saw ya," he said with a laugh.

"Feel a lot better. Thanks."

"How about some breakfast?" He pointed to a coffee pot and rolling cart with silver-covered trays with small burners underneath to keep them warm. I walked over to look under the lids and found eggs, bacon, sausage, and French toast. I guess I still hadn't totally recovered from my hangover since the look and smell made me a little nauseous.

"Think I'll stick with coffee for now," I said as I grabbed a cup and poured coffee blacker than oil.

"Thought we could work at the dining room table," he said as he pulled out a chair to sit.

I placed my briefcase on it and took out my folders to start going over my ideas and discussing our objectives. We needed to develop at least three-thirty second spots to pitch, so we had to keep them short, funny, and concise. For example, AT&T was cheaper and more effective than other long-distance business services. Mickey kept nodding his head in agreement. We decided that the entertaining aspect was easy with one of the hottest comics in the country making the pitch. I thought that the best way to grab the viewer's attention and to hold it was to place him in an environment where they wouldn't expect him to be seen. We could put him in a tux at a fancy restaurant, a cocktail party in a lush penthouse, the opera, or driving a Rolls Royce – all of which are now affordable because of the savings he's acquired using AT&T's long-distance services. When we first meet him, he would be speaking in a pretentious voice; then he would revert back to his Mickey Green voice where he would talk about all that he has saved and mention AT&T's long-distance plan a few more times to hammer the brand name into consumer's heads. Of course, he would use his trademark eye-popping, collar tugs, and his "give me a break" line when he reverts into his Mickey Green persona.

Mickey liked my ideas and said he would write new jokes to put into the scripts.

"That is," Mickey said, "if I can find any in here." He reached over for a large black folder that was next to him on the table. It was thick as the Bible, maybe thicker.

"I have all the jokes I've written, or written with others, in here," he said, patting it.

"All your jokes? How far back does it go?"

"Since the beginning -- at least thirty years. Back when I started doing stand-up in shitty dives in Jersey. Yep, they're all here, and some are real pants wetters – you know, so funny they make you piss your pants."

"Great. Hope we can use some."

He started stroking the book gently like it was a dog.

"This isn't the only copy. I have another in a safe deposit box in case I should ever lose this, which of course, I won't."

The way he looked at it, it might actually be his Bible or at least jokes he believed in. We decided to work on a script for the expensive restaurant. I'd get it going, and Mickey would begin looking through his folder for some jokes that might fit in. I was feeling excited and optimistic that we just might pull this off. There was a typewriter set up in the other bedroom where I would start knocking out the script. As soon as I completed a few pages, I would go over it with Mickey to make sure he was comfortable with it and make any necessary changes. Since I wasn't quite sure how to write a script, I'd end up completing three slighting different approaches and show each to Mickey. I was relieved to hear that he thought the agency just didn't send out a hot young writer but also a perfectionist. Most of the jokes in his folder were too crass and rude for TV and had to be changed or softened. He ended up writing different versions of the same jokes, those he could use in his stand-up act and sanitized versions for possible use in our TV spots. Our working together fell into place almost immediately. It was organic and couldn't have gone smoother. I'd work on the scripts in the bedroom, Mickey worked on jokes in the living room, and then we'd meet at the dining room table to cut, paste, and assemble all parts. We followed this system over the next four days, only stopping to eat a quick lunch and dinner sent up by room service. We would quit well after midnight and then start the process over again at nine the next morning.

Mickey did catch me a little off guard when he called me away from putting the finishing touches on our first script.

"Hey, Kid, come in here for a moment, will ya?" I realized I needed a break anyway and walked into the room. "What's up?"

"Have a seat. I want to run these jokes past you."

"Sure. Fire away." He read a joke that was so funny; my immediate response was uncontrollable laughter.

"You laughed, so I guess it's funny, but is it a pants-wetter?"

"I don't know. I just found it funny."

"Okay, here's another."

I found that one funny as well, but he wasn't sure if either were truly funny. I found it strange that one of the biggest comics in the country couldn't really tell if a joke worked or not. I would have thought it was second nature to him by now. It gave me hope that if I were still writing copy, scripts, or anything else in 30 years, I'd know the difference between what was good and what wasn't.

"You must know what's funny by now."

"Well, I do, and I don't. Let me run them by you again."

The first time he read them, it was straightforward, and in a normal tone that could've been anyone if I closed my eyes, then he read them in Mickey Green's tone with all of the famous mannerisms. The jokes were infinitely funnier the second time, and I laughed a lot harder.

"Ya see, the jokes work or kinda work when read straight, but when Mickey delivers them, they are homeruns," Mickey said, smiling victoriously.

I had to admit that the jokes were funnier with the Mickey Green delivery.

"But Mickey is your creation too," I retorted.

"You bet he is, and his timing is impeccable. I'm talking about the good joke in its purest form. Writing the joke down and knowing it's a good one before you even bring it in front of an audience. When I first started doing stand-up, I relied just on the joke. I knew it would work coming out of the mouth of any comic if he perfected his timing and delivery. Then, I started perfecting Mickey and relied on him to put the joke over, even when I knew my material wasn't up to my standards. With more and more gigs coming my way as a result of Mickey, I couldn't keep writing the stuff I was capable of producing; there wasn't enough time."

"You had to take on writing partners."

"Of course. A few of those guys were good, but most of them sucked. I always enjoyed writing my jokes. I knew what was needed, but it became impossible."

He stopped and looked at the table for a second or two, then at me again. "And that movie? Fuhgeddaboutit. There was a team of writers that I thought would be good, who, in the end, weren't. I added a few of my other jokes and ideas, but mainly signed off on what the studio wanted. It was basically Mickey Green going through the motions." He paused, half laughing, then adding, "I swear to God, Kid, I ended up sleepwalking through it and made sure I got high before doing every scene. I fucking hated every minute of it."

This famous, successful, wealthy comedian who seemed to be living the life he wanted, was actually unhappy on a very basic level. He had a pained look on his face, and though I hate to admit it, I was feeling sorry for him. I felt like I was watching a clown without his face painted on.

"You created Mickey, who everyone loves, and the movie made millions. That's no easy task to pull off. Fuck, you're the hottest comic in the country, and with your talent, there's no reason you won't be for a long time."

I thought he might say, *you're right, Kid, you're right. I've accomplished more than I ever thought possible.*

Instead, he asked as if he didn't hear me, "Do you like poetry?"

This question caught me off guard. "Can't say that I do, although I never really read it except for the stuff I had to read in high school and college."

"Well, don't let this get around, but I like it. Especially Robert Frost. Ever read him?"

"In school once. I do slightly remember the poem about the woods and snow. Liked that one."

"Yeah, it's great, but I've read all his stuff and realized that he and I have a lot in common."

"How so?"

"Writing a good joke, I mean a really good joke like I used to write in the beginning is a lot like writing a good poem. They're both short, compressed, entertaining, and can heal you. See what I mean?"

"I never thought of it that way, but I see what you mean."

"I used to think of myself as the poet of jokes, the poet of laughs. I even thought about calling myself Mickey Frost, but, like I told you before, Green just sounded funnier for some reason, and it's the color of money."

"Never heard of any poets who made a lot of money."

"That's true. Just don't tell anyone about this, my liking poems and Frost. It would be bad for Mickey Green's image."

I smiled. "And yours."

"Yeah, mine too."

"Okay, it's a deal."

"Ya know, when you first started working on the scripts, you pissed me off."

This startled me a little since I thought we had been working great together from the get-go. "Really? How'd I do that?"

"You were never satisfied with anything you wrote and showed me at least three different approaches to every scene. The sign of a true perfectionist."

"And that pissed you off?"

"Yeah. It reminded me that I used to be a perfectionist, too, when I started out. It made me realize that I got to get back to being one. Get the control back."

I was glad he confused my not being sure of what I was doing with being a perfectionist.

"So, I was really pissed at myself. Not you." He paused for a few seconds, then said, "Do me a favor, Kid."

"Sure, what's that?"

"No matter how successful you get, never lose what you got."

I nodded. I knew what he meant, but being a perfectionist meant nothing to me. All I wanted was to learn how to do it better – the rest would take care of itself.

"Since you're happy with this script, I'm going to clean it up, format it properly, and send it off special delivery to my boss at P&G."

"Clean away."

"I'm hoping we can complete another by the time I have to leave next Tuesday. That gives us more than enough time if we start it tonight."

"Tonight? Not so fast. We're going out for dinner tonight. I feel like having a hobo steak."

"Never heard of a hobo steak. What is it?"

"A steak that only Chasen's makes. In fact, they invented it. No one else makes it."

"Chasen's is a steakhouse?"

"You never heard of Chasen's? It's a restaurant that's been around since the thirties. It's famous. Movie stars, celebrities, and even presidents have been going there for years. You'll love it, and it's on me."

Mickey's car picked us up, and within three minutes we were on Beverly Blvd, which was a quick change from the opulent area around the hotel. It was generic from what I could see with its office buildings, stores, and gas stations. If it didn't have palm trees, it could've been any street in any city in the U.S.

We stopped at Chasen's, which was on the corner in a one-story white building that looked like it might have been taller, but melted down and spread out in the hot West Hollywood sun. There was a large portrait of Queen Victoria with W.C. Fields' face near the door as I walked in. Mickey stopped in front of it.

"When I first came here and saw that painting, I knew I was in the right place. One of the greatest comedians of all time." He kept looking at it and asked if I had seen any of his movies. Before I could answer, the maître d' rushed over.

"Mr. Green! How nice you can join us tonight!"

"Julius, how are you, my friend?" Mickey then introduced me to Julius, who was of average height with a German accent and wearing glasses the size of windshields you might find on a sports car. He seemed pleasant and friendly.

"I have a great booth for you, Mr. Green. Please follow me."

We headed towards our booth in the front room paneled in dark wood with red leather seats matching the others cozied up to the walls. All the tables in the center of the room were filled with men who looked like they worked on Wall Street; the kind of guys who could afford all the jewelry their wives or girlfriends were wearing – women with hairdos that a hurricane couldn't destroy. Waiters in short red jackets were hurrying around to the other rooms, bringing trays of food and taking orders. At some tables, there were different waiters dressed in black tuxes and cooking in large metal trays with blue flames underneath and spooning sauces over whatever was being cooked. I spotted celebrities everywhere I turned: Clark Gable, Jimmy Cagney, Errol Flynn, Groucho Marx, Gary Cooper, Michael Jackson, and Elton John, but they were all in photos or headshots covering the walls that were signed or inscribed. I tried to look around the restaurant to catch a glimpse of even one of these people in real life but didn't see anyone notable.

"You know what booth this is?" Mickey asked, excited.

"Haven't a clue."

"It's the Hitchcock booth."

"As in Alfred Hitchcock?"

"The one and only. And it's a Thursday too."

"I don't follow."

"Every Thursday, Hitchcock and his wife come here for dinner and no one is allowed to use it but him.

It's also the most important room for all the heavy hitters. There are other rooms to the side and in the back, but this is *the* room."

"Well, it's Thursday. Hitchcock isn't coming, and you're important too, or you wouldn't have been given this booth of all booths."

"I like the way you think, Kid. Now you're in for a great fucking meal."

A waiter in a black tux came to the table and greeted Mickey with a German accent.

"Claude, this is my friend, Benjamin Kissel." The waiter nodded politely towards me and turned back to Mickey.

"Are you having the usual, Mr. Green?"

"Yeah, we're going to share it. Is Pepe at the bar?"

"Yes, he is."

"Great. Have him make me a Flame of Love."

"What's that?" I asked.

"It's a drink he created with vodka, sherry, and an orange peel. Half the fun though is watching him make it. It's a real show."

"That's the first time I've heard you use the word love, and of course, it has to do with vodka."

Mickey smirked. "What can I say? It appeals to the romantic in me. Want one?"

"I bet. I'm good, thanks. I think I'm going to pass on the booze for the next ten years or so."

"That hangover still haunting you, Kid?" he asked with a ball-busting tone.

"It's only been four days, and yeah, it still haunts me." I looked at Claude, "I'll just have a Coke, please."

"Wonderful," Claude responded, then he looked at Mickey, "Perhaps cold cracked crab for an appetizer?"

Mickey nodded and said, "Make sure there's enough for two."

Claude smiled, "I'll make sure there's enough for four."

"This place is something else," I said to Mickey with a touch of amusement in my voice.

"And it has been something else for years, and I hope it continues forever as long as forever exists."

"A place that invents its own food and drinks has a good shot. I bet the only thing you can't get here is chili."

Mickey's eyes bulged. "What're ya kiddin' me? They're famous for their chili! Everyone gets it here! Gimme a break."

That sounded strange to me. "Really? Chili?"

"You never heard of Chasen's Chili?"

"Before today, I'd never heard of Chasen's."

"It's Liz Taylor's favorite dish here. When she was filming *Cleopatra* in Italy, she'd always have about ten gallons flown over to the set every two weeks."

"For some reason, I can't picture her digging into a bowl of chili."

"A guy I knew who worked for the assistant director told me she and Burton would often have the chili with beer for breakfast. Once, during a love scene, Liz was farting so much that Burton backed up and fell down a flight of stairs in his fucking toga."

We were both laughing when Claude brought our drinks, cheese toast, and a large metal bowl with the cracked crab resting all over ice, which looked as high as an igloo. We started working on the crab, which melted in my mouth and went phenomenally with the toast. Claude whisked by again with a rolling table that had a large tray and a mini stove with a pan beside it. He started cutting into a thick piece of salted steak that lay on a separate cold plate. Then he dipped each piece carefully in butter before placing them on a hot plate, which radiated steam. He turned to the pan, and dropped an entire stick of butter into it, and placed two thick cuts of steak inside, gently spooning the melted butter over the fillets. The sight of all that butter made me nauseous – I never liked butter, not even on toast. Looking at an entire pan full of pure butter swishing around and knowing that I would have to eat it, made me swallow hard. I looked at Mickey, who was watching so intently and impatiently that I thought he might reach into the pan and eat it raw.

"I have to tell you, I got this thing about butter. I'll be sick as hell if I eat this, and I only have a few days. We still have more work to get done, and I don't want to waste time being sick."

Mickey had no problem understanding my aversion to butter. "If you feel that way, we gotta order you something else. You do like meat, though, right?"

"Sure. Of course."

"Okay, got it." Mickey turned to Claude, who was immersed in his butter display. "Claude, bring my friend here an order of the deviled bones. He's going to pass on this."

"Certainly, Mr. Green," Claude whispered to a passing waiter and continued preparing the steaks. After he placed the filets on pieces of toast, my order arrived.

Staring at my plate, I was convinced Fred Flintstone was in the kitchen, butchered a dinosaur, and placed three huge bones covered in meat on my plate.

Mickey said, "Think you can handle those?"

"Yeah, but I might need a crane to lift them."

The meat was tender, sweet, and enough for a family of four. I could only finish one and took a couple of bites from another before throwing in the napkin. An order of chili also arrived, and Mickey motioned for me to take a bite.

"Now I understand why Liz had 10 gallons flown in."

"And blew Burton down the stairs."

We were both too full to laugh this time. "Yeah, that too."

"Want dessert?"

"Are you kidding? I can't move."

What I really wanted for dessert was Marla. I pictured her sitting there instead of Mickey and thought about being with her last week. Suddenly, I felt anxious about getting back to New York to pick up where we left off.

"Just as well. There's a dessert back at the hotel that I want you to try."

"Sounds like a good idea since I want to kick around ideas for another script and hopefully knock it out before leaving on Wednesday."

"You sent the other two to New York?"

"Before we left for dinner."

"Don't worry, Kid. They're gonna love 'em."

I hoped he was right.

Chapter Sixteen

There was a knock on my door. When we got back to the hotel, I told Mickey I'd go to my room to change then meet him at his suite to go over ideas for the next script in about half an hour. I opened the door, and there stood Mickey, smiling with two girls - one blonde, one brunette - who looked to be in their twenties.

"May we come in?"

Before I could answer, they walked past me and stood near the bed. I closed the door and walked over to them.

"Benjamin, I'd like you to meet Cindy," he said, motioning to the brunette, "and Mindy" as he touched the arm of the blonde.

The brunette giggled and said, "I'm Mindy," and the blonde said, "I'm Cindy."

"Yeah. Whatever. You may remember seeing them at Bob Evans' bash the other night."

Of course, I didn't. "Yeah. Sure."

They went over to sit on the couch. Mickey looked over at them. "Ladies, show Benjamin what we brought." The blonde reached into her pocketbook and took out a small plastic bag with white powder in it. She dangled it like it was a carrot, then put it on the small coffee table in front of the couch.

Mickey grinned. "That's the dessert I told you about at Chasen's."

"Is that cocaine?"

"Sure is." He looked over at the girls who seemed to be waiting patiently for their orders. "Get some lines ready, ladies." The blonde sprang into action, pouring some of the powder on the smooth surface of the coffee table.

"Hey man, I don't do that stuff. I once tried hash that was probably laced with other shit, and I thought I killed my parents."

"Relax, Kid. This isn't like any of that crap. There are never bad reactions to this. It just makes you feel great, and there are no hangovers like you had the other day."

"Can't you get hooked on it?"

"No, no. Coke's not addictive. It's all-natural, organic. It's practically health food. I bet ya in a few years it's found to be so healthy by the AMA that moms will be feeding it to their kids as part of a healthy diet."

I smirked. "Doubt it."

"I'm dead serious. Can't you see some mom saying to little Jimmy, 'You can't go out and play until you finish every line of coke on your plate'? Mark my words – the day is coming."

Cindy or Mindy, whoever the brunette was, said, "It's just like Mickey says. We've used it a lot. It's nothing but a way to make you feel really, really good."

The blonde one added, "It is natural, and no one ever gets hooked on it."

"See, Kid, even the girls are backing me up on this," Mickey added.

"In that case, it's gotta be true," I said.

"Look, for the last couple of days, we just worked on scripts and turned out two that I know are going to fly, right?"

I nodded. "I think they're good."

"They are. The next one we will work on tomorrow will be even better because now we're going to kick back and relax. You know what I mean? I don't want to have to explain it again in front of the girls here."

"Got it."

"Good. Now try some blow and hang with these two lovely ladies. I promise you there won't be a hangover tomorrow, just the opposite, in fact. You'll be full of energy and ready to go. And we'll start first thing in the morning just the way you like it."

Obviously, I wasn't going to get out of this, and he wasn't suggesting that I try it – he was telling me. I decided it would be easier just to do it since I really wanted to knock out one more good script for insurance before heading back in a few days. I walked over to the girls to sit between them. I looked at the five lines on the coffee table, then up at Mickey, and said, "Let's do this."

The girls seemed excited. Mickey gave Cindy (or maybe it was Mindy) a hundred-dollar bill. She rolled it into a small tube then stuck it up one nostril while pressing the other shut. She leaned over the coffee table and sniffed up a line. She handed the bill to me, but I leaned back and said, "Ladies first."

She smiled. "You are a gentleman," then handed it to Mindy (or Cindy), who sucked up a line and handed it back to me.

I looked at the line that supposedly had my name on it and thought, *here goes nothing*. I leaned over it, and snorted it into my nose, which went numb. I couldn't feel my throat either. Mickey came over and did a line.

"Gotta get going," he said.

"You're not staying?"

"Nope. I got two other friends waiting for me upstairs. Don't worry, Kid, you can handle this. You're going to have a great time."

He must have thought I was nervous about his leaving, but I didn't give a shit. I was already feeling amazing. I watched him go, and the girls said they'd see him later or something like that. I rested my head back and closed my eyes. I never felt so good. I was happy, elated with a really good time, and ready to go. Every bottle of Dom Perignon in L.A. had nothing on the high

I was feeling right now. When I opened my eyes, I wanted to know more about the girls, and they were eager to tell me. I stopped using their names since I couldn't keep them straight. They both came out here to be actresses from towns in the Midwest that are even too small to be named on road maps. The brunette ended up doing some modeling in men's magazines – nothing racy, just cheesy photos. The blonde said she could land some extra background work on *The Six Million Dollar Man* and *Maude*. They both held part-time jobs until they got into some fancy parties attempting to meet people in the industry and have been taken care of by actors like Mickey Green ever since. Mickey promised them some work on his next film in exchange for some small favors. I knew what the favors were, but I wondered how many times Mickey and actors like him had made those same promises.

"So, you girls go to a lot of parties out here?"

"Sure," the blonde said, "That's how I met Warren Beatty. He was a spectacular lover."

"Just so you know, I have nothing to do with the movie business."

The blonde started rubbing the back of my neck, which felt like a massage that I could never afford. "Mickey says you're a new hot writer and you're working on movie scripts."

The brunette scooted closer to me. "Maybe you could keep us in mind, you know, even for a minor role." She began rubbing my leg.

I felt so good that creating parts for them in a movie script that I would never write actually made perfect sense. "Of course, I will."

They both squealed with delight as one went for my mouth and the other started rubbing the iron pipe between my legs. As she started pulling down my zipper, the other pulled back from my lips. "Let's finish the blow and get on with it. Whaddaya say?"

I wasn't quite sure what she meant about "getting on with it," but I was feeling great, like a changed man, a true believer, and wanted to finish the blow. After we snorted what was left, they took me by the hands towards the bed like we were three happy kids on our way to play in a sandbox. That's when it hit: A surge of energy I had never felt before invaded me as if pushing past my kidneys, bladder, and liver to get to my heart and pound it against my ribs. The heat was turned all the way, up and I was going to fuck anything that moved. Luckily, Cindy and Mindy had the same plan and were out of their clothes faster than I could get out of mine. They were making out with each other since I was already late for the party. When I got into the mix, I quickly made up for the valuable seconds I lost, making them one person, Cindy-Mindy, the girl with two of everything. I slid into one and then the other and everything else they wanted me in. Hands grabbed and rubbed, and if there was an opening, I filled it. We were doing ninety – we were a blur. I lost who I used to be and was glad. Now I was a superhero. I was goddamn Superman.

At some point, it wasn't so much that we stopped; it was more like we gave up, and I ended up falling asleep between the girls with the dead weight of their legs resting on mine. A knock on the door woke me. The room was washed in sunlight as I looked over the shoulder of one of the girls at the clock and saw it was 9:15AM. I felt tired, but Mickey was right – I didn't feel the least bit hungover. I rested my head for a few minutes until I heard a knock. I eased my way out between the girls, found my pants on the floor, zipped them up, and went over to open the door, thinking it was Mickey. I was wrong. "Marla!" She was standing in front of me in a short white dress with a large pocketbook hanging over her shoulder.

"Surprise!" She said in a low voice, smiling.

I was thrilled to see her. That feeling quickly left as a type of panic rushed through me like a brushfire. I couldn't let her into the room with two naked girls sleeping in my bed. I had to come up with something quick.

"This is a surprise," I said, not moving from the door, which I held open just wide enough to make sure she couldn't see behind me.

"The last trade show finished late, and I missed my flight out of Seattle. The next one I could get on had a layover in L.A. So rather than sitting around LAX for the next five hours, and since I knew where you were staying, I thought we could hang out a bit if you had time before I head back to NY." She leaned back slightly as if to examine me for a second. "You look tired, although I really like the shirtless look."

"Oh yeah. I was working late and thought it was Mickey at the door." *Why couldn't she have come by tomorrow or yesterday? Why fucking now? Shit!* If those girls weren't in the room, I would've had Marla in bed with me by now. I could sense that she was wondering why we weren't in bed yet either.

"So maybe this wasn't a good idea."

"No, no. It's a great idea." I was trying not to sound nervous and needed a plan in a hurry. "I want you to come in, but the place is a wreck and probably smells a little since Mickey and I have been working here instead of his place upstairs. So let me shower and I'll let the maid in to straighten things up. In the meantime, why don't you meet me downstairs in the Polo Lounge for breakfast? I hear it's great and I still haven't gotten there with all the work we've been doing. How does that sound?"

"Okay, sure. Sounds good."

It was a tremendous spur-of-the-moment plan that would give me enough time to get the girls up and out, straighten things up, then meet Marla for breakfast and bring her back to the room. It would have worked too if the phone hadn't started ringing and it kept ringing. I just ignored it and hoped that neither of the girls would wake up nor make any noise.

"Are you going to answer your phone?" Marla asked, perplexed.

"Nah, it's probably just Mickey. He's always calling." I heard rustling behind me, and the phone was picked up. I could feel myself perspiring and my skin moistening. I held my breath.

"Benjamin, it's your mother," one of the girls called out from behind me. I stared into Marla's eyes. For the first time, there was nothing behind them. Her face went cold and I could feel the chill on my bare chest. She might have been standing in front of me, but it was clear she had already left.

"I can't believe this! You're disgusting! Don't even bother trying to call me ever again!"

I watched her turn and walk towards the elevator as she disappeared around the corner of the hallway. There was nothing I could have said to stop her, so I didn't even try. I felt wounded and out of breath knowing that it was over between us before it even got going. I stood there for a couple of moments – which felt like a couple of hours – staring at the empty hall, and then I remembered that my mother was on the phone. I walked back in confused as to why my mom was calling me. She'd never call me unless there was an emergency. For a second, I hoped it might be Mickey fooling around to see how things went last night and had no idea of his poorly timed call. The girls had fallen back asleep and left the receiver on the end table. I grabbed the phone and pressed it to my ear. It was my mother.

I could tell immediately from the tone of her voice that something was wrong. It was about my father: He had a stroke that was more serious than the first. He was resting comfortably, but the doctors wouldn't know anything until further tests were done. It happened at home as they were eating breakfast together, and she had him rushed to Lawrence Hospital in Bronxville. She was still at the hospital and assured me that he was doing fine and our neighbor was with her. I told her I loved her and would be on the next flight home. She said everything would work out and to try not to worry so much since everything was in God's hands. I got off the phone and stared at my own hands, which wouldn't stop shaking. Just a few minutes ago, I thought the worst thing that could've happened was Marla walking out of my life. She wasn't even out of the building and she was already the distant past. I knew I needed to be with my parents and see my father immediately.

I had to make plane reservations, pack, and call Mickey, but I had to get the girls out of the room before I did. "Ladies!" I almost yelled. They stirred, and the blonde sat up. "You both gotta get going. I have to leave in a hurry." The brunette got up and rubbed her eyes.

"What's going on?" She asked.

"He's leaving. We gotta go," the other answered.

"Sorry, it's an emergency. I need you out of here in two minutes," I said, grabbing my suitcase and beginning to pack.

The brunette said, "Okay, okay, we're going, but I gotta use your bathroom."

"Go ahead, but make it fast." I wanted to call Mickey, but I needed them gone.

They slid into their dresses and combed through their hair in record time. As they walked out the door, the blonde turned and said, "Don't forget parts for us in that script of yours." She blew me a kiss and closed the door behind them.

I called Mickey's suite. "Hi, Mickey, it's Benjamin."

"Hey, Kid. Good time last night?"

"Yeah, good. Listen, I have to leave. Fly back to NY right away."

"Why? What's going on?"

"I got a call from my mom. My dad had another stroke and is in the hospital."

"Jeez, sorry. How is he?"

"They're not sure yet. They have to do more tests, but my mom says he's resting comfortably."

"That's good, that he's resting."

"Yeah, so I have to be with them."

"Of course, you do. Listen, I'll have my people get you on the first plane back and I'll have my car take you to the airport. It will all be taken care of. Just pack up and I'll call you as soon as the flight is booked."

"Thanks, Mickey. I really appreciate this."

"It's nothin'. It's the least I can do."

"Sorry we couldn't get the third script done, but the two we did are really good. I'm sure my creative director will go for them, and so will AT&T."

Of course, I wasn't sure of anything, and right now, I didn't even care. It didn't seem important with my father thousands of miles away in the hospital.

"They're homeruns. I'm sure you'll be out here again when we film them and working with me on some more scripts."

"I'm sure you're right."

"Okay, Kid. My people will call soon. Let me get on it."

"Thanks, Mickey."

"Good luck. I know your old man will get through this. Keep me posted."

I was grateful to Mickey for booking my flight and letting me borrow his car. Very grateful. I took a quick shower, dressed, and packed. Within twenty minutes, one of Mickey's secretaries called to say that I was booked on a noon flight and there was a car waiting for me downstairs to take me to the airport. I couldn't get out of that hotel fast enough.

Chapter Seventeen

Mickey booked me in first class. It was a large, comfortable seat, but I couldn't take sitting next to Marla, who was screwing the pilot as the copilot stood next to them with his pants off, waiting his turn. Every once in a while, Marla would breathlessly say, "How do you like it?" I couldn't tell if she was talking to the pilot or me. I started yelling at her, telling her to stop until Father Cavendish came out of the cockpit and sprinkled them with holy water. For some reason, most of the water missed them and kept hitting me in the face, then splashing on me as if it were being poured out of a bucket. I began coughing and gagging, feeling like I would drown, but then the plane hit some turbulence and rattled me awake. I was relieved it was a dream and that no one was no one sitting in the chair next to me. I had dozed off into a feverish nap for no more than ten minutes. I was perspiring heavily. My back was wet and my hair stuck to my forehead. A passing stewardess must have thought I looked sick since she wanted to know if I was feeling okay and offered to get me something. I told her I was fine and asked for some coffee. I wanted the caffeine - there would be no more naps.

I wasn't tired. I was exhausted from being stressed out and worrying about my father. Marla had something to do with it, but I couldn't think about her and what had happened. I had to concentrate on getting to the hospital to be with my parents. I looked out the window, thinking that this had to be the longest flight ever or that I was riding on the slowest jet in the fleet. I imagined getting on the intercom to ask if a New York City taxi driver was on board to take over for the pilot. With the cabbie at the wheel, he'd tailgate a few clouds until they moved out of the way and then zigzag around other jets to get us into Kennedy airport at least an hour earlier. The thought made me smile a little, although I couldn't wait to get off the plane and felt more anxious with each passing minute. After the stewardess brought me coffee, I decided to get up and walk. I had to move and couldn't sit any longer. The plane looked only half full, so I slowly headed for the bathroom in coach since it was at the other end and would keep me on my feet longer. I didn't need to use the john, but I needed a destination, and since it was the farthest from where I was now, it was the only logical destination.

It felt good to be on my feet. I walked slowly down the aisle past quite a few seats, even more than I originally thought, and surprisingly, there wasn't even a cloud over the smoking section. I would've thought a flight from L.A. to New York would've been packed, but what did I know? This was only the second flight in my entire life. I was learning there's a lot I didn't know. When I reached the bathroom, the lights outside of it were off. I could go in, though I didn't. I waited because if I went in, it meant I'd have to go back to my seat that much sooner. I stood there staring at the door when something I didn't plan happened: I stopped thinking. My mind went blank as if it had hopped on another plane and flew away from my head. Every thought I was trapped in during the last few hours took a vacation from me. It was a welcomed relief to leave myself behind for a couple of minutes, and then someone behind me asked if I was going to use the bathroom. I half smiled, nodded, and went in. I turned the lock to switch the light on and leaned over the sink towards the mirror to examine my face. It was clear that I looked the way I felt. I splashed some water on my face and ran a comb through my hair, and walked back out. I noticed a small TV screen on the opposite wall that showed a map of the U.S. and a small red "V" representing our plane and the route we were taking. We still had a long way to go. I slowly turned and walked over Utah to go back to my seat.

I must have been followed because a girl plopped down next to me, startling me a little as soon as I sat down.

"Hi," she said, "Anyone sitting here?"

"You are." My reply made her smile, although she seemed full of energy regardless. She was around my age and dressed in a one-piece black mini. She had shiny black hair that was cut like Rod Stewart's.

"There are a lot of empty seats on this plane. I fly back and forth between New York and L.A. a lot and it's never like this." She spoke rather quickly as if she weren't choosing her own words. They were simply escaping from her mouth.

"I wouldn't know. This is only my second time flying."

"Wow! Really?"

"Yep. Number two."

She stared at me for a few seconds as if she were sizing me up before introducing herself.

"My name is Mo," she said, extending her hand.

"Benjamin," I reached out and shook her hand awkwardly.

"Hi, Ben."

"Benjamin."

"Mo is just a nickname for Maureen. My last name is Moe, spelled with an 'E' so everyone calls me Mo Moe."

"Nice to meet you, Mo Moe."

"Are you working or in school?"

"Working."

"What do ya do?"

"I'm a copywriter. Was in L.A. on an assignment."

"Cool. I'm an assistant to Peter Max."

"Wow! He's huge! He even made the cover of *Life* a few years back."

"Yeah. He's as big as it gets and as nice too."

"How'd you get to work with him?"

"I was taking classes at Parsons. He was friendly with a professor teaching my painting class and asked if she could recommend a student to intern for him, and here I am. Of course, we slept together. How could I not? You have to sleep with a genius if you get the chance, right?"

She looked at me, examining my reaction to see if I agreed or not.

"Sure. Guess so."

"Yeah. We had a romantic thing happening for about a year until he got another intern and slept with her."

"And you stayed?"

"Oh, sure. He offered me a full-time assistant gig, so I dropped out of Parsons. I learned more about painting and art working with him over the past three years than I would ever have at Parsons."

"Sounds like it."

"I was in L.A. to oversee an installment of one of his exhibitions. Anyways, would you like to know why I'm sitting here?"

"Sure. Why's that?"

"I was in my seat in coach near the bathroom and noticed you standing there staring at it, and I thought, 'Now there's a cute guy.'"

"Oh. Well, thanks."

"I wondered, 'Is he waiting to go into the bathroom when there's obviously nobody in it?' Then I thought, 'Maybe he's waiting because he's a member of the club and is hoping another member is waiting to join him.'"

"Club? What club? Who would I be waiting for?"

"You know – The Mile-High Club."

"You mean when couples go into the bathroom and have sex?"

"Yeah. Am I wrong?" A look of concern spread across her face. "Oh no! I'm totally wrong. Right?"

"Right. You're wrong."

Her concerned look turned into embarrassment. "Oh. Wow. I'm so, so sorry."

There was something innocent about her, even if what she was proposing wasn't innocent at all. She was also attractive, and I had to admit I was a little flattered, but there was no way in hell that I could be a club member today of all days, or even on a good day for that matter. I found myself trying to console her for not wanting to fuck her. "You are very attractive and sexy, and on any other day I would've definitely joined the club with you, but today has been awful for me so far. The girl I'm in love with will probably never talk to me or see me again over something I did and I cut a business trip short to get back home to see my dad who is in the hospital."

"I'm so sorry," she said, almost whispering as she reached over and touched my hand. "I hope you can patch things up with your friend and that your dad makes a speedy recovery."

"Thanks," I said as she got up and walked back to her seat. I turned and looked out the window, thinking about how I finally admitted that I was in love with Marla, even if it was to Mo Moe. I realized that I fell in love with Marla the first time I saw her in class. I had heard and read about people who said they fell in love at first sight and never believed it until now. But it didn't make any difference. It was too late. I took care of that.

Chapter Eighteen

As soon as we landed at JFK, I grabbed my bags and hurried off the plane and into the first taxi waiting in front of the terminal. The cab flew onto the expressway and then Van Wyck. Most of the two and three-family homes along the expressways looked drab and tired, dressed in their brick and stucco facades under the gray sky. The apartment buildings were the kind that didn't have a doorman in their lobbies and were no taller than Mickey Rooney. But today, I preferred to think of them as cheering crowds lining up along the parade route to welcome me home. When we headed over the Whitestone Bridge, I gazed to my left and saw the City in the distance, looking small enough to fit in my hand. I opened my fist and slid a flat palm underneath the entire city, balancing all of it – the World Trade Center on my thumb and the Empire State in the center of my palm. Even though my dad was sick, it felt good to be riding home towards Bronxville with L.A. behind me.

As soon as we pulled up in front of the hospital, I paid the driver and didn't bother waiting for my change. I grabbed my bags and hurried into the lobby. The receptionist at the front desk told me that my father was in room 210 on the second floor. Instead of waiting for the elevator, I ran up the brown staircase and walked to the end of the mint speckled hall, where I saw my mother sitting on a couch. She was talking to a nurse who was standing and speaking in a gentle tone. My mom glanced up at me, hurrying towards her and automatically got up and headed my way without speaking to the nurse. I could tell by the look on her face that something was wrong, and she'd been crying. I dropped my bags as she embraced me. She quietly spoke in my ear, "Your father is with God." It was clear what she meant, but I went numb as a strange heat engulfed my entire body, and an invisible clamp tightened around my chest. I needed more – more time to process, more of a goodbye, more clarity.

"He passed away about an hour ago," she said, still hugging me.

"An hour ago?" I asked, pulling away from her but still grasping her arms as I studied her face.

"Yes. It was another stroke."

"But he was supposed to be alright."

"We thought he was, but often God has other plans."

The nurse came over and introduced herself to me, but I didn't catch her name. She said something about how sorry she was and told my mother she would come back a little later. My mother was surprisingly in control, or maybe she was still in shock like me.

"Where is he?" I asked.

"He's still in the room. Do you want some time alone with him?"

I nodded my head slowly. "Are you okay here by yourself?"

"Of course, I am, dear. The nurse will be back in a few minutes with some forms to sign. Go ahead."

I went before she could tell me that he's with God again. I didn't want to hear that. I kissed her on the cheek and squeezed her hands before slowly walking down the hallway towards room 210. I had a difficult time lifting my feet since it all seemed so surreal. I was mad at myself for not getting there an hour earlier. At the same time, I was angry at the small part of me that didn't want to be at his bedside, the cowardly me who didn't want to witness the conclusions of a life in the form of a gasp.

By the time I reached his room, I felt like I had been walking for days. I pushed open the heavy door that was slightly ajar and was shocked at what I saw. I took the comb from my back pocket, hurried over to the side of his bed, and began combing his hair back. I had never seen my father with a single hair out of place or falling over his forehead the way it was now. He would have been appalled to let anyone see him not impeccably groomed. I wasn't about to let anyone see him like this either. It was bad enough that he was in a hospital gown and not wearing his own monogrammed pajamas. I kept combing his hair gently, wishing I had some gel to stiffen it back the way he always did. I noticed some gray that was peeking through around his ears where the black dye ended. If I had some root touch-up, I would've applied that too. Finally, I stopped to inspect what I was trying to accomplish. "That's the best I can do, Dad." I put the comb back in my pocket. I pulled up a chair, sat down, and just stared at him. He appeared as if he was just sleeping, and I noticed there wasn't a line or wrinkle on his face. I picked up his heavy hand and pressed it against my face. I began sobbing.

I don't know how long I sat there holding his hand before getting up to leave. At the door, I turned to look at him once more before letting the door shut behind me. I went to the waiting room, where I found my mother talking to a woman I recognized immediately. It was the tall blonde showgirl I saw him leaving the restaurant, Knickerbockers, with last winter and who hurried into the hospital the next day. She had been sitting and holding my mother's hands. As I entered, she stood to greet me. She was a couple of inches taller than me and dressed in a conservative, dark pants suit that made her look even more attractive since she wasn't competing with a short, sparkling party dress like she was wearing the last night I saw them together.

"This is Dr. Sage Mindy, your father's cardiologist," my mother said.

Weird. Another Mindy in less than twenty-four hours? Could she have been my dad's girlfriend?

"I so wish we could've met under different circumstances," said Mindy, as she reached to gently touch my arm.

I nodded as I inhaled her perfume that smelled cleaner than seductive. I still needed to know more. I didn't quite understand why it was necessary; maybe I simply wished that I had known my father better and didn't want this to be a secret he took with him.

"My dad was your patient?" I asked. As soon as it came out of my mouth, it felt wrong. It wasn't because I wanted to know if anything was between them; I referred to him in the past tense.

She nodded slowly. "I played golf with your dad in Pelham and offered my services when his cardiologist retired." A few moments of silence followed. "He was a wonderful golfer."

"Yeah, he played all the time."

"You know; I feel as if I know you." She said.

"Really?"

"Your dad talked about you all the time."

"He did?"

"He was extremely proud. He told me about your scholarship to The New School and all about your copywriting position at Pruit and Gray. He was so excited that you were in Los Angeles working on a campaign for AT&T with Mickey Green."

I was emotionally drained, exhausted, and now shocked once again. *My father bragged about me? He was proud of me?* I remembered how I felt when he told me how proud he was when I won the scholarship, but hearing he was proud of me from someone else placed it on another level. I had no idea. I did know that I was grateful to Dr. Mindy for telling me. Still, for whatever reason, I wanted to know if something was going on between them.

"You know, I'm positive I saw you with my father once."

"Oh, really?"

"It was last winter. I saw you both coming out of Knickerbockers down on University."

I didn't want it to sound like I might have been suspicious of them being together, so I added, "I called out to him as you two got into a town car, but I guess he didn't hear me over the traffic noise."

"Yes, that was the night of the retirement party for one of my colleagues in the Cardiology Department. Your dad attended since they had become good friends since they played so much golf together. I ended up leaving a bit early. I wasn't quite over a bout of the flu. My husband stayed to make a presentation, and your dad was gracious enough to escort me home before being dropped off at Grand Central."

Aside from a touch of foolishness, I was too full of grief and wiped out to feel much of anything when it was clear that she wasn't my father's girlfriend.

"Of course, that was the night of his first minor stroke. He seemed fine at the dinner and later in the car. I did race over to the NYU Hospital the next morning. We had already placed him on a special diet."

"He obviously didn't follow it."

"I'm afraid not. We also placed him on Coumadin after the stroke. It was important for him to take it at the same time every morning, but he admitted last week that he only took it when he remembered."

"He was impossible," my mother interjected, sounding exasperated, her voice shaky. "If it wasn't in a cream sauce or at the bottom of a glass of wine, he wouldn't take them."

Dr. Mindy looked at my mother sympathetically.

"I'm going to go to the ladies' room," my mother said, rising to her feet.

"Would you like me to come with you?" asked Dr. Mindy.

"Oh, no, I'm fine, dear. Thank you so much for all you've done. I really appreciate you coming down here and for all of your time."

"Sorry I couldn't have done more," Dr. Mindy said, embracing my mother. "If you need anything, please don't hesitate to call."

"I will," my mother nodded.

When she left the room, Dr. Mindy said, "Your father adored her. The way he spoke about your mother would have made any woman envious of her. I know I was."

Something else I didn't know about him. He just didn't love my mother, but he "adored" her. He would never have cheated on her with this beautiful woman standing in front of me or any other woman for that matter. What made me think he would? On the list of regrets that I'd been piling over the last twenty-four hours, I added, not really knowing my father the way I should have and always easier to finding fault with him.

"Yeah, he was crazy about my mom."

"Well, I should get back to my office, but I will see you in a few days."

I assumed she meant she'd see us at my father's wake. "Thank you for helping my dad."

She smiled warmly and placed her hand on my shoulder, and left.

I stayed in Bronxville to be with my mother, who continued to be what I didn't expect – in control of her emotions. At least she seemed composed and didn't cry in front of me the way I expected. I figured she was still in shock, or her faith was coming in handy, convincing herself that my dad was with God and she would be with him later. I was beginning to understand how a strong belief in God was necessary for times like these. It could bring comfort the way it did to my mother; the kind of comfort I could never give her. Catholicism was a type of roof over your head that kept you dry during a storm. I never did buy into any of it and had no idea where my father was or that I'd ever see him again. There was no roof over my head – my clothes were drenched.

The one conspicuously absent person was Father Cavendish. I was sure he would have been at the hospital, calling and coming by to comfort my mother. When I asked where he was, she said he had called from Rome. He was at the Vatican on church business and wouldn't be back for another week. She was disappointed that he wouldn't be able to say mass at the funeral but seemed upset over the sound of his voice. She said it sounded very raspy and almost didn't sound like him, though he assured her he had a bad cold and was fine. I was a little annoyed she was worried about his cold when we hadn't buried my father yet. I told her we should concentrate on getting through the next few days and she could worry about Cavendish's cold later. And that's what we did – we got through the next few days.

The wake at McGrath's Funeral Home on Monday night was surprisingly crowded, not with family since my parents didn't have siblings, but with friends of my parents and many of my father's patients. Once again, I was surprised how much so many people knew about me and how proud they said my father was of me. It was humbling to hear.

I was talking to an older couple when I noticed Dr. Mindy walk in with a man who seemed to be her husband. He was as good-looking as his wife was beautiful. They looked like they might have walked off the top of a wedding cake as they went over to my mother, who was only a few feet away from me. I had been keeping my eye on my mother, who continued to act strong and hadn't really cried in front of me, except for her eyes watering up. I guess I was waiting for her to have a total breakdown and collapse. However, she continued to greet people and keep her emotions inside. What I didn't know was that I was about two minutes away from something I would have to take to my own grave and never tell anyone about. I talked to a couple with hair the color of clouds whose names I didn't hear. After expressing their condolences, Dr. Mindy walked towards me while her husband was still talking to my mother.

It was as if she was moving in slow motion. She was all white and gold like a spotlight was hitting her for a red carpet event. She was Hollywood in Bronxville. Every time I saw her, she was more stunning than before.

"I'm sorry, Benjamin," she said in a low, warm, honey-soaked voice before embracing me.

That's when it happened. Standing there in her embrace, I began to stiffen. I got an erection. That's right – a hard-on at my father's funeral! I just kept my arms at my side and immediately pulled back from the waist down just in case. As I looked into her eyes, my face turned red and exploded into flames as I hurried off to find the men's room. In front of the sink, I quickly turned on the water and splashed it against my face to douse the flames and the utter disgust and embarrassment I was feeling. I grabbed a paper towel, dried myself, and then stared into the mirror. "You're a sick bastard," I fumed in a low growl at the guy in the mirror. "What the fuck is wrong with you?" I looked down at the sink and closed my eyes, "I'm sorry. I'm sorry, dad. It was involuntary – just a reflex action. I had no control. It just happened." I didn't know if he could hear me, but I just knew I had to apologize.

I walked back into the crowded room where my father lay in the casket. I was hoping that this was all a bad dream, and someone else's father would be lying there. But there he was, looking like he was sleeping, except for some makeup that made his lips a little too red. I was relieved that Dr. Mindy and her husband were gone and noticed more flowers were delivered while I was in the bathroom. I went over to read the cards. One was from Jack Sera, who I had called to tell about my father's passing. He told me not to hurry back to work and to take all the time that I needed. At the moment, I didn't feel like ever going back. The biggest flower arrangement was almost the most impressive; the buds were vibrant and alive. The card read: "My condolences to the Kissel family – Mickey Green." I had no idea how he found out about my father's passing, but it was gracious and thoughtful of him, or his people, to send something.

After everyone left, my mother knelt next to the casket and said a prayer. The room smelled of the perfumes many of the older women had marinated themselves in as well as the flowers from the various arrangements. The smells blending was beginning to make me nauseous, and I wanted to leave, but I also knew that I'd never lay eyes on my father again unless it was in a photograph. Looking down at him, I thought he'd probably have a window open in here if he could ask. He was a rather warm-blooded man, usually wearing the lightest of coats even on the coldest winter days and detested summer heat. I remembered how warm his hand was when he shook mine since shaking hands was usually his way of expressing physical contact with me. I couldn't even remember ever hugging him. He always thrust his hand out almost as a guard against a more intimate hug. I couldn't remember ever kissing him. It just wasn't in my realm of possibilities. What would be the reason for that? I found one now. I leaned over and gently kissed his forehead. It felt cold like ice, and the lack of life startled me. Nothing so cold had ever touched my lips.

Chapter Nineteen

It was Black Friday, and for the first time, it felt like the appropriate name, considering how I had been feeling. I was on a crowded train heading back into the city packed with Christmas shoppers – hunters anxious to track down bargains. For them, it was the opening day of hunting season. I hadn't been in my apartment since before I flew out to L.A. The funeral was on Tuesday, and my mother and I weren't in the Thanksgiving mood, so we just ate a little of the food our neighbors had brought over for the reception at the house after the funeral. I told my mother I'd be back on Sunday to help her go through my father's clothes. She wanted to see what I would keep then donate the rest. I didn't want any of the clothes. They simply weren't my style, and even if they were, I'd have to pack on 50 or 60 pounds just to fit into them. What I wanted to keep was one of his pipes that he smoked on occasion, its tip stained from resting in his mouth, and the cigar he didn't finish smoking that was still resting in the ashtray near his chair. I planned to wrap it in foil and keep it until it disintegrated and disappeared. I didn't want anything else.

Grand Central Station was filled to its walls with commuters, shoppers holding Christmas bags hurrying towards exits, stairs, and trains. If you tripped, you might be trampled to death, and no one would notice, or they'd pretend not to notice. I made my way over to the exit ramp that led out onto 42nd Street and, once outside, let the crowd push me along towards Park, then Lexington, as if it was a river with strong currents. I couldn't swim against them if I wanted to. I waded towards Times Square. I passed the smell of roasting chestnuts, the ringing bells of the Salvation Army, the endless honking of horns, and the hundreds of faces I glimpsed as we passed each other – just happy that I didn't recognize any of them. I thought I enjoyed walking with Mickey and having people notice me and wondering who I was, but I realized that was false.

I was in Mickey's orbit, his reality, not mine. Here on these streets, I was nobody again, but felt like a celebrity of my own making, basking in my invisibility. It was good to be home. Three weeks ago, being pushed along by these crowds would've annoyed me, and I would've avoided them at all costs and opted for the subway. But now, I wasn't even heading towards my apartment. Instead, I was floating along down 42nd. It felt good to be among all of these strangers. The noisy streets are how the city breathes. I thought about my parent's house. It felt much bigger, even with my mother in it. She never had the type of personality to fill a room with her presence, let alone an entire house. Knowing my father wouldn't come through the front door again, made the house feel enormous and empty with his absence. Until I got off the train, I didn't realize that I needed to be around people, lots of people. I didn't need to know them, of course. I just needed to know they were alive.

I found myself walking under the marquee signs of porn theatres on the West side of 42nd. Their titles always struck me as funny rather than sexy. Across the street was "Cock or Two Will Do," next to it was "A Cock Work Orange," and the timely "Tricky Dick in the Watergate." I passed the occasional whore standing in the doorway of a dingy walkup in high platform shoes or boots, under wigs that always seemed to be a little crooked. I headed up 7th Ave, more as an explorer than the resident of a city I've lived in for a little over four years. The truth is, I tended to stay away from this area, leery of what I might find there or what might find me. The papers and the local TV news stations constantly reported someone being attacked or killed in this area, along with drug busts and prostitution raids. Bumby told me a friend of his was stabbed four times on 45th Street one night on his way back from a bar. The doctors said the only thing that saved him was that he was too drunk for his body to go into shock. Bumby said it proved two things, "Never be in Times Square late at night, and getting shitfaced is good for you."

I figured walking around during the day was safe enough, and it seemed that way. The buildings looked as if they hadn't been cleaned in years. They were caked dark with soot. Neon signs were doing their jobs over topless bars, parlors, and burlesque joints. Little round lights framed pictures of strippers who were appearing there that night. It all seemed rather safe in the bright sunshine as long as I continued to look and not touch. Mayor Beane has been saying he wants to clean the whole area up. Still, I couldn't imagine that happening unless he kicked everyone out before coming in with a pail and detergent, then getting down on his hands and knees and scrubbing until it shined.

I was going to turn around and go back to grab a subway downtown when I spotted another topless bar. It was different from the others I had seen since it looked new and clean. I was like a kid who saw a shiny coin in the middle of the sidewalk and headed over to it. Perhaps because it looked so new and I had never been in a topless bar. I went inside on a whim to check things out. A huge bald guy in a tight tee-shirt that looked as if it was painted on opened the door, smiling. He could have been Mr. Clean's twin if they sold 8-foot bottles of the stuff. "Welcome," he said stiffly. The room was large and looked cleaner than its outside façade. It was on the dark side, but bright enough to see everything. In the center was a large circular bar wrapped around a stage where three girls were nude, except for G-strings, and were dancing to the Stones "Honky Tonk Woman."

From time to time, one of the girls would jump up and grab onto one of the three poles and spin around with their legs open. There were small tables around the room where a few more girls in their robes talked and laughed with guys in suits. Uncorked champagne bottles were in the middle of the tables, looking like large candles. The "suits" might have been business execs on their lunch breaks dropping a lot of money on cheap booze and hoping for a chance to talk to one of the girls they just saw naked. The girls dancing had bills stuck in their G-strings, and the drooling guys were sitting at the bar, continuously adding to their bill collections. All of it was what I expected when I decided that I had enough, turned, and headed for the door. Before I could make my way out, Mr. Clean stepped in front of me.

"Where are you going, my friend?" He asked.

"If you must know, I'm going home."

He had a strange, forced smile. "Really?"

"Yep. Haven't been home in over a week."

"Wow. A week."

"Yeah. Seven days."

"I want you to go home too, but didn't you see what it says on the sign?"

"Nope. Must've missed it. Wait, wasn't it called 'Topless Joint'?"

"It says, 'Gentlemen's Club'."

"Catchy name."

"Yeah, it is, but you're not acting like no gentleman."

"How do you mean?"

"Well, at the very least, a gentleman would buy a drink for himself or one of the girls."

After he said that, he folded his arms across his chest, looking even more like Mr. Clean. It was clear that I wasn't going to get past this muscle-bounded fuck, and I wasn't about to try.

"Know what?" I said, looking at the bar.

"No. What's that?"

"You're absolutely right. I think I'll get a drink before I go."

"Great idea. I knew there was a gentleman in there somewhere."

I might have looked calm, but as I turned and headed back to the bar, my heart was racing. I took a seat and ordered a beer I didn't want. A girl was dancing almost directly in front of me who kept looking and smiling at me, and every once in a while, she would wink. I figured she was just doing her job – working for tips I might place in her G-string, which was already so full of bills that she seemed to be losing money as it spilled underneath her feet. She had muscular legs and a perfect round butt. She'd jump up on the pole, spin, then slide down. I heard the guy sitting nearby say loudly to his friend, "Before, when she opened her legs, I swear I could see the Lincoln Tunnel!" The girl faced me, leaned up against the pole, slid down against it until she was squatting, opened her legs, and kept them open, so I could get a good look. She winked once more, got up, and as she started walking off stage. A voice over the loudspeaker said, "Gentlemen, a nice round of applause for Cassie, the girl with the classy chassis." There was a smattering of applause, and as soon as she got off of the stage, another girl came on and took her place.

I sat there for a few minutes, afraid that if I left too soon, Mr. Clean might think I still wasn't gentlemanly enough and ask me to stay longer. I was staring at my expensive glass of beer the way I should have been staring at the dancers. I was listening to Elton John singing "The Bitch is Back" when I heard a woman behind me. "Hi, there," she said. I turned around to find Cassie, the girl with the classy chassis, dressed in a short, thin robe and beaming at me.

“Mind if I sit next to you?” She asked, not giving me a choice as she pulled a stool closer to me and sat. “How about a drink? It’s not because I’m thirsty. It’s just that if you don’t buy another drink, you’ll annoy Ben over there by the door.”

I turned to glance at Mr. Clean, looking in my direction. “Wouldn’t want to upset him,” I agreed.

“I didn’t think so.” She leaned over to the bartender, who lent his ear in her direction. “Jimmy, a Diet Coke, please.”

“Driving home later?” I asked.

“Hardly.” She smirked.

“I gotta tell you, I’m a little annoyed that big fucker by the door has my name.”

“Not really, since you prefer Benjamin.” She cocked her head, waiting for a reaction.

“How’d you know that?” I asked, my voice cracking a bit from the shock.

She sat up straight. “You really don’t know who I am, do you?”

I examined her face for a few seconds. Her hair was cut short and brown, her eyes were probably naturally beautiful without all of that makeup, and she had a perfect, tiny, turned-up nose. I was stumped.

“No, I don’t!”

“I thought sliding down the pole and opening my legs the way I used to in your parent’s basement would ring a bell.”

I almost fell off of the chair. “Holy shit! Flora?”

She laughed. “I don’t blame you for not recognizing me.”

“You look so different!”

“Well, my hair is short and much darker than the last time I saw you.”

Her hair was almost black, straight, and cut short with bangs framing her face like a flapper from the roaring twenties. The biggest change was her nose. It was shorter and turned up slightly at the tip. Before I could mention her different nose, she tapped it with her index finger.

"This, of course, is the biggest change and probably why you didn't recognize me."

"Yeah. I guess. It's totally different."

"Well, about three years ago, I got a nose job. I always hated my nose."

"I remember."

"It was too much like my father's."

Times have changed, I thought. She actually admits to something she didn't like about her dad. Although the new nose was perfect, the problem with the old version was that it made her look too much like him. I hadn't thought about either of them after I left their house for good. My dislike for her father, however, came rushing back as if I saw him yesterday.

"You did end up with the perfect nose, although I thought the other one was cute too."

"Thanks, but I'm glad I did it," she said, taking a long sip of her soda.

I was getting used to the new nose along with the new look. She was becoming Flora again.

"So, how's your father and mother anyways?" I asked, resting my elbow on the bar.

"My dad passed away about a year ago."

I instinctively placed my hand on her leg. "I'm so sorry to hear that. Was it sudden?"

"No. It was cancer. Lung cancer."

No surprise there, I thought. He smoked like it was going out of style and always smelled like an ashtray.

"Hope he didn't suffer."

"Oh, he suffered alright. It was awful." Her eyes began to well up. "I always begged him to quit smoking.

He would smile and say, 'Don't worry,' he was going to be fine."

Before she could continue, Big Ben came over and said to me, "Take your hand off of her leg."

I took it off in a hurry.

"Is this guy bothering you, dear?" He pointed his thumb towards me.

"No, no. He's an old friend."

I looked up at him and gave him my best 'screw you' smile, adding, "Yeah. We go way back."

Big Ben huffed and turned to go back to his post by the door.

"Sorry about that. He's just doing his job."

"Yeah. He's good at it. Anyways, how's your mom holding up?"

"She quit smoking, thank God, and moved to Florida. Boca Raton. She's doing fine, I guess. Of course, she still isn't over my father. How could she be?" There were a few moments where we sat listening to the loud music on the speakers before she asked, "And how are your folks?"

I didn't want to tell her about my dad. It just didn't seem right to talk about in a topless place in Times Square. I didn't want anything from Flora, especially her sympathy. "They are doing fine."

"They're still in Bronxville?"

"Yep. Still in Bronxville." I didn't want any more questions about my parents, so I changed the subject before any more questions came up. "So, how long have you been working here?"

"Are you surprised?"

"I mean, yeah, a little bit."

"I've been here for about a year, but it's just two days a week. I also work at a craft store and do temp work – you know, typing, answering the phone – that kind of stuff."

"Wow. Three jobs?"

"It's necessary to support my painting."

"Great! You're still painting! I was going to ask."

"Never stopped. I inherited some money when my father passed away – not much, but enough to have this fixed." She tapped her nose with her finger again. "Then, I met another painter, a really good guy who's very talented. We found a huge loft in SoHo for a hundred and fifty a month. Most of the other lofts in the building are just as cheap; that's why they're so many artists that have moved in. The space is amazing, and the sunlight is even better. There's no heat, and the bathroom is on the second floor, which is inconvenient, but..."

"How do you guys stay warm?"

"There is a large cast-iron stove that heats the entire place, and the loft is large enough to use as a gallery to display our work. Most artists who can't get into the galleries and live there exhibit their paintings in the hallways throughout the year. We are going to have an opening in about a month. You should come!"

"Sounds great! Glad you found a way to get your stuff shown."

She smiled approvingly. "And what about you? Are you married?" She asked good-naturedly, looking at my left hand. "I don't see a ring. And what are you doing to pay rent? More importantly, why are you here on a Friday afternoon?"

"Am I married? No, absolutely not. I work as a copywriter, and I came in here because it looked clean, and I'd never been into a topless bar before."

"Never?" She asked, shocked as if she didn't believe me.

"Nope. Never."

"So, what do you think?"

What I had been thinking was how strange it was to be talking to her in a topless bar where she dances. It bordered on surreal. "It's fine," was the best I cared to come up with. She started talking about something else, but I stopped listening. I remembered how the sound of her voice would begin to irritate me and how her mannerisms often got under my skin. A new nose, haircut, heavy makeup, and all couldn't keep that from resurfacing. It was time to leave. She was in the middle of saying something about living in the city and I felt the immediate need to interrupt her and leave abruptly.

"I should really get going," I said as I reached for my wallet.

She seemed a little surprised. "Sure. Of course."

I placed the money for our drinks on the bar.

"You really should come to the opening at our place. I'm going to be exhibiting some new pieces I've been working on." She said this so quickly that the words seemed to tumble into each other.

"Sure. Maybe I will." I resisted the urge to shrug.

"Where can I send your invite? Do you live in the city?"

"Yeah, on Eighth Street. I'm in the phone book."

"Okay. I'll be in touch when we figure out a date."

"Sounds good," I said as I got up from the chair. We looked at each other for a very long second, then at the same time, we said, "Take care."

I turned and headed towards the door where Big Ben was standing. I wasn't sure if he'd say something to me or if he'd even let me leave. I knew I had to get out of there no matter what; even if I had to run between his legs. As I got closer, he just nodded his head and opened the door to the bright sunlit city waiting outside.

Chapter Twenty

After leaving the bar, I realized what a complete fool I was to simply let her walk out of my life. Why didn't I stop Marla? I just let her walk out of the hotel without saying a word. Now that the dust was settling a bit from last week, I thought about her a lot. As I made my way over to Lex to take the subway downtown, she was all I thought about. I had to accept my father's death, but I could not accept the death of a relationship with Marla. I could resurrect this one if I could figure out a way to make it happen. I kept arguing with myself about what I should have said but kept answering and losing the argument. *Maybe I should have told her to let me get dressed, and I'd meet her downstairs. But you would have had to ask her into the room eventually, and she would have seen those naked girls.*

How about the truth: "Yeah, I was doing blow and was completely out of it."

She might've responded with, "So the first thing you do is fuck not one, but two chicks?"

"Mickey forced me to do it. Kind of."

"What are you, a fucking child? Aren't you an adult? What if Mickey wanted you to kill someone? Would you do it? Grow up!"

If I couldn't convince myself, how was I going to reason with her? I just wanted to talk to her and plead my case. I simply didn't have a case yet. I needed something that, if not the truth, then something that could pass for it.

I was getting hungry and stopped off for a slice of pizza on University since I knew there would be nothing at my place. I happened to pass Knickbocker's on the way. I stopped to imagine re-watching my father and Mindy come out of the front door again, the way they did that night that I thought he was having an affair. A feeling of guilt rushed over me as I apologized once more for thinking that. I hoped that the apology in my head was loud enough for him to hear. After I had a slice, I stopped at a deli on 8th to pick up some staples: Coffee, soda, beer, and chips. I don't remember much about doing any of it because all I was really thinking about was trying to get in touch with Marla.

When I entered my apartment, the same apartment that started becoming too confining and alienating, it looked just the opposite now. It was welcoming, spacious, and safe. It was a familiar place for me to lock out the world and to think. I needed to figure out how to contact her. I could call, but I knew she screened her calls, so she more than likely wouldn't pick up if I did call. I clicked on my own answering machine, hoping for a miracle that she might have left a message. Of course, there wasn't anything from her. There was only a few hang-ups and older calls that I had already dealt with before. I went through all of the messages again just in case I somehow happened to miss it. When I got to number eleven, I erased them all.

I crashed on my bed, thinking the only way I'd be able to talk to Marla about that morning was bumping into her. The only way that I could do that was to hang out near her apartment. I knew that if she wasn't traveling, she usually got home between 6 and 7 in the evening. All I had to do was be there and wait. Would that make me a stalker? I remembered Humphrey Bogart in so many of his movies would wait outside of a building until he saw Lauren Bacall or some other sexy babe and pretend he just happened to bump into her, and they always ended up together. I wouldn't be only a fucking stalker; I'd be Bogart. I was getting better at reasoning with myself, although it still sounded rather desperate. Even if it did, I knew I'd be there every evening until I saw her.

At the same time, I wanted to get back to Bronxville each night, at least for the next week, to ensure that my mother was transitioning as smoothly as possible in her new life without my father. I also wanted to discuss with her the possibility of selling the houses in Bronxville and Mt. Vernon and moving into an apartment in town near the train station. It would allow her to walk to the shops (since she was a nervous driver), give her easy access to the city, and most importantly, more money in the bank from the sale of a house too large for one person anyways. Convincing her to sell might prove difficult, although it was worth a try. I had no intentions of going back to work the next week; Jack said that I could take all of the time I needed, and that's what I intended to do. I didn't want to think about the scripts I wrote with Mickey or what our creative director thought of them. I didn't want to think about Mickey at all since he was the main reason I was in this predicament with Marla.

I thought I'd start playing Bogart on Monday evening. It was the weekend, and I'd have even less of a shot seeing her. I began to get up when the phone rang.

"Hello?"

"It's me," my mother said.

"You alright?"

"Oh, yes. I just wanted to call to tell you that my friend, Missy Print...Did you meet her at the wake?"

"No."

"Well, she invited me to her home in Pleasantville for a few days, at least until Friday. She thought it might be good for me to get away a little, and I think it might be a good idea."

"So do I. Got her phone number?"

"I do. I have it upstairs and will call you with it or leave it on your answering machine."

"Okay. I was going to come back tomorrow, but since you won't be there, I'll wait until you come back."

"There's no need to come here. Stay in the city, and you can come up next weekend."

"Guess I'll stay put then."

"What about work?"

"What do you mean?"

"When do you plan on going back?"

"I'm not sure yet."

"Well, don't rush. Take your time."

"I am. By the way, how are you getting there? I don't want you driving."

"Missy's coming to pick me up."

"Good. Don't forget to call me with her number please. I'll call you during the week."

"No need to do that."

"I know. I will anyways."

"Yes, dear." I heard her say that thousands of times to my father over the years.

"Okay, then. Relax and enjoy your time with Mrs. Print. Like I said, I'll call you and come home at the end of the week."

After I hung up, I was pleased she was getting out of the house for a few days and that I wouldn't have to go back each night after waiting for Marla. Of course, if I saw her on Monday and said what I needed to say, I could stop my nightly treks to the Upper East Side. I knew what needed to be said; I just didn't know how to say it, at least not yet. I did know that whatever I would say to her could never be totally true, yet it had to be something close to passing for it. I kept thinking about it over the weekend, writing scripts in my head in between watching television and sleeping. I didn't realize how tired I was and how little sleep I had gotten over the past two weeks. I didn't want to talk to anyone and screened my calls, including a few of the guys I worked with who were checking in to see how I was doing or wondering when I was planning on coming back to work. Naturally, Bumpy wanted to take me out for a drink. I didn't want to see anyone or return their calls. Even though I planned not to think about it, I did wonder how the scripts were going over with my boss and the account group. Were they as good as Mickey and I thought? I quickly let it go and thought, *Screw Mickey. Screw him.*

I slept most of Saturday away, ordering Chinese food in for dinner and listening to the radio after putting leftovers in the refrigerator that more than likely would be there until spring. On Sunday, I decided to do something I had never done before. I went to the movies alone. I always used the buddy system, when I went before, but since I didn't want to deal with anyone, this had to be a solo project. *Chinatown* had come out in September and was still playing in a theater near 6th Avenue. I figured it had to be good since Jack Nicholson and Faye Dunaway starred in it. Forty minutes into it, I discovered even they couldn't save the movie. It was too political for my taste – all about corruption and depriving counties in L.A. of necessary water – or something like that. Nicholson was good, as usual, and his clothes were even better. He played a private detective in the 1930s who has a weakness for expensive threads. He looked like he walked out of the pages of GQ magazine in every scene. Dunaway was good too, but her hair was dark brown and curled, making her look nothing like the way she did in *Bonnie and Clyde*. With the dark hair, she did nothing for me. When she was killed at the end of the movie, I thought they should have shot her earlier and shortened the movie by a half hour.

Monday afternoon rolled around quickly, and I took the subway up to 59th Street. I was nervous about not knowing if I'd even see Marla and get a chance to talk to her, and I still wasn't sure what to say if I did. I was pretty sure that if she didn't walk away, I had to try to convince her or place the idea in her head that what she saw and heard that morning wasn't what she thought it was. I might just have a few minutes to get it out quickly. It felt like an athlete who practices his routine and has only a few minutes to impress the judges. However, in this case, just one judge.

As I walked out of the subway at 59th and Lex in the shadow of Bloomingdale's and headed towards her place, I remembered the diner across from her building. It was where I went to kill time before going to her apartment. That was back in the good old days, which was just a little over three weeks ago.

I took a seat at a booth near the window with a clear view of her building and the front entrance. I ordered a cup of coffee, and cherry pie, which I recalled was pretty good. I checked my watch and realized I was there an hour earlier than when I wanted to be. I guess I was anxious, even a little nervous, but I didn't want to miss her if she got back early. The traffic light on the corner of 3rd was the last one before the 59th Street Bridge. As rush hour got closer, the traffic kept getting heavier and heavier, with everyone trying to get onto the bridge. It was as if 2nd Ave was putting on weight and stuffing itself on cars and trucks. I'd get nervous on occasion when a large truck would stop, blocking my view of the sidewalk across the street and the entrance to her building. I would stand up to see if I could peer over it, and if not, I'd walk to the other end of the diner window for a clearer view until it moved, then go back to my booth. Every once in a while, the waiters would come by and ask if I wanted anything else. I ordered another slice of cherry pie, and the waitress would automatically stop by and fill my coffee cup whenever I took even a sip. It went on like this until 6:30 pm. At one point, I had so much coffee that I had to take a major piss but held it in. I was afraid that if I went to the bathroom, it would just be my luck that I'd miss her walking by. I stuck to my cut-off time before I hurried into the bathroom and pissed until even my eyes went dry. I paid my check and then headed back downtown.

The next evening, was more of the same, with a little less coffee.

On Wednesday, I felt discouraged while gulping down my fourth cup of coffee, thinking that she must be on a business trip. Who knew when she would get back? I glanced at my watch. It was almost 7 p.m. when I heard, "Benjamin?" I looked up at Marla standing next to the table, looking a little perplexed and, perhaps, slightly annoyed.

She was annoyed, all right. "Yeah, um, hi. I was in the neighborhood and decided to stop in for a coffee and hoped I might see you walking by."

"Just in the neighborhood, huh?"

"Yeah. I needed to talk to the owner of the furniture store two blocks up. You know, Golds? I'm working on a radio spot for them."

Before she could say anything, the waitress came over and said, "Hi, Marla. The usual?"

"Yes, thanks. I'll take it to go, though."

"Sure, honey," she said smiling, then looked down at me. "Can I get you anything else? Coffee, perhaps?"

It was meant to be an inside joke. "No, thanks. I'll just take the check."

Marla wore a black coat, jeans, boots (the brown ones that I thought were sexy), and a large black shoulder bag.

"I was hoping I'd bump into you and could talk to you for a few minutes about our last meeting," I said, a little quieter than I intended.

She shrugged her shoulders. "Nothing to talk about." She looked over at the counter. "Tina, I need that sandwich. Got a business call in fifteen minutes." She said it as if she were thinking out loud.

I stood up. "It will only take a couple of minutes."

"There's nothing to say, Benjamin." She emphasized my name in a razor-sharp tone.

Before I could retort, the waitress called out from behind the register, "Here's your sandwich, honey."

Marla walked over, said something to the waitress, and turned to head for the door. I slapped a ten-dollar bill down onto the table and hurried after Marla. The traffic light turned red, helping me out. Marla had to stop at the corner.

"Please just listen to me for a moment."

She rolled her eyes. "What?"

When I followed her out of the diner, what I wanted to say came to me finally. When she was at the door of my hotel room, I realized that she heard a woman's voice saying that my mother was on the phone, but Marla never saw her. She just heard the voice, so there was only one person in the room as far as she knew. She didn't have any idea that another woman was there too.

"I want you to know that the woman's voice who answered the phone was Mickey Green's secretary who was working with me on that script. It got too late, so she crashed on the bed and I crashed on the couch. Our plan was to continue working first thing in the morning, but we were so exhausted that we overslept." I noticed the tension in Marla's face dropped a little after hearing this bit of information. I was making headway.

"You came to the door without a shirt on."

"Yeah, I was on the way to shower, and Betsy was still out cold."

"I guess I should have called."

"No, I should have invited you in. I just wasn't thinking clearly after working all night and basically napping rather than sleeping. Also, when Betsy – who is ancient, by the way. She's at least fifty – answered the phone; you had this look on your face."

I thought Marla was going to say something, but she nodded her head slightly in agreement.

"I should have told you to stop when you walked away. The thing was, my mother would never have called me unless it was something serious. It turned out to be very serious. So instead of looking for you, I had to book the first flight home that I could get on."

"Is everything okay?"

"No. My father was sick and in the hospital. He had a stroke, and they thought he would be okay, but he died an hour before I got there." This was the only truly honest moment of my story.

"Oh my God. I am sorry. So, so sorry." She reached over and squeezed my arm. "Your poor mother. How is she doing?"

"Better than I could have ever imagined. She's away at a friend's house for a few days, but I'll be going up and will spend most nights with her for a while."

"Of course. Again, I'm so sorry."

We stood for a few seconds, and I noticed that the traffic light had changed a couple of times, and she didn't leave to rush across the street.

"I certainly know what it feels like to lose a parent."

"I know you do."

"If it's any consolation, I know from experience that your relationship with your dad won't end. It will just take on a different configuration. He'll always be here for you when you need him."

"Thanks."

"I really do have to get going. I have an important conference call in a few minutes."

"Sure. Sure."

"Well..."

"Look, I just needed to clear up what took place, or what you thought took place that morning in the hotel. It was just a big misunderstanding. That week we spent together before was great. It felt like everything was coming together for us. You and what we have are too important to me to let go of. I'd love for us to pick up where we left off before L.A. I promise I won't try to contact you and you won't find me in this diner again. Just...just think about what I said, and if you would like to meet and talk when you have more time, simply call me. I'll come running."

I'd always been an avid reader, but reading her face to find out what she thought was difficult. A few seconds followed as I waited for her to say something, although it felt like an hour.

"Again, I'm so sorry about your father. If your mother knows who I am, please send her my condolences."

It wasn't the response I was hoping for. "Sure. Thanks."

"I really have to go. Take care."

She turned. I watched her hurry across the street and disappear into her building.

Chapter Twenty-One

By the time I got back to my apartment, I was convinced I'd never see or hear from Marla again. I gave it my best shot; it's just that it wasn't good enough. Still, I kept analyzing what I said, what I should have said, replaying her facial expressions, and more importantly, thinking about what she didn't say. I knew she would never call me to meet and talk some more like I'd suggested. I remembered Mickey Green saying that years before he was famous, he was at a party and finally got up the nerve to ask a beautiful girl for her phone number. She told him she never gave her number out but would take his and call him. When I asked him what happened, he said every time the phone didn't ring; he knew it was her.

I had spent a sleepless night tossing and turning, pulling the covers over me, then kicking them off, and started to doze off when the phone rang. There is something frightening about a phone ringing in the middle of the night. It doesn't break the silence – it shatters it along with an accompanying feeling of alarm. If something can't wait until daylight, it must be bad news of some sort. Good news can always wait; bad news can't. The only other option is a wrong number, and if that is the case, you are too rattled to go back to sleep. As I went for the receiver, I looked at the clock and saw it was close to 5 a.m.

"Hello?"

"Benjamin, it's mother." She said, sounding upset as if she were crying.

I sat up and threw my legs over the side of the bed.

"Are you alright?"

"I'm sorry for calling so early."

"That's fine, fine. Are you alright?"

"Well, not really. I need to see you today."

"Sure. Sure."

"Please come home as soon as possible."

"How did you get home? Thought you were staying with Mrs. Print until Friday or Saturday."

"Missy drove me back." She started to whimper and then sob.

I tried to comfort her. "Mom, you're upset. After all, dad just died last week. Now that the shock of it is over, it's all catching up." I was almost relieved that she was sobbing. I was surprised she hadn't broken down before this. She was always remarkably composed at the hospital and throughout the funeral. Even later, when we were alone in the house, she pretended to be fine. Still, I hated hearing her cry.

"I just need you to come home. Please. We have to talk."

"Of course. I'll be on the next train, and we'll talk. Anything you want. Okay?"

"Yes. Okay. See you in a little while."

I felt awful hearing her cry but knew it was healthier to grieve and not hold it in. I needed to get home and comfort her the best I could. I showered, dressed quickly, and hurried out the door. Eighth Street was so empty and quiet that I could hear myself breathing a little heavier as I rushed to the curb to hail a cab, which was easy since most of the city was asleep. It would be more difficult to get one when more of the city woke in another hour or two and started to move. By eleven, it would be almost impossible since all of the city would be racing through the rest of the day.

One of those large checkered cabs picked me up. I had never been in one before. It was so big and spacious inside that the entire Lower Eastside could fit in it and still have legroom. I sat back and looked out the window.

I had almost forgotten that it was the holidays. I had loved the season and even more so living in the city. I almost missed the Christmas trees being sold on street corners and their smell, which I always inhaled so deeply that a pine forest filled my lungs. The holiday lights twinkled on the buildings as if they were stars that fell out of the night sky. I certainly didn't feel the spirit that went with it this year. The only thing I felt was loss. I had graduated a little over six months ago, but there was so much more out here that college didn't prepare me for. It certainly didn't prepare me for what had taken place over the past few weeks. I knew that there was no way it really could, but if this was somehow part of maturing, then maturity is overrated. By the time I got to Grand Central, I had figured the only thing I could do moving forward was expect the unexpected since everything I didn't know was what I knew best.

I got an express into Bronxville and took a cab from the station to get home faster. I rang the doorbell a few times in rapid succession to let my mother know it was me. When she opened it, her eyes were two red dishes that needed to be dried, and her shoulders slumped over with the extra weight of grief she was carrying. I hadn't ever seen her look so distraught.

"Hello, Benja," the rest of my name got lost in her throat.

"Mom," I said as I put my arms around her and hugged her. She seemed small and frail in a way she hadn't before.

"We have to talk."

"Of course."

She turned and walked into the living room, then sat on the couch. I looked at my father's leather smoking chair and pictured him in it. I pulled over another chair and placed it across from where my mother sat. I sat down and took her hands in mine. I knew she needed to talk about my dad – the realization that he was gone and, perhaps, what her plans were now that she was alone.

I hated seeing her this way but still felt it was positive that she was grieving openly and not hiding it. She removed her hands from mine to search for a hanky in her pockets, then buried her face in it.

"I have to tell you this," she said, looking into the hanky and then squeezing it.

I leaned in closer, gently touching the side of her legs. "It's okay, Mom. Take your time."

"It's Father Cavendish."

I was surprised to hear his name. "What about him?"

"He's very sick."

"How sick is he?"

"It's cancer." She buried her face into her hanky again, her shoulders trembling as she cried.

This made me pull back and sit up in my chair. She was more distraught over Cavendish than she was about my dad. I assumed that it was because more bad news was coming so soon after my father's death, a kind of piling on. It made perfect sense.

"I thought he was in Italy at the Vatican or something like that."

"As did I. Then I called the rectory to see when he was coming back, and they let it slip that he was battling cancer. He didn't want me to know and said he was at the Vatican on business when he was really at Sloan Kettering."

"You mean, in the city?"

She nodded her head and started crying again.

"Why would he lie to you about it?"

"He didn't lie. He was protecting me," she said, sounding defensive.

"Okay. He didn't lie, but what was he protecting you from?"

She blew her nose. "Because we are very close. We've always had a special relationship, and with your father dying, he didn't want to upset me further."

I found myself getting annoyed. It wasn't because of their special relationship, but rather that she seemed more upset about Cavendish than she was about my father.

She dabbed her eyes with her hanky to try to compose herself, then looked me in the eyes and said, "There is something I have to tell you and I hope you will try to understand."

"I'm sure I'll understand anything you have to tell me."

"It began before you were born. As you know, from that day in the attic, my father was a priest."

"Of course, I remember."

"I grew up believing that I was closer to God because of his being in the priesthood. He also told me that the church teaches that once you are a priest, you are always a priest, as you know. On Sundays, he would say Mass for my mother and me in our basement and give us communion. He would also hear our confessions."

"You and your mother went to him for confessions?" I asked incredulously.

She nodded her head.

"You do know how unhealthy that sounds, right?"

"It was how I was raised," she said, searching my face for some sort of understanding. "Later, when I was eighteen, I told him I wanted to become a nun. It was about a year after my mother died, and he said it was too late to enter the convent because they were polluted with lesbians."

My mother never talked about her parents and had to tell me that her father was a priest only after I found that photo. Now that she was finally talking about her family life, I hoped she would stop. It was clear that the Fig family was strange. Grandpa Fig was nuts, and he did his best to ensure his family followed his twisted theology. I thought I knew my mother, but there was nothing that could have prepared me for this. Somehow, I knew it was just the preamble to what she was about to tell me. I realized that I didn't know my mother at all. She was transforming into a stranger in a black dress sitting on my parent's couch.

"Just before your grandfather died, he told me to contact a young priest in Bronxville, New York who would help me find a job, a place to live, and guide me spiritually."

"Father Cavendish?"

"Yes. He did all those things my father said and more. He got me a secretarial job at a realtor's office in Bronxville and helped me find an apartment." She kept looking into her hanky, dabbing her nose, and then looking back at me. "In time, as I said, we became very close, and I told him about wanting to become a nun and what my father thought about it."

"I hope he told you how destructive your home environment was."

She looked at me with a somewhat confused expression. "Oh, no, it wasn't destructive at all. It's how I was raised and I was fortunate to have a father who was a Catholic priest. Very fortunate."

I knew then this woman in front of me was not the mother I thought I knew. She really was a stranger. I found myself getting agitated and wanted her to get on with what she needed to tell me.

"So, what did Cavendish have to say?"

"He said those were my father's beliefs, and I should continue to pray for his soul."

She said something else that I missed because I kept thinking about her father saying Mass in the house and hearing their confessions. It sounded more twisted the more I thought about it. How could she feel fortunate about all of it? I let it go for a moment to focus back on what she was saying.

"He would meet with me regularly, and he prayed with me for God's guidance."

"Where?"

"What do you mean?"

"Sorry. Where did you meet with him?"

"Sometimes at the rectory or at my apartment in town. During one of our meetings, I told him that I still wanted to enter the convent, but I also had a strong desire to be a mother."

"Well, I'm proof that you didn't become a nun."

She didn't acknowledge my comment and continued.

"Father Cavendish clarified things and offered a solution for me to stay even closer to God and still be a mother." She looked up at me. "I had always prayed that when the time came to explain it to you, you would understand."

I started to get even more annoyed and anxious. "Explain what?"

"The miraculous way I had you."

"Go ahead. I'm listening."

"Father Cavendish showed me how unique my Catholicism was since my father was an ordained priest, making me even closer to God than the typical Catholic."

"Okay. What did he have in mind?"

"To have a child."

"So, he told you to marry dad and have a child. Doesn't sound too unique to me."

"Yes, he did tell me to marry your father, who I was dating when I was pregnant."

I really did not want to hear this, but she was going to tell me whether I wanted to hear it or not.

"Mom, that's not so unusual. That happens a lot more often than you think."

"This is what you have to understand: Father Cavendish was the father." She said it quickly, as if in a rush.

I'm pretty sure I might have stopped breathing for a few seconds. I felt like someone sucker punched me in the stomach. I heard what she said but wanted to make sure there was no mistake.

"Cavendish was the father?"

She nodded her head.

It sounded surreal at best. It was then that the impossible occurred to me.

"What happened to the baby?" I asked, almost praying for the answer I needed to hear.

She looked at me squarely in the eyes. "It's you, Benjamin. Father Cavendish is your biological father."

Hearing that zapped all the life out of me. I leaned defeated against the back of the chair and stared at nothing for several minutes. I gazed up at the ceiling, then at her again. I needed some sort of hope that she may be mistaken.

"But you were dating Dad at the time, right? So maybe he really is my biological father?"

She shook her head no. "I wasn't having sex with your father. We weren't married, and like any good Catholic, I don't believe in pre-marital sex."

I started raising my voice. "Do you know how messed up that sounds? You won't have sex with Dad because you weren't married, but you screwed a priest!"

Hearing me say that was as if I threw cold water in her face. She stopped sounding emotional and seemed to gain her composure.

"I've explained all of that to you and my connection to Father Cavendish."

I leaned forward. "You've explained nothing! Nothing! Don't you see how you were brainwashed first by your sick father, then by another one hiding behind a collar? Your priest was a sexual predator, and your father got you ready for him. He paved the way."

She started shaking her head back and forth.

"I was afraid of this. You would never understand, but I had to tell you. I had to tell you now."

"But why?" I asked, almost pleadingly. "You waited twenty-four years. You should have waited for another twenty-four."

"Father Cavendish might not last the week, and he asked me to tell you. He wants to meet and talk."

"Talk? Why? To tell me what?" I jumped up from the chair. "My father. Are you kidding me? The bastard's a sperm donor who seduced my mother and broke every law of the church. We buried my father last week – the man who raised me. Did he know about this?

"No, never. Father Cavendish introduced us."

"Of course, he did, that sick fuck." I had never cursed in front of my mother, but times had quickly changed. "It was part of his sick plan."

It was as if she didn't even hear me. "Please see him. He's at Sloan Kettering."

"Did you ever love Dad?"

"Of course, I did."

"How do I know you are not lying? You've lied to both of us my entire life. In fact, my entire life is one big fucking lie."

"You will have to trust me."

"Trust you? Trust you? How could I ever trust you again?"

She started to cry again and seemed to look even smaller, drowning in her black dress three sizes too big for her. I remembered seeing my mother cry when I was a kid and how much I hated it and tried to comfort her then. Now, I didn't care. I was always drawn towards my mother and her needs, but now, I needed to get away from her. I got up from the chair and started to pace back and forth across the room. I started feeling like the walls were closing in on me. They were getting closer and closer, and if I stayed, they would crush me. She said something else, but I didn't hear her. I felt my heart trying to burst through my chest. I had to leave.

"...please visit him."

"I gotta get going," I said, not looking at her as I headed for the door.

She called after me in a pained voice, "Benjamin..."

I couldn't look at her or answer as I slammed the door behind me.

I walked through town stunned and numb as I thought about Cavendish. I kept getting angrier and angrier until I felt like I could burst into flames – a large ball of fire walking along Pondfield Road. Christmas shoppers avoided me as I passed. If anyone got burned, it would be their own fault. A mix of ice and snow started falling and put out most of the flames by the time I reached the station.

Looking out of the train window, I saw Cavendish's face covering the drab buildings of Mount Vernon. No wonder that prick looked at me the way he did every time we met. He was examining me to see if I resembled him. I never liked him, but now I hated him, and I never hated anyone before. There was no way I could visit him in the hospital. For what? To make him feel better for what he has done to my mother. My mother! How ironic. She was never the saint I made her out to be. The problem was that I was the one who made her a saint. I canonized her. I didn't want to accept that she was human. Why was I always ready to find fault with my father to the point of convincing myself that he was having an affair. I couldn't have been more wrong. It was my father who adored my mother and it was my mother who adored Cavendish.

She actually thinks these two bastards, Fig and Cavendish, brought her closer to God instead of being victimized all of her life. Because of it, I've been living a lie this whole time. At the moment, I didn't feel real.

I was so angry that I started to tremble. I felt like I was going to ignite again and set the train on fire. My thoughts were racing and banging into each other. I wished I could erase the last three weeks and start them over by pushing some kind of restart button. My head began to spin and I expected Rod Serling to walk up and say, "Your next stop is the Twilight Zone." Then for a brief moment, I felt closer to my father. We had both been living a lie created for us. Not one size fits all, but individual, custom-made lies for each of us. Why would Cavendish want to see me now? To tell me that he is my biological father? To make a last-minute connection before he kicks, looking for absolution? Does he expect me to open my arms, hug him, break down, and cry with him? Father and son united at long last? My father just died. We just buried him. The man who raised, clothed, and fed me – the only man I knew to be my father and who will always be my father just died. I pictured grabbing Cavendish by his black suit and throwing him to the floor, or worse. The truth was, I never physically hit anyone and wasn't about to now. Fantasizing about it felt good though. I was even feeling a little winded from throwing him around.

When the train pulled into Grand Central, I followed everyone until I reached the Tiffany clock that sits on top of the information booth. I was going to take the subway to my apartment since there was no way I was going to the hospital. Something my mother said on a few occasions over the years that never meant anything popped into my mind, and suddenly, it meant a whole lot more. She said that Cavendish baptized me. I'm sure my mother's father baptized her, which made me another link in their twisted, theological chain. I suddenly felt the urge to tell Cavendish what I thought of him, and I didn't give a fuck how sick he was. I wasn't going to do it for my father or even my mother. I needed to do it for myself. I hurried over to Lex and grabbed a cab to Sloan Kettering.

Chapter Twenty-Two

I didn't know where the hospital was located, but it was well known, so all I had to tell the cabbie was "Sloan Kettering," and he got me there within ten minutes. It was on East 69th Street, not far from Marla's. The receptionist behind the lobby desk was shaped like a keg of beer, and she looked annoyed when I asked for Cavendish's room number. I felt like saying to her *no one wants to be here, patients or visitors, so the least you can do is fucking smile*, but I held my tongue.

She checked a piece of paper, frowned some more, then looked over another paper and, without looking up, asked for my name. I gave her my full name.

"You and one other person are allowed up. It's room 315."

I went over to the elevator, wondering whose other name was on the list. When the doors opened, I followed the room numbers posted on the wall across from the elevator on the third floor and made my way. I was sure of what I was going to say; in short, I was going to give him hell.

His room was located in the center of the hallway. As I walked in, I stopped as if I had hit an invisible wall. I turned around and walked back out to make sure I was in the right room. I was. I slowly went back in and stared at the man in the bed. I thought for a moment that maybe it wasn't Cavendish, but I saw his name printed on the foot of the bed. I walked closer, looking at him in disbelief or what was left of him. The once good-looking priest was now more of a skeleton with a layer of skin covering it. His full lips had almost disappeared and formed a rubber band that pulled tightly around his protruding teeth. His thick black hair was nothing more than a few white strands sticking up towards the ceiling like smoke rising from tiny campfires.

I had never witnessed what cancer was capable of and how it could take a body and gnaw on it like some ravenous animal.

"You must be Benjamin," a voice from behind me said.

It startled me as I quickly turned to face a nun sitting in the corner of the room near the door. With all of my attention and shock on Cavendish, I hadn't noticed her sitting there as I walked through the door. She seemed short and was wearing a white habit. She had a very pale complexion and a warm smile. She got up and walked over to me, placing a rosary in a pocket inside her habit.

"Just you and your mother are allowed up, so it wasn't divine intervention or a lucky guess that I know your name. Father said the only visitors he wanted and expected were you two."

I wondered how he was expecting me when I wasn't even convinced I was coming until twenty minutes ago.

"By the way, I'm Sister Celia from St. Joseph's. I've been here for the past three days talking to him and praying with him. Be here if he should need anything. Of course, their nursing staff, as you could imagine, is extraordinary, but we want to take care of our own, and Father Cavendish is such an amazing priest."

I said nothing and nodded in agreement.

"So, I'll leave you here for a bit with him." She gazed over at him. "He's been sleeping on and off for most of the afternoon. A nurse should be in to change his IV, but when he awakens, he'll be surprisingly clear-headed. So..."

I turned to watch her walk out of the room as if I were being left alone and didn't know what to do next. I moved closer to the bed to look at him and started examining his face like he used to examine mine every time we met. Of course, I know now he examined mine to see if he could find himself in my facial features. I was just looking to see if I could find the face of the man I knew in this ravaged man. I had a difficult time until I found bits of the face I remembered around his eyes, but nowhere else. Then they opened, which unnerved me for a moment before I relaxed again.

"Benjamin?"

He said my name as if he wasn't totally sure it was me and wanted affirmation. I was surprised he recognized me at all. "Hello, Father."

"I'm so pleased you came. I knew you would."

The nun was right – he did sound clear-headed.

"I hadn't planned to."

"Still, here you are." A faint smile appeared on his face. "Please pull up a chair."

"No, thanks. I'm fine. I'll just stand."

"Did your mother speak to you about the three of us?"

"Yes, she did."

"Then, I'm pleased."

At that moment, I thought about football, specifically Joe Namath, the guy Cavendish disapproved of because of his lifestyle. I remember reading what Namath said in the second half of the Super Bowl. He had a play he was going to call but then looked out at the Colt defense and knew his play wouldn't work. He changed it at the last minute and called an audible instead. I knew what play I was going to call, what I was going to say, but when I saw Cavendish, I too had to call an audible. Seeing him changed everything I had planned to say. I was still angry but was not expecting to find what was left of him. How could I tell him to go to hell when he was already there?

We were quiet for a few moments before he spoke. "So, you know the truth finally."

Maybe it was because he sounded so clear-headed and lucid when he spoke, that his face before cancer reappeared, allowing me to say, "You mean to finally know the lie."

"I'm sorry you feel that way. In time you'll understand your mother's unique closeness to God."

"You mean because she grew up with a nut for a father. Fig was crazy."

"I don't think he was crazy at all. He was a priest, and once a priest..."

"Yeah, yeah. I know. Always a priest."

"He was a unique man who I knew when I was a young priest and kept in touch with after he left and married. He created a religious foundation and forged a path for your mother to travel. Before he died, he contacted me to ensure that she stayed on that path."

"So, you took an emotionally unstable young woman direct from the Fig nut house and continued to take advantage of her. You broke your vows of chastity, went against church teachings, and became a predator." Although I was churning inside, I had no choice but to say it rather calmly.

"It is obvious you haven't thought this through as I had prayed you would."

"I've thought it through alright. You are just a man who uses spiritual power to manipulate the weak and bends church teachings to fit your own purposes. You impregnated a mixed-up young woman to fit into your own theological reality."

"Her father set this in motion. He was a spiritually devout Catholic with issues concerning church teachings, as did I. He contacted me to help ensure that your mother would continue on the unique path he helped create. After much contemplation, I moved forward."

"That's what you call it? 'Moving forward.'"

"As you can see, I'm at the end of my earthly life. You needed to know who your father is."

I still had my coat on, and after he said that, I began to feel how hot the room was. I moved a little closer to his bed. "Just so you know, I have always known who my father is: Bruno Kissel. He died last week. I'm proud to be his son. Always will be."

Cavendish stared, then closed his eyes. I waited for a second before I turned and walked towards the door. I stopped, suddenly feeling like I needed to say something else, although I wasn't sure what that would be. So, I went back toward his bedside as he opened his eyes.

"Yes, my son?"

That was a phrase priests used for all guys no matter how old they were, although now it felt more specific, personal. I found it insulting. Hearing it forced me to say something I never thought I would. I leaned close to make sure he could hear every word. "I just want you to know one thing: I forgive you." I waited for him to say something, but he didn't. He just closed his eyes. I waited there for a few moments in case he wanted to respond. I felt like some major weight was taken off of my back as I turned and headed once more for the door. Sister Celia was standing there with a slightly perplexed expression. As I passed her, I said, "He knows what I mean."

It felt good to be outside in the cold air. I had been sweating in Cavendish's room, and when the wind hit my back and chest, it felt like they were covered in ice. It started to flurry, and on the corner across the street from the hospital, they were selling Christmas trees as carols played over the loudspeaker. I stood there for a few minutes listening to "White Christmas." However, Bing Crosby couldn't compete with the traffic moving up 1st Avenue. I hadn't decided if I should take the nearest subway home or a cab downtown. Before I did either, I wanted to grab something quick to eat since I hadn't eaten anything all day. I saw a Bagel Nosh, a place that sold coffee and sandwiches that were all made on bagels. There were a few of them around the city, and the bagels were quite good. I had never had one until I moved into the city. They weren't that popular in Bronxville and the rest of Westchester County. Still, they were a staple, almost a necessity in the city. The entire city rolled on them. I can remember hearing a tourist, whose accent I didn't recognize, asking his friend what a bagel was. His friend explained that it was a hole with dough around it. I always thought that was the perfect description.

I sat down by the window and took a sip of coffee as I looked out at 1st Ave, where the traffic and snow were getting heavier. Without any real wind, it fell evenly like the flour my mother used to sift when baking. My mother, I'd have to sort through all of my emotions before seeing her again. Of course, I was angry with her for not telling me about my connection to Cavendish sooner, but how could she have if she couldn't even tell my father. Telling him would have been disastrous. Her telling me was unrealistic. I just didn't want her confessing a week after my father died. It was piling on my grief, so why tell me now? Maybe living a lie is fine if it's not your lie. I guess that's just another way of saying ignorance is bliss, and in this case, ignorance had its advantages. She really wasn't telling me for her own purposes. It was for Cavendish, who didn't want to die without me knowing our connection. It made me think even less of him since he made her tell me because now he had nothing to lose. He was a coward on top of everything else. Of course, I would work things out with my mother; I loved her too much in spite of everything not to. I also knew I couldn't see her until after

Cavendish died. I just couldn't comfort her over his death when she didn't need consoling after my father's.

I took a bite out of my sandwich and another sip of coffee. I felt like my life in the real world just got started, and all kinds of obstacles were hurled in my way. I had to find ways to avoid them, get around them, and keep moving forward. Maybe all you can do is keep moving forward. I also realized that some of these obstacles came out of nowhere, like my father's death and finding out about Cavendish. I had to blame myself for some of the others, though, like screwing things up with Marla. Maybe I took advantage of my mother not in the way Fig and Cavendish did; that doesn't even come close, but why did I have to make her into something of a saint? If I simply viewed her as an ordinary mom, maybe I wouldn't have found so many faults with my father. As far as I was concerned, he had all kinds of flaws that were even more obvious because my mother didn't have any. My thoughts were interrupted by a guy in a Bagel Nosh t-shirt walking around to various tables and picking up trays or whatever else anyone left behind. When he could, he would chat, or try to chat, with customers. I hoped he'd pass by my table without a word since I wasn't in any mood for small talk. No such luck.

I looked up at him. He may have been in his fifties and was slightly overweight. "Hey."

"Are you finished with your tray?"

"Yeah. Take it," I pushed it in his direction.

"Hope you don't mind me saying this."

"That depends."

"You look kind of annoyed. Hope everything is okay."

"I'm not annoyed," I said, sounding annoyed.

"Good. I'm glad."

I wanted him to walk away.

"I'll just take your tray and wipe the table clean for you." He took out a cloth from his back pocket and started to wipe the table. When he stopped, he said, "Mind if I share a little advice with you?"

If it meant he'd leave me alone, I wanted to hear it. "Sure. What is it?"

"At an AA meeting, just had my anniversary, ten years sober," he said, proudly and displaying a large gap between his two front teeth.

"Congratulations."

"Thanks! Anyways, when I first started meetings, I had all this anger that was obvious to everyone but me. You seem angry too. Saw it on your face when you came in."

I just wanted to go. "Guess I'm a little angry."

"Well, I wanted to share with you what they told me. Carrying around anger and staying angry at someone is like peeing your pants – after a while, only you feel it."

"Thanks."

"Good luck!"

"Yeah, you too."

After he left, I thought about what he said. It actually made sense. I turned to see where he went. He was in back of the counter pouring coffee. I turned to face the window again and watched the snow fall once more. I thought about how angry I was at my mother today and how angry I was at Cavendish. If holding onto anger is like peeing in your pants, I had to admit that my pants were a little wet. I knew if I wanted to move forward, I suppose I had to make peace with it all. Telling him that I forgave him was like putting out those flames. There was no way I could totally forgive him, especially so quickly, but I knew it was a step in the right direction.

A bag lady, who looked like she was wearing two or three coats and an old cowboy hat, stopped outside the window of where I was sitting. She placed her bags on the sidewalk, then started yelling and arguing with herself. I couldn't help but watch her. A guy sitting across the way from me said something about the street being filled with nuts, then went back to reading his paper. She stopped yelling as if she sensed I was looking at her, then stared at me for a few moments before walking over to the window, and started yelling at me.

"Stop looking at me! Call your mother! Call your mother! I'm not your mother; she is! Don't be a little shit. She loves you!"

I didn't mind her yelling at me. I just wished she yelled something else. I gulped down the rest of my coffee, and as I headed out the door, I caught the eye of the AA guy and thanked him again.

He gave me a big grin so the gap between his teeth looked like a small cave. "Sure. Pass it along!"

I nodded. "Will do," I said then headed over to 59th and Lex to take the subway downtown.

I was glad to get back to my apartment. It had gotten colder, and the snow on the ground was as thick as a Russian novel, making it difficult to walk since many of the sidewalks hadn't yet been shoveled. After I took off my coat and hung it up, I saw the light on my answering machine blinking. I kicked off my wet shoes and hit the button. The first person had hung up, the second was a wrong number, and the third was my boss.

"Benjamin, it's Jack Sara. Hope you are feeling better. Again, sorry about your dad. Well, you did it, kid – these scripts are great! The account group loves them too. We are sending them on to AT&T. There's no way they will turn them down. More than likely, we'll be sending you back to L.A. sometime next week to start filming. I will need you here tomorrow morning for an important meeting. I know it's a difficult time, but maybe getting back to work would be good for you. It's important that you are here at 9 a.m. Congratulations! Great work, kid!"

I pushed rewind to hear it again. Finally, good news. Actually, great news. I had been thinking over the past week how I didn't care about the scripts or copywriting, and maybe not even going back to work at the agency. That way of thinking had more to do with blowing it with Marla and, of course, the shock of losing my dad, which clouded everything. It was a way of protecting myself against failing. It was safer to think that the scripts probably wouldn't fly. It was a wall I'd built against the shrapnel of rejection. Now, after hearing the call and with a little clarity, I didn't have to kid myself any longer. I definitely wanted those scripts to work, especially since Sara and everyone else at the agency didn't think I had any real chance of pulling it off originally. This changed everything. This was validation. I would no longer be the low man on the *scrotum pole*. I'd be given high-profile campaigns, more strategic responsibility, and a higher salary. He wanted me there in the morning at 9 a.m. I'd be there at 8.

I tried watching a little TV, but after about ten minutes, I turned it off. I was too excited about the meeting to concentrate on some TV show. I headed to bed so I'd be well-rested at the agency in the morning. I looked outside to see if it had stopped snowing. The street was already plowed and I could hear someone outside shoveling the sidewalk in front of the building. Coming home earlier, it felt like a major storm, but now it looked like only a couple of inches had fallen and was already melting. It would make it easier getting uptown in the morning.

I woke before the alarm went off at 7 a.m., made a quick cup of coffee, and put on the TODAY show, letting John Hartz's voice fill the room with stories that I didn't listen to. I do it more for the company, but I stop to watch it every once in a while if I hear a story that captures my attention. I heard him say that unemployment was rising at 6.5%, the highest in thirteen years, reminding me that I was lucky to be working.

I took a long hot shower then shaved, wishing I had a heavy beard so I could grow one like Jim Morrison had in the photo on the cover of *Rolling Stone* when he died. That kind of thick beard totally changes your appearance, and you can hide behind it. I tried growing one in college, but it grew in thin and patchy and just made me look dirty. I gave up after about two months and shaved.

I went into the bedroom to get dressed. As I walked back towards the kitchen to get another cup of coffee, I saw the answering machine blinking. I must have gotten a call when I was showering and didn't hear the phone ring. I pushed the volume up to hear it as I walked into the kitchen, but stopped as soon as I heard who it was. I spun around, and hurried back to play it from the beginning.

"Benjamin, it's Marla. I was thinking about what you said the other evening and wanted to let you know that I do want to talk some more. So that's what I would like to do, talk a bit more, at least that's what I'd like to do now before I change my mind. I'm off to Seattle for work today for at least two weeks. I have a flight out of LaGuardia at 10 a.m. I'm going over to the diner across the street first for breakfast and should leave there by 9:15 a.m. to get to the airport. So, if you get this message and want to meet me there to talk, that's where I'll be. It's now 8 a.m. and I'm heading over. If you can make it, we'll talk. If not, well...okay...bye."

I was completely surprised that she would call or even want to meet to talk. I was convinced that I blew it with her the other night. I looked at my watch – it was 8:10, which meant that if I grabbed a cab uptown, I could get to the diner by 8:30 and that would give us about forty minutes to talk. Hearing her voice made me forget about my 9:00 a.m. meeting. Once again, Marla's timing wasn't the best. I needed to be at that meeting and I needed to see Marla. If only I could split myself in two and make both. I had to get to that meeting – a junior copywriter selling TV spots to the agency's biggest clients is almost unheard of and I was that copywriter. It was a fluke that they even sent me out to L.A. After I go out to film commercials with Mickey and all goes well, I'll be writing more with him. Even I can't believe it. I had to be there. So, I'll go to the meeting and have to miss Marla at the diner. I decided I'd call her and leave a message that I was in Bronxville and didn't check my calls until later. I put on an overcoat and, instead of feeling excited, I was feeling down about not seeing her. I grabbed my keys and headed out the door.

It wasn't as cold, and the snow had now been cleared off of the sidewalks or had melted into the cracks. I went to 6th Avenue, hailed a cab, and told the driver to take me to 57th and Madison. I sat back and thought that Marla probably wasn't totally convinced about us picking up where we left off. There was hesitancy in her voice, as if she wanted to see me and talk, although it might be best to let things go. Calling me at the last minute and wanting to meet at the diner, a neutral spot, before having to catch a plane was fraught with chance and all kinds of restrictions. Still, she called and was rethinking everything after I met her on Wednesday and made my pitch. I'd have some more convincing to do if I met her, and that's what I should be doing to fully gain her trust back. I knew I was in love with her, and I really enjoyed being a copywriter so far, but love didn't come into it. So why was I on my way to the agency and not on my way to see Marla? I had a chance to really set things right and to start over. How many times will I have the chance to do that? Finally, something I needed surfaced from the last two weeks and was there for me to embrace. I leaned forward and said to the cabbie, "Forget about 57th and Madison. I'd like to go to the Star Diner on 63rd and First." *Marla is waiting*, I thought. *The agency will have to start the meeting without me.*

Kevin Pilkington is a member of the writing faculty at Sarah Lawrence College. He is the author of ten collections: *Spare Change* was the La Jolla Poets Press National Book Award winner; *Getting By-* won the Ledge chapbook award; *In the Eyes of a Dog* received the New York Book Festival Award; *The Unemployed Man Who Became a Tree* was a Milt Kessler Poetry Book Award finalist. His poetry has appeared in many anthologies including: *Birthday Poems: A Celebration, Western Wind,* and *Contemporary Poetry of New England.* Over the years, he has been nominated for four Pushcarts.

His poems have appeared in numerous magazines including: *The Harvard Review, Poetry, Ploughshares, Iowa Review, Boston Review, Yankee, Hayden's Ferry, Columbia, North American Review,* etc.

He has taught and lectured at numerous colleges and universities including The New School, Manhattanville College, MIT, University of Michigan, Susquehanna University, Georgia Tech.

His debut novel, *Summer Shares* was reissued in paperback. His collection *Where You Want To Be*: *New and Selected Poems* was an IPPY Award Winner. A new collection entitled *Playing Poker With Tennessee Williams* was recently published. This is his second novel.

Made in United States
North Haven, CT
27 February 2023

33271760R00159